PRAISE FOR BRACKEN MACLEOD

"Bracken MacLeod writes dark, human stories of horror and modern noir. Absolutely one of the brightest stars of the next generation!"

—Christopher Golden, *New York Times* bestselling author of *Snowblind* and *Ararat*

"MacLeod's stories begin with a familiar sense of normalcy—the night out at the club, the visit to a friend's home—but quickly nosedive into the sublimely weird and horrific, leaving his reader breathless and dazed. These tales are jagged, sharp, and will definitely leave a mark."

—John Mantooth, author of *The Year of the Storm*, *Shoebox Train Wreck*, and *Heaven's Crooked Finger*

"Beauty, anger, and the grotesque. These are the three ingredients I demand as a reader of dark fiction, and they are three that MacLeod provides in just the right amounts in this collection. An absolute stunner."

—Adam Cesare, author of *The Summer Job* and *Zero Lives Remaining*

"*Stranded* is a smart, surprisingly moving, first-rate thriller that chucks Martin Cruz Smith's *Polar Star* down a *Twilight Zone*-esque rabbit role. Don't mind my mixing metaphors because me fumbling around for proper words of praise is what the talented Bracken MacLeod has wrought."

—Paul Tremblay, author of *A Head Full of Ghosts* and *Disappearance at Devil's Rock*

FIRST EDITION

13 Views of the Suicide Woods © 2017 by Bracken MacLeod
Cover artwork © 2017 by Erik Mohr
Cover and interior design © 2017 by Samantha Beiko

Distributed in Canada by
PGC Raincoast Books
300-76 Stafford Street
Toronto, ON M6J 2S1
Phone: (416) 934-9900
e-mail: info@pgcbooks.ca

Distributed in the U.S. by
Consortium Book Sales & Distribution
34 Thirteenth Avenue, NE, Suite 101
Minneapolis, MN 55413
Phone: (612) 746-2600
e-mail: sales.orders@cbsd.com

Library and Archives Cataloguing Data

MacLeod, Bracken, author

    13 views of the suicide woods / Bracken MacLeod.

Short stories.

Issued in print and electronic formats.

ISBN 978-1-77148-411-4 (softcover).--ISBN 978-1-77148-412-1

(PDF)

    I. Title. II. Title: Thirteen views of the suicide woods.

PS3613.A2739A613 2017   813'.6   C2016-907551-6

C2016-907552-4

CHIZINE PUBLICATIONS
Peterborough, Canada
www.chizinepub.com
info@chizinepub.com

Edited by Brett Savory
Proofread by Leigh Teetzel

 Canada Council Conseil des arts
for the Arts   du Canada

We acknowledge the support of the Canada Council for the Arts which last year invested $20.1 million in writing and publishing throughout Canada.

 ONTARIO ARTS COUNCIL
CONSEIL DES ARTS DE L'ONTARIO

an Ontario government agency
un organisme du gouvernement de l'Ontario

Published with the generous assistance of the Ontario Arts Council.

Printed in Canada

13 VIEWS OF THE SUICIDE WOODS

BRACKEN MACLEOD

ALSO BY BRACKEN MACLEOD

Mountain Home
White Knight
Stranded
Come to Dust

13 VIEWS OF THE SUICIDE WOODS

ChiZine Publications

for . . .
KL PEREIRA, ADRIAN VAN YOUNG,
and GRUBSTREET
Who taught me how to write short stories

"And perhaps many will, like myself, recall how amid the dangers and terrors of dreams they have occasionally said to themselves in self-encouragement, and not without success: 'It is a dream! I will dream on!'"

—Friedrich Nietzsche, *The Birth of Tragedy*

TABLE OF CONTENTS

STILL DAY: AN ENDING

The morning breeze passed between the blanched, lifeless trees rising like fractured bones jutting from the forgotten marsh. The only sign of its passing, a light and silent ripple on the surface of the shallow water. The clear sky reflected brightly, blue above and blue below. The facets of the wind on water sparkled like diamonds in the light. A lone blue heron sailed from its nest, searching for something to eat, unconcerned with the line of traffic creeping by a hundred yards away. Drivers sat in their cars with the windows up and radios tuned to the recap of last night's game at Fenway or NPR or empty morning talk, paying no attention to the wetlands beside them, staring ahead, squinting against the rising sun as they ate, shaved, checked e-mail, made calls, and put on makeup. All focused on the road ahead, the day ahead, the growing anxiety of sitting still with so much to be done. Not a single one looked toward the trees or the water. They were blind to the calm and elegant wood that had once been living trees growing up over a hundred years. Before they were born, before the road was built, there was the fen and the trees and the water and sun above shining on it all.

The heron flew back to its nest unnoticed.

The woman lay in the water, unseen.

She rested on the far side of the fen, as bright as the day and silent as the water. As beautiful and broken as the trees. A gentle halo of algae that would eventually overtake the entire surface danced around her bare shoulders and thighs. It caught in her golden hair and the deep red cuts rent in her flesh. It gently painted her pale skin green. The sun warmed her and kissed her with quiet light. Her body accepted the gifts it was able to receive.

Traffic inched forward. A radio announcer explained that an accident on a different road, miles away, was causing a delay getting into the city, but made no mention of the delay on Route Two. The voice described the weather, but made no mention of the great blue heron preening its feathers in a nest built in the bare branches of a tree high above the body of a dead woman. It made no mention of a human life ending in a scream of terror and pain and longing for another chance for a different outcome.

The radio voices moved on to other subjects and traffic crept forward and she lay still in the water as life all around her thrived. The algae in the water grew. The bacteria in her gut started the process of breaking down her organs. Insects waking to the growing heat of the day lazily crawled over her skin searching for a dark, fertile place to lay eggs and give life to new generations that would need what the woman offered to thrive. A fish slipped through the water near her, catching the sharp eye of the heron above keeping watch. And the people in their cars breathed warmed air and ate cooling food out of paper bags never thinking that tomorrow and tomorrow and tomorrow again might never come for them. That a truck might crush their bodies, a sudden disease could lay them low, that another one of them might open their skin and veins to the air and let life leak out onto a lonely mattress in a dark room, unseen and secret. No one woke up thinking that all there ever would be in their lives was behind them—not unless they had already been dying for a long time. The day and the city and the drive home that night and the next commute to work the morning after were always ahead. The sun was always in their eyes.

A small snake slipped past her, gliding into the water mirroring a line of ink in her skin. The blurred gray design arced into a once graceful feather curving along the small of her back as if the last of her wings had fallen away leaving only the hint of the light being she had once been. A woman who flew in her imagination, dreaming of a life above the clouds, living in the stars shining brightly, sparkling for the people below gazing at her beauty and radiance. But the once crisp and delicate lines had fattened with age and her airy feather became a leaden reminder of the years.

The day grew long and the sun moved above her before falling behind. The heron ate and rested and then worked its nest. The snake swam and slithered and warmed itself on a rock. The algae spread, bacteria fed, and the insects made a home for their children in and all around her.

And she lay waiting for that one set of eyes to glance toward the teeming life all around and see her.

All her life waiting to be seen.

And still invisible.

SOMETHING I SAID?

for Miah

It took a minute for my eyes to adjust to the dim light inside the bar. This wasn't a gastropub where people would bring their kids for lunch and sit near the front to people-watch while they sipped particularly resiny double IPA. The windows were painted black a generation ago and the smoked mirrors installed above the booths in the 1970s were beginning to distort with gravity. Walker's Pub was a place for townies to come after work to down a few before they went home to face whatever it was that made them want to stop off at a bar in the first place. And I served them drinks five nights a week. Not tonight, though. It was my night off.

When I could finally make out more than the familiar shapes and shadows within, I looked around to find who I'd come looking for. He was sitting on a stool near the register chatting up Valerie.

I am not a tough guy. I never have been. I maxed out at five foot eight in middle school and am a soft hundred and sixty pounds in middle age. I like food and sex and watching TV, and I get a lot of both food and television since my wife left me for another man nine months ago. Scott, on the other hand, was ten years younger than me and built like an action figure with acne. We sometimes joked behind his back about him forgetting the steroid hypo still sticking out of his ass.

I wasn't sure how I'd get his attention if he was sitting at a table in the middle of the room or, worse, in a booth, but it was a safe bet he'd be at the bar. From my experience serving him, Scott was the kind of customer who liked to talk to his bartender. It's not that he was all that friendly or wanted a confessor—the opposite on both accounts, actually—he was one of those skinflints who thought if he made friends, at some point in the evening his new pal would start comping him drinks.

No one ever did. Jerry, the owner and grandson of the original Walker, would unceremoniously shitcan anybody he found giving away alcohol. It was one thing to pour free Cokes for the rarefied DD, but booze? Never! Hell, he almost fired me for *selling* a customer an empty thirty-year-old cognac bottle he thought gave the place class, even though the guy paid enough for it to buy half a case of the stuff. Still, having never scored a free drink in the past didn't keep Scott from trying. That Valerie was serving him tonight was icing. She had all the qualities men like Scott desired. Except the ability to say "Yes." Again, that sweetened the deal for him. He was one of those "pick-up artist" assholes. Even had a blog offering a "coaching" service for it. He saw flirting as a competition against a hostile adversary. Sex was the spoils of being an effective combatant, not something another person agreed to because it was enjoyable for them.

He'd start out "negging" a target, wrapping an insult in a slight compliment meant to undermine a woman's confidence and drop her defenses. If the target recognized what he was doing, he'd move on to gaslighting or some other petty torture he thought was master-level hypnosis but was really just exploiting people's insecurities. At his core, he was a predator. And while he claimed to get more pussy than a veterinarian, I never saw him hook up. Not at

Walker's anyway. His routine definitely wasn't impressing Val. She didn't give half a shit what his opinion of her tattoos or Madonna piercing was. But then, to put it in his parlance, she wasn't "about the D." That was not an obstacle in his world.

She set a Red Devil—what people in the rest of the country called a vodka cran—in front of him and swept his exact change off the bar top. Scott, in addition to his other flaws—and they were many—was also not a tipper. I'd listened to him hold forth one night with another customer cribbing almost the entirety of Mr. Brown's soliloquy from *Reservoir Dogs* on the subject. Unlike in the movie, his barstool buddy didn't argue the point, but grunted and nodded as he slurped a 'Gansett out of the can, trying not to fall off the steady seat beneath him. Tonight, he sat alone. Even better.

Val tried to busy herself at the other end of the bar drying glasses from the shelf drainer. He knew she'd be back as soon as someone else put in an order. She had to work the till. And when she did, he'd work her. I took a seat three stools down from him. Not so close he'd accuse me of being a fag, but close enough he could hear if I said something. Val nodded at me, smiled, and set to mixing a dry Manhattan. She set the cocktail in front of me, poured herself a shot of shitty cinnamon whiskey, clinked my glass and threw back the fire. "Hey, Abel. It's your night off," she said. "Admit it. You just can't get enough of me, can you?" She slapped a hand on her skinny ass and flipped her purple bangs away from her forehead.

"I don't know how you can drink that sugary shit."

"My sweet tooth is a demon that demands sacrifice."

"If that sacrifice is your stomach lining, it ought to be happy enough." She poured herself another hit and threw it back while I sipped my drink, enjoying it. Although the selection of spirits at Walker's was curated with the intent of offering an affordable, quick buzz to people less interested in taste than effect, she made an excellent cocktail using what we stored below the bar—a personal collection paid for with our own money, without Jerry's approval—so we wouldn't have to suffer. Val should have been working in one of the upscale waterfront bars in the city. Instead, she was up here in the industrial Revere hinterlands. She claimed to like it better in townie bars. No one tried to make her feel like shit for "only" being a bartender, or treated her like the help. I suspected she preferred to work off the books more than she liked the atmosphere. Whatever her reasons, working with her was like a master class in being a badass behind a Boston shaker.

"So, for real. What's up?"

I shrugged. "Just thought I'd drop in and say hi. Since Katie left, I'm bored on Thursday nights."

"God, I hope I never get that bored." She didn't acknowledge the departure of my ex-wife. She was a good friend, protective and loyal. She'd been my best man at our wedding. Thinking of Katie made her angrier than it made me sad. Her jaw flexed as she gritted her teeth. She let out a long breath and patted the back of my hand, giving me the kind-eye invitation to stay as long as I wanted.

A guy I'd never seen come in before took a seat at the far end of the bar, and she put the candy rotgut away before sashaying over to serve him. He didn't know she was queer, and she knew how to earn her tips. She left her glass sitting in front of me. Val was meticulous about her bar; it meant she was coming back. I secretly wished she'd left the bottle behind along with it. I could have used a little more liquid fire in my belly than was left in my own glass. I took a big swallow of the Manhattan and tried to settle my nerves. It didn't work. My blood thundered in my ears as my pounding heart tried to kickstart my legs to get me to stand up and walk out the door. Even my Dutch courage was weak. I sat where I was and pulled my phone from my jacket pocket. I checked the time: quarter to ten. Late enough.

Scott was scanning the place for other marks, not having made the kind of headway he'd hoped with Val. I took a quick look around and saw there wasn't a single unaccompanied woman in the place. That meant Rhonda had come in with her husband. Time was short before Scott killed what he had in front of him and decided to take it on the heels looking for prey in the city.

"Cunt."

"What was that?" Scott said, turning to look at me.

I held up my phone and said, "Someone sent me a link to this guy's blog. It's called 'Female Sexual Motive' or some shit."

"And what did you say about him?" He stood up from his chair and cocked his head at me like I was hard to see under the yellowed lightshades. Maybe I was. Or maybe he was just trying to figure out why I looked familiar. Since I wasn't behind the bar wearing an apron, he seemed to be having some contextual confusion. I hoped he was lubricated enough to want to fight, but not so drunk he couldn't put his back into it.

"Who? My friend?"

"No. The author."

The author. I almost laughed. In hindsight it might have sped things up if I did. I shrugged again and went back to looking at my phone, dismissing him.

Scott took a step toward me. "I said, did you call me a cunt?"

I shook my head and pointed at my phone. "No. This guy. But I take it back. Calling him that implies he'd be worth a fuck. Reading this dogshit, my bet is he isn't deep enough to hold a tampon—"

He came at me like he'd heard the bell before the hammer even bounced. His haymaker took me in the side of the face and a blossom of heat spread across my cheek. My head whipped around and I staggered off my stool, tripping over another trying to keep my feet beneath me. The tall chair I'd been sitting on clattered to the floor while my phone slipped out of my hands, skipping once like a flat stone on a lake before disappearing behind the bar. He punched me in the kidney, making the muscles in the left side of my back cramp and my spine twist. He shouted something I couldn't hear over the ringing in my ears from his first hit. I did hear his voice crack at the end, making him sound as hysterical as he claimed all women were right under the surface: emotionally driven and borderline hysterical at all times.

I turned and tried lifting my fists to put up a guard. He hit me again in the gut right between my elbows. I dropped my arms to protect my midsection and he whipped around with another bent arm hook into the other side of my face, hitting me in the jaw this time. I spun and staggered away from the bar, both sides of my face numbing and growing tight with swelling. I stumbled into the middle of the bar and stood, trying to shake the haze out of my head. It wouldn't do any good to get knocked out too fast.

Blood dribbled out of my mouth and I stuck a finger in to assess the damage to my aching back teeth. Touching my molars caused pain unlike anything I'd felt before. They weren't loose. They were gone. He'd broken off at least two that I could feel. I tried to blow a kiss at him, but my mouth hurt so bad all I could manage was to let it hang open while blood and saliva drizzled down my chin.

Once upon a time I took karate, or something the instructor called karate. He'd made up his own style and named it after some piece of kanji he found in a book, the way teenagers pick their first tattoo. He told us it meant something poetic like "lunar eclipse," and waxed esoteric about appearances versus reality and what real warriors did and didn't do. I found out later he'd never bothered to ask someone who could actually read the language, and the symbol he'd named his art after was Japanese for "restaurant." Admittedly, it's a tough language. But he never double checked. Anyway, that was the guy who taught me how to fight. Against guys who'd also learned how to fight from him, I was good. In the Way of The Restaurant, I was Jim Kelly cool. Against a guy who spent all of his free time in a gym lifting and doing MMA, I was a punching bag; I just couldn't hit back.

Most of the time, I skirted around conflict with humor and a fast-talking reason that calmed even the most hotheaded guys down enough to not pummel me. But I really thought I might be able to block at least one of this dick's hits. Just one, so I felt like I was a participant in the fight. Scott, however, was fast and motivated. I had nothing in my repertoire of three-step slo-mo techniques and pseudo-religious platitudes about honor to counter a whip-fast hook or a rabbit punch. Learning that hurt worse than any of his punches.

It was hard to breathe. My stomach was cramping. Another slam in the guts and I crumpled. The floor was where I wanted to be, actually. Lying there, I felt none of the uncertainty of being rocked on my feet. Lying on the floor, I knew which way was up, which was down, and where I was. Definitely down, on my side, smearing my blood in the tracked-in dirt and road salt from the previous winter. The other thing being on the floor told me was he would have to change it up from fists to feet.

"Was . . . it something I . . . said?"

He kicked me in the back. Scott wasn't wearing work boots, but they weren't fluffy bunny slippers on his feet either. It didn't matter. Legally, almost any "shod foot" is considered a dangerous weapon. I felt the pointed toe of his Rockport against my ribs and heard the snap of bone echo in the shocked silence of the bar. The only other noises I heard were my ragged breathing, his cursing, and Val in the background shouting for him to stop. *Bless you, Val*, I thought. *But let him go*. I knew she'd already called the cops.

I rolled over to protect my back and he gave me a final shot in the face. Right where I wanted it. Where it would count the most. I felt my lips shred around the remains of my front teeth and I choked. I was done. He could stop any time. *Please Val*, I wished. *Make him stop*. But he hadn't exhausted himself yet, and I'd worked what I knew was his rawest nerve. No one treated him like a woman, or even suggested he was one. Calling him what I did was the same as threatening his deepest seated personal identity. And with a few in him, he didn't respond with anger. It was pure fury I'd tapped.

That's what my step-daughter—ex-step-daughter—Cory, told me about him. She's best friends with his daughter, Ginger. Goes over to his house for sleep-overs sometimes. She'd seen him go nuts at "Ginge" because he thought she called him a pussy. "She said he was 'being pushy,' but he wouldn't listen. He just screamed at her until his face turned all red. I thought he was going to stroke out right there in front of us," she told me. "He scares me, Abel."

A couple of days later, she sent me a link to his Pick Up Artist blog. He bragged about "railing some chick" in his daughter's bed because he was "about keeping it fresh (and his wife was napping in their bedroom)." I read through all the entries until I found the one where he "experimented" with his technique on one of his daughter's friends. *Fifteen and almost hot*, he'd written, *the little bitch acts like she already knows she can make any Beta "Male" do whatever she wants by even hinting at the* idea *of spreading her legs. She's probably got all the boys in her school already twisted up with promises and blue balls. But I'm A Man. So that weekend I set out to teach her an early lesson about the truth behind Female Sexual Motive using the techniques of the Alpha Male Plan. I got her AMPed up and when I was done, she was curled up in my lap and purring like a nice little kitten.* He added a disclaimer at the end saying he never followed through with his AMPlan because he wasn't "into felonies." Adding, *She'll be legal in six months. I can wait. ;p*

The blog post was date-stamped July 19.

Cory's birthday is December 21.

His sentencing is next week on February 15. Aggravated Assault and Battery with a Dangerous Weapon. Arrogant as ever, he spun the wheel on a trial instead of taking a plea and lost. I left my false teeth out when I testified. Fucking up my mouth was a cherry on top since it's a disfigurement and increases the penalty. He's looking at fifteen years. The irony is not lost on me.

I am not a tough guy. I never have been. But I'll do anything to protect my kid.

PURE BLOOD AND EVERGREEN

Pyotr cel Tinar long ago lost the ability to distinguish between falling snow and ash. The memory of sticking out his tongue to catch a cold, white flake only a single winter ago sent shivers of revulsion through his body. He had no desire to taste the crematory snowfall.

Outside the double fences surrounding the camp, the snow-covered meadow and evergreens beyond beckoned. The clearing and the trees each silently promised in his imagination to both betray his escape and conceal his flight. But the fantasy was pointless; the fences surrounding Block A were topped with concertina wire. The small razor daggers punctuating the elegant, overlapping coils gleamed in the moonlight like silver rose thorns in a fairy tale. In a perverse mockery, the guards had strung garlands of small, red flowers among the barbs.

Pyotr tried pretending that he was only dreaming the camp, the guards, the razor wire. But it was no dream, no fairy tale. No one would brave the metal brambles to wake him. No savior in a sky blue UN helmet was coming to liberate him or anyone else. He would have to be the author of his own salvation—a story not easily written, since the snipers in the guard towers would stop him in the No Man's Land between the fences well before he made it to the meadow. Instead, he sat fondling the small religious fetish his grandmother had smuggled with her into the camp. Now that she was gone, it was his. His very last possession—his last empty hope.

The fences also separated him from the second half of the camp. Block B was the mirror image of his own home in Block A—two prisoner barracks, communal commode, no showers, and a guard tower in opposite corners to watch over them. Between the towers and patrols through No Man's Land, there was nowhere a person could disappear from sight entirely. The space directly beneath the corner eaves nearest the middle tower was as private a place as there was left in Pyotr's world. He was in sight of only one tower, but could still keep an eye on both sides of the camp while preserving a clear view of the distant trees. Sometimes, he imagined he could hear their branches rustling in the breeze—when the thought of it didn't make him despair too badly.

Standing around the oil drum in the center of the Block A courtyard, the surviving members of his village huddled close to a fire built from the broken remains of empty prisoner bunks. Although it was warm near the others, they took their chances standing in the light. Time was short; a bored sniper could shorten it further. From where he sat, if a guard began shooting, Pyotr could be inside and hidden before the others could even remember which way to run.

There was a plan in place for their *cleansing*, and it was proceeding quickly. It had started with the healthiest men of the village—the army had destroyed the last remnants of the Resistance while they still lived on the Reservation. Then they opened the camps and proceeded to collect the sick and the old—the ones who would be of no use in the New Republic. That was when they still pretended that there might one day be a reintegration. No one believed those lies any more. The last adult led to the medical center took hope with her, leaving only the children and despair behind.

And when the last of the children are gone, what then? I guess they turn the camp into a museum. Or maybe they'll raze it and plow it over. Let the evergreens take it back, and leave no trace we ever lived in the Democratic Republic of Srpskepoje.

Remembering the photographs from his history texts, Pyotr felt he might have slipped back in time a hundred years. His country had never kept up with the times, however, and the world had turned a blind eye to Pyotr's little corner of creation. Breakaway independence had given way to a military junta and then to anarchy before being restructured as what? *As the camps? What else is there?* The movement within the tiny nascent nation to preserve the people of Pure Blood was all Pyotr knew of governments and order—all he knew of humanity and homeland. The ethnic cleansing that had once been a subject in school—an abstraction—was now his reality. *School. How long since they burned the school?* Pyotr did not know. Time was another luxury that had abandoned him. Now he measured his life in days remaining, not years lived. *One less today. Maybe tomorrow. Maybe one more after that.* He'd taken to staying up as much of the night as he could—lengthening the conscious hours of the day as a way of extending his life. It was a small act of rebellion against a counting clock.

Pyotr turned away from the evergreens and stared back at Block B. His last living friend, Vlaicu, sat defiantly in No Man's Land, fingers laced through the links. He wore a haunted, hungry look.

"Pyotr, come closer. Come sit with me." The withered young man beckoned him with a skeletal finger. His friend's appearance grew more frightening with each passing day. More withered. Paler. Whatever grudge the guards held against Pyotr's tribe paled when compared to the treatment Vlaicu's received. The leaders of the revolution proclaimed themselves to be people of Pure Blood, but they'd never said what made them superior to any other ethnic group. They only said that they were better than the "ticks and leeches." Vlaicu would not speak about where his people came from or why he thought they were segregated from Pyotr's tribe.

"What do you want, Vlaicu?" he hissed. "You're not allowed there. If they see you, they'll shoot you."

"They'll shoot me no matter what. Come here."

"If I move they might see me."

"They *always* see you, Pyotr."

Pyotr briefly considered staying put and letting his friend call to him from the fence. But Vlaicu was the last person who would still talk to him. He stuffed the fetish in the waistband of his pants, huddled up under his blanket and moved cautiously in a crouch toward the fence. "I was warm over there," he said.

"I am starving."

"So is everyone. So?"

"I would not ask, but . . ."

"But what? I have nothing to share. I can't afford to give you any more than I already have."

"Give me your hand," Vlaicu said. He wiggled his fingers. The flickering firelight reflected in Vlaicu's maroon eyes. Pyotr noticed flecks of gray at Vlaicu's temples. *That's not ash. His hair is turning gray! How old is he? My age? Older? Seventeen?*

Pyotr raised his hand, hesitating before grasping his friend's skeletal fingers.

"Please," Vlaicu begged. "I want to die holding hands."

Six months ago, Pyotr would have been shocked by his friend's statement. But he had learned much about death since then. Death came as a pair of dour men in white lab coats, dragging a sleeping woman from her bunk. It floated down upon them, belched into the sky from the top of smokestacks. No one died with dignity holding on to warm, comforting hands. He reached for Vlaicu's hands and held on.

"Why do you think you are here?" Vlaicu asked.

"Because the Avarkhur hate us. They say we steal babies and drink blood and—"

"Are these things true?"

"Of course not!"

"Would it make a difference if they were?"

Pyotr shook his head in frustration. "What does it matter? They're destroying everything *but* the stories."

Vlaicu closed his eyes as he held Pyotr's fingers. "So warm," he whispered.

Pyotr felt something draining out of him. He'd never touched Vlaicu before. It was forbidden. With the double fences and guards always watching, it was impossible. Yet, he realized he needed it. He wanted to feel a connection to something living. Instead, all he felt was the cold biting harder through the layers of tattered clothes he wore, stolen from corpses before they were dragged off by guards in thick woolen coats and heavy boots. Vlaicu's grip hurt.

"You're so cold. You need to build a fire or else you *will* die." Vlaicu's fingers tightened and Pyotr felt his hands draining of the meager warmth they'd stored up while inside his pockets. He tried to pull away.

Vlaicu's head dipped forward. "So hungry."

"Stop. You're hurting me. Please stop squeezing." Pyotr's hands were so cold that he barely felt his friend bite into his middle finger. Blood leaked from between Vlaicu's ragged, yellow teeth and dribbled down his chin dripping down onto the ground. "Stop! Vlaicu, STOP!"

A spotlight zeroed in on them. The shaded side of Vlaicu's head flew apart, spraying black patterns in the white snow. A rifle crack resounded in Pyotr's ear a half-second later. Vlaicu's limp hands slipped away from the fence as he fell back into the snow. Rolling out of the boy's slack mouth, the mangled remains of Pyotr's severed finger came to rest near the far fence—too far for rescue.

A siren wailed in the yard. Underneath its plaintive howl he heard the other children from his village running for the shelter of the barracks. He lay on his back clutching his hand, stifling his screams. Pain shot down the inside of his arm.

Blood trickled from the wound and dripped warmly on his neck. Sitting up, he caught a glimpse of the other members of Vlaicu's tribe huddled together, scraping at the snow and dirt with talon-like fingers to get under the barrier to get to his dead body. A boy stuck his spindly fingers through the links and teased Pyotr's severed digit closer. He eased it through the fence and studied it for a moment, red eyes reflecting in the spotlight. The boy leered with a maw full of black teeth as he popped it in his mouth like a candy. More gunshots. They scattered. A couple of Vlaicu's tribe fell down dead and the survivors dragged their bodies off, biting and tearing.

Pyotr's reverie broke and he pushed backward with his heels and an elbow through the sloppy, half-frozen mud and slush. From under the eaves of his barracks, he watched the guards in ripstop hazmat suits quell the chaos in Block B, snatching pieces of bodies from the hungry mouths of children. *How could they do that to their own?* In his fist, Pyotr gripped the leaking stump of his middle finger, trying to staunch the bleeding. He thought it should have hurt more, but mostly his hand just throbbed in time with his racing heart. Pulling his legs up he tried to become as small as possible. The bare bulb above the barracks door and the fire from the oil drum threatened to expose him. He needed to find a place to hide until the camp calmed down. Hide and not freeze.

As heavily armed guards cajoled the villagers back into their barracks, men in clean-suits appeared and started to sanitize the area where Vlaicu's remains had fallen, packing the bloody snow into barrels, laying down sawdust and salt. *Is that it? Is everyone in Block B infected with something? Did Vlaicu have it?* He looked at his bleeding hand. *Do I?*

He was starting to feel sick. His stomach cramped and the muscles in his neck tightened, sending pain creeping up the back of his skull. He squinted as the night grew brighter.

Light infected everything, making his head throb. Each flake of falling ash glowed as though it was a tiny floating ember. Closing his eyes, Pyotr imagined himself back in his village, safely nestled between his father and mother, his grandmother in the front pew of their ancient church wearing a blank mask and saying her prayers.

"It's through the barrier! There's one on the other side," one of the cleanup men shouted, his voice amplified by the speaker in his plastic facemask. The spotlight circles began tracking along the ground again, meeting, merging, and moving on, searching for someone to burn. Searching for him. "Contain it! Contain it now!" Men with machine guns ran for the gates separating the patrol zones from Block A.

Pyotr pushed himself harder against the building, trying to melt into the shadows, to slip into the liminal gap between the camp and black oblivion. A loose board behind him shifted and creaked as he pushed backwards. Turning around, he stuck his remaining fingers through a hole and pulled, ignoring the pain. His knuckles scraped across the rough wood; splinters jabbed into the backs of his hands. He pulled the board away from the building a few inches, wide enough for him to wriggle his emaciated body through and into the crawlspace beneath the barracks. He shoved the board back into place, sacrificing what was left of his ruined hands. Guards ran past barking at each other. He held on to hope that it was too dark to see the blood he'd spilled in the snow. He knew, of course, that hope could only last until the dawn or until they let loose the dogs. The inevitability of his capture moved a step closer with every throb of his pulse.

The retreating villagers' footsteps thundered on the floorboards above him as they were herded out onto the parade ground by guards. Muffled shouts and screams floated down like the dust falling between the cracks. All around, the howls of sirens and alarms screamed, and in the distance, one more sound—a low howl he could feel moving through the ground beneath him.

Pyotr dropped his head and prayed. He pulled the fetish out of his waistband and, closing his eyes, pictured him standing at the edge of the forest—the god's black, bearskin cloak absorbing the moonlight as he cast his lupine face upward and howled under the magnificent branches of his antlers. Snow fell from the pine needles as his voice shook the roots of the earth and made the trees tremble with longing and fear. He prayed to the god of his ancestors to deliver him—to raze the camp and deliver his people from captivity and destruction.

Standing impossibly tall in the low crawlspace, a vision of the god beckoned him to the rear of the building, away from the pounding footsteps and commands of his captors. It drew him to the wall closest the fences and pointed toward freedom. *Come now.* He felt the words tremble in his guts. *Come be with me.*

Pyotr fell on his back and kicked at the boards until one came loose, letting the night wind howl into the crawlspace. He squeezed out and scrambled for the gates. The night was bright and glowed with the snow and ash still hanging delicately in the air like distant stars in space. He pushed through, stumbling for the fence where he would die.

The gate in the far corner hung open, neglectfully abandoned by a guard rushing to contain . . . him. Pyotr dashed through it into No Man's Land. A spotlight washed his world in white oblivion. A voice crackled in a loudspeaker: "Target acquired. Southeast quadrant. Assemble in the gap. Assemble in the gap!"

Off in the distance, near the trees, the Wild God stood, waiting.

Pyotr leaped up the fence, scaling with a burst of panicked strength. From behind, he heard the muffled sounds of German shepherds being released from their leads. They cut the dogs' vocal cords to stifle barking, but he still recognized the hungry snapping sounds of their jaws. At least he thought it was the dogs, and not Vlaicu's people. He caught a whiff of a faintly familiar odor—a corrupted perfume. His stomach cramped again. *Go!* He heard the rattling of the guards opening the fence gates. The dogs would be on him. He'd seen this play performed before.

He tore at the fence links, pulling himself up to the concertina wire topping the barrier. He paused, imagining what the razors would do to his hands. *It'll be less than the dogs will do if I fall.* On the other side were the field, the tree line, and freedom among the sheltering cathedral of evergreens. Where He waited.

Another wave of nausea hit him as the stench of the flowers woven from brace arm to brace arm floated down upon him in the light breeze. He tried reaching up above the lines of blossoms beaming in his eyes like powerful red lights. Pyotr's naked wrist brushed against a bloom; the velvet petals burned. He fell backward off the fence back into the ashen mud in No Man's Land. The impact stifled his cry and he heard the dogs' clacking teeth getting nearer.

The sirens took on a sharper, more painful shrieking—a disorienting new sound that gave him vertigo. The world swam, and he lost his balance as the ground pitched like the deck of a boat in stormy seas. He pushed back up the fence as fast as he could in the yawing, slick yard.

He leaped up the fence, pausing just below the wire before vaulting himself over the top, grazing past the flowers and cutting razor barbs. His sleeve caught in a barb and tore free as his weary body went over. Behind him, he heard another gate angrily creak open. Looking back, he saw the black dogs clotting through the narrow opening, snapping and quietly snarling at each other. He sprinted for the evergreens, howling along the way as though he were leading His Great Hunt, running down apostates and heretics to be devoured by wolves and shat into Hell.

Halfway across the meadow, the dogs broke his ecstatic dream. He fell with them in a heap of fur and claws and mouths with teeth-ripping wounds that seared and burned. *The guards put the flowers in their food! It's in their food!* Pyotr howled above it all. "Have mercy! Have mercy, Dziki Bożewojtek!"

Dziki Bożewojtek was not a merciful god.

The guards came upon him and pulled away the hounds. Pyotr tried to move; the flesh of his arms and legs burned and sizzled with the dog's stinging saliva, and he was paralyzed. A man stood over him, the bore of his gun a blind, black eye staring down. Another pushed past the dogs and knelt beside Pyotr, his ruddy, soft face shining like a gilded icon reflecting in the sun. He plucked the fetish from Pyotr's fingers and threw it away into the night. He looked down at his prey with disgust.

"I am not this," Pyotr whispered. "I am not a monster."

"Yes you are. You're a fucking Radeszenie." Pyotr felt something sharp sting his chest, right above his heart. The guard leaned down on his bayonet. *"Soli Deo gloria! Amen!"*

The horned god's howl silenced. Pyotr heard the rustle of the pine branches in the wind. He turned his head to see the first hint of the blinding sunrise burning the horizon. Ashes fell on his face. He scattered in the light and blew away with them, descending the mountainside on the breeze, cast about the dying night on cold winds that couldn't be held back by fences and flowers, by men or gods.

CIUDAD DE LOS NIÑOS

The child leading Martín down the path looked back over her shoulder at him and, despite the summer heat, he shivered. An oily drop of sweat trickled down her temple, streaking the painted flower design outlining the blackened pockets of her eyes. Martín couldn't tell if the girl was pretty through the la calavera catrina death mask, but the blankness of her stare was clear enough. Her eyes were solemn and old and she looked at him the way a butcher looks at a Corriente cow—with a little pity, but mostly boredom. She frightened him. He would have dropped her sweaty little hand if she'd let him, but the girl held on tightly. She guided him through the rows of half-sized candy skulls set along the narrow dirt road. The calaveras de azúcar were baking in the hot sun, scenting the air with caramel. "Is it far, niña?" The girl smiled cheerlessly. The teeth painted around her lips framed her own tiny white incisors. *She looks like a shark*, he thought. *Dia de los Muertos isn't for another five months.*

Farther up the path, he saw more children in unseasonable corpse paint. Martín had always assumed the name of the place she was taking him—Ciudad de los Niños—was poetic, not literal. He had yet to see a single adult, however. He got his own start as a twelve-year-old working the secuestro express in Mexico City steering gringo tourists toward his partners' taxicabs. Like the girl was doing to him, he'd drag turistas by the hand through a confusing maze of alleyways, warning them along the way that it was imperative to be careful choosing how to get around the city. The drivers would then take the marks to Tepito and demand that they withdraw as much money from an ATM as they could if they didn't want to be left in the barrio bravo. As he got older, Martín graduated to extorting supplemental money from the families of secuestro express marks before breaking out into his own business for an entirely other class of victim— the kind who came to a trade with a suitcase full of money instead of an ATM card. He considered himself a legitimate businessman now—a broker—willing to serve as a neutral party to bring family members home alive and untouched. For a fee. But he'd never been called to work the Ciudad de los Niños. That didn't happen. They didn't bargain. If you went missing there, you were simply one of los desaparecidos— The Disappeared. That's what he'd always heard. Then his daughter disappeared, and he heard differently.

An image of Luz's mother, Narcisa, flitted through Martín's mind as he made his way to trade a briefcase full of money for his daughter. He remembered her panicked voice, yelling about how *her* daughter had been taken to Ciudad de los Niños. She told him some bruja—some witch—was holding her hostage. His ex-wife wasn't the only woman trying to take what was rightfully his. *Narcisa was the one who let her get snatched in the first place. No. No more Narcisa in our lives!*

Martín and the painted girl walked past a small band of young boys lounging against the side of a red adobe building. Their faces were also ornately decorated with flowers and spider webs, black tears and spades transforming their round babyish features into leering reflections of death. The boys stood guard with Kalashnikov rifles, their eyes tracking Martín as the girl led him by. He felt sized-up and categorized like they were deciding between pasture or killing floor. They let him pass, clearly put into the category of not-a-threat by the casual indifference of hardened soldiers. Not one of whom was older than fourteen.

A blast of hot air buffeted him with sand, carrying away the caramel smell. In its place he smelled something else.

Rot.

Martín refused to look down again, not wanting to know why the skulls were getting larger or why they no longer smelled like caramelizing sugar. He stared instead at the back of the girl leading him over the next hillock. Her bare shoulders were brown from the sun and coated with pale dust kicked up from the dried river bed that encircled the encampment. She looked like she hadn't bathed in weeks and carried a heavy scent of corruption along with her which the unmerciful wind swirled around him. He marched forward, toward his meeting, clutching his suitcase, reminding himself that it was only business.

Over the next rise, a small chapel surrounded by a series of smaller outbuildings appeared. Two more boys with Kalashnikovs guarded the entrance while other children milled about in the street. *So many.* Drawing closer, the guards sized him up. This time, he did not feel dismissed. He felt cowed. Itching sweat ran down his back in a constant rivulet like rain on a windshield. He wanted to rub at the small of his back, but he kept his hands at his sides where the children could see them, knowing beyond certainty that the gesture of reaching for the small of his back would get him killed. Normally he would have his gun nestled in the small of his back. But in his haste to get the ransom for Luz to the drop, he'd forgotten it in the car. *Everything's different when it's your own child.*

The guard to his left looked no older than eleven—the one on the right, maybe thirteen. Both boys were slender and wiry, dirty like his guide, their round faces padded with baby fat, and half his height. Still, they exuded the kind of menace he had felt from dealing with cartel soldiers and guerillas—the willingness to commit an act of violence was just a single misstep away—except these kids seemed without the limitation of conscience. *Life isn't cheap to them. Cheap still has some value. Life here is worthless. Even if I had my gun, could I kill a child? These children. Yes, I think I could kill them if it came to it.*

Around a corner appeared a group of girls and boys playing with a black and red soccer ball. As a boy kicked the ball toward Martín, another intercepted it, punting it away. The ball careened into the side of an outbuilding, bounced back and sent one of the painted skulls lining the street lolling out into their path. The boys squealed with delight and abandoned the ball for the head. Another kicked it in front of Martín. The group stopped and waited, staring silently at the adult in their midst, looking expectant like they wanted him to kick the new ball back into play. He looked down at what had been offered to him. The head was painted white in the same Dia de los Muertos style as the children's faces. It was not made of sugar, however. A roughly hewn neck, caked brown with dried blood and mud faced him. The ivory color of a budding vertebra peeked through behind the collapsed fold of a trachea. Martín's guide scowled disapprovingly and kicked the severed head back to the boys, barking in a little girl's squeak, "¡Ponla donde estaba!" They immediately did as they were told and put it back before returning to their game.

"Por aquí," the girl said. "La Bestia le espera adentro."

La Bestia! Martín wanted to ask if he couldn't just give the girl the money instead. But he kept it to himself. *¡Sé hombre!* he told himself. *Be a man! You'll pay, and you'll get Luz back and everything will be fine because you were a fucking man and you did what it takes to protect what's yours.* "Por aquí," his guide repeated, pointing with the machete she held in her other hand. *Jesus! Was she carrying that the whole time? Why didn't I see it?* She still hadn't let go of him, and Martín wondered whether he'd be able to break her tiny grip if she tried to pull him into a machete swing.

Willing his legs to work, he took a step forward. The girl nodded, commanding the boys standing guard outside the chapel to open the doors. Together they walked through the portal and up the aisle like a father leading his daughter to her waiting fiancé. Except, the girl was leading *him* toward a wooden throne atop the dais where, in any other church, there would be an altar. She was pulling him toward the woman who held his daughter captive. Delivering him to La Bestia.

The woman's head was framed in a garland of red roses woven into the thick black hair cascading down her bare shoulders and over her red ruffled bosom. Thorns scraped tiny crimson lines in the skin of her exposed alabaster cleavage. Martín's gaze would have lingered at the buxom chest that rose and fell softly with La Bestia's breath if it weren't for the fact that her tattooed face terrified him and kept him in thrall. Delicate white lines like the outlines of teeth were permanently drawn on her full lips. Her nose and eyes were tattooed black, while around them soft swirling lines drew attention to the intricate roses tattooed on her chin and at her forehead where her hair parted. Cold blue eyes stared out from the black holes.

"Bienvenidos." La Bestia held out a lace-gloved hand to Martín. The girl gave him away, placing his hand in hers. Martín did his best to hold the contents of his bladder at the rough scratch of the woman's grip. "Me complace que usted está aquí," she said. Behind the death mask, she actually did look happy to see him. *As happy as a wolf about to eat a jackrabbit.* Without releasing her hold on him, La Bestia leaned back in her chair forcing him to half-kneel on the step in front of her if he didn't want to sprawl across her lap. He definitely did not want to touch any more of the woman than he had to. His guide pried the suitcase from his other hand and stepped back to the first row of pews.

"Tengo t-tu dinero."

"Si. ¿Y por lo tanto . . . ?" She challenged him to ask her for something. To beg.

"Please. I do not . . ."

"Do you know who we are?" she asked.

"You are The Beas—"

"Who *we* are." She tightened her grip, grinding his knuckles painfully against each other.

"Esta es la Ciudad de los Niños."

"And what is the City of Children to you?" she asked. Kneeling near her legs, Martín's senses were overwhelmed. She was all he could see. He smelled the roses in her hair— her sweat, her sex. He felt caught in a web next to a sac of eggs waiting to hatch.

"This is where the lost—"

"None of my bebés are lost," she said. "They are all seen and heard."

Martín wanted to fall back—to scramble away—but she held tight. He winced at the strength of her hot dry grip. "But this place . . ."

"Is the womb of a new nation. Every child here is a wanted child."

"The heads . . ."

"Each one is a birth from death." La Bestia gestured to her left at a painted head resting on a shelf beneath a reclining porcelain doll. "That is the head of Padre Marcial Evaristo. From that óvulo I gave birth to my sons, Raul, Ricardo, and Carlos. Evaristo was scheduled to be sent back to Rome, but instead, he resides here where he can watch my sons grow." She pointed at another skull on a shelf beneath Evaristo's. "This cabeza belonged to a pimp named Israel Fonseca Moreno. He gave me the girl who stands behind you now and a half a dozen others. All baptized in blood. All risen from the graves these men and women dug for them and reborn from my body. All of the men and women who decorate my

city are paying the price for betraying la sangre de la Raza."
She took a deep breath and cocked her head at an angle,
considering him for a small moment.

"Just like you," she said.

Martín's heart raced. A spike of pain shot through his left
armpit. *Better to have a heart attack or my head chopped off?*
"I haven't betrayed anyone," he protested. "I get people back
to their families. I get them back alive. I'm a neutral broker."

"After you extort them for their life savings and leave
them destitute. You think you are a predator. But you are
just a parasite drinking la sangre de la nación."

"I brought you money."

"And for that you want what exactly?"

"The deal. To leave here. To take my daughter and leave."

"That she is the second thing you mention explains why
you will never leave." La Bestia released Martín's hand and
gestured toward the rear of the chapel. The guide who led
him tossed aside the suitcase and opened the door. On the
other side waited a congregation of children who filed into
the building, taking seats in the pews. Martín considered
making a run for it, pushing through, but he knew that the
boys with the rifles waited just on the other side of the door.

"Are you ready to pay for your sins?" La Bestia asked.

"I brought you the money you demanded."

"And the tribute is apreciado. Your money will buy food
for the children and ammunition for their weapons. But
money is not the only debt you owe."

Martín looked over his shoulder at the child approaching
him. He barely recognized his daughter dressed in a delicate
white dress with her face painted in a death rictus like the
other children. "¿Mi Luz?"

A pair of children marched behind her holding a white
silk pillow upon which rested a gleaming new machete. La
Bestia stood up and spread her arms wide in a gesture of
welcome toward her soldiers. Martín tried to feint sideways,

but three children from the front pew leaped up to stop him. He wondered how many kids it would take to hold him. He couldn't wait around to find out. He bucked off their small hands, grabbed Luz by the arm, and rushed toward the front doors plucking the machete off the pillow as he passed. A howl of anger went up among the children. He swung the machete menacingly, but none of them backed away. They could not be intimidated.

Glancing back over his shoulder, expecting La Bestia to be coming for him with her own blade, he saw her standing in place, smiling. Martín wished she would make some kind of threat, show that she was concerned that he would get away with his daughter. She didn't. That worried him more than the children with the rifles.

She already knew how this would end.

"I got your confession, puta! I know what you did. I'll bring the Policía Federal back here and show them the heads and they'll shut down your revolución before you can—"

La Bestia kicked a head from the top step of the dais down the aisle at Martín. "Tell this one. Él va a escuchar." Martín shuffled back away from the head that stopped in front of him face up. The man's badge glinted up from where it had been pinned to the skin of his forehead.

A shirtless young boy with ribs Martín could count through his skin lunged forward with a knife, clumsily stabbing toward his guts. Martín dodged and got stuck in the hip instead. He yelped in pain. Beneath the paint, a dark look of amusement showed on the boy's face as he drew back to stab again. Martín swung the machete, chopping into the skinny boy's shoulder. The child went from a hardened soldier with a death-dealer's stare to a shrieking infant in the time it took for the blade to open his arm up. Horrified, Martín's guts threatened revolt. *I can't fucking do it! She's using children because no one can do it. They'll do the terrible things she wants because they don't know any better, and she'll win because that sound . . . that sound!*

Luz struggled to break his grip on her arm. He swung his daughter up in front of him, betting that the cult wouldn't take the chance of hitting the girl. She howled in protest, kicking her feet, as he clutched her tightly around the waist. "Come at me and you'll hit her." Shoving through the children, he kicked at the doors, swinging them open, startling the guards outside.

Turning to take another look back, he saw La Bestia's placid countenance break. Her glare sent a shiver through Martín's body despite the summer heat. He began to run backward as best as he could, hoping the first band of children he'd seen leaning against the stucco wall had chosen to attend the service instead of waiting for him over the rise. Relief danced at the edges of his panic as he crested the hill and they weren't there.

Hefting his daughter up over his shoulder, he turned and sprinted the rest of the way to the car. The stolen machete slipped from his sweaty grasp as he went. *Fuck it! I just need to get to the car. We'll get away in the car. We'll head toward Texas and we'll disappear. Just you and me, Luz.* He didn't feel the bite of the blade in the back of his leg at first—just warmth. It wasn't until the second, deeper cut that the pain reached his conscious mind and his brain replied with the command to fall. Martín crashed face first into the dirt, landing on his daughter. Her knees drove into his chest, pushing all the air from his body. He gasped, inhaling a lungful of dirt instead of air, drowning on dry land. She kicked at him and scrambled out from under his weight. "Luz," he choked, spitting mud. The car was only meters away. He could see freedom.

His daughter stood over him staring down with the same blank look that his guide had given him less than an hour earlier. She waited, loosely holding the wet blade at her side like a favorite blanket dragged everywhere. Martín started to pull himself toward the car. Luz stood still. The footsteps of the congregation soon followed as children came running over the hill, surrounding him. They encircled him wordlessly, each one sharing his daughter's quietly malicious gaze. When La Bestia walked into the ring, two boys jumped in after her and roughly flipped Martín over onto his back.

With the sun behind her, La Bestia's garland of roses framed her corpse-white face in a bloody red halo. She gently positioned Luz in front of Martín. The girl raised the machete over her head. She hesitated a moment, looking to the woman with an expression of concern. "Igual que con mamá, pero esta vez será más fácil," La Bestia reassured her. The girl smiled sweetly.

"No, Luz! I'm your papa! Don't do this. I don't care what she's made you do. I love you!"

"Niños, ¿Qué el amor?" La Bestia asked the children.

A chorus of voices answered, "¡Amor es lo que hacemos por los demás!"

"Muy bien. Love *is* what we do for others." She smiled and Martín lost hope.

"You're insane," he said.

La Bestia looked into Martín's eyes. "Don't despair," she said. "I only want your head. I'll leave your heart for Luz. Because she loves you."

THE BLOOD AND THE BODY

Em leaned in through the open window and gave her boyfriend a kiss, leaving a black impression of her thin lips on his cheek. "Why are we driving, Jay? You too good for the T all of a sudden?" Joshua's car was rusting, noisy, and cold, but it was paid for and reliably started in any temperature above freezing. While she didn't date guys based on what kind of car they drove, she preferred the subway to his rolling tetanus-mobile. It wasn't the car as much as the freedom. If they took the subway, she didn't have to rely on anyone but herself for a ride home.

"It's a limo kind of night, doncha think?" he said, winking. She stared at him for a moment through narrowed eyes. On the other hand, if they drove, they could stay until closing instead of having to leave early to catch the last train. Dressed as she was in Dr. Martens, ripped tights, a corset top and black dancer's shrug, she looked like a crazed cyberpunk ballerina who'd kicked her way out of the Matrix, and not the kind of person psychologically capable of the girlish skip and hop that carried her around Joshua's car. She jerked open the car door with a crunch and a loud screech and plopped into the passenger seat. Before she was able to pull her door completely shut, he hit the gas and pulled into traffic.

"At least let me get in the car, okay," she said, leering at him with her easy, black-lipped smile. He grunted and steered into the far lane without looking back. She pulled her feet up onto the seat and sat quietly for a couple of minutes bobbing her head to Dinah Cancer's crazed screech on the 45 Grave CD. When he didn't turn the corner where she expected him to, she began paying attention to the passing scenery instead of the music. After the third set of lights it was clear he had no intention of reversing course toward Central Square. "What the hell, Jay? You promised we were going to ManRay."

"Don't freak out. We gotta make a stop somewhere else first." He was bouncing his knee to a different, faster beat than the song on the stereo. She had never known him to get spun out before they went out, but it *was* a special night. Em supposed he was as excited as she for their last trip to ManRay. Difference was she'd planned on sharing her scores; she wasn't a selfish prick.

"Come on, turn around! I have to work every night for the rest of the week; this is my last chance."

"You've been a million times. Tonight isn't going to be any different. Trust me. This is going to be way better."

She leaned over and traced his arm with a black polished nail. Blowing her warm, cinnamon-scented breath on his neck, she cooed, "I'll make sure you remember this trip more than the other million put together." She darted her tongue in his ear and let out a long sigh meant to tickle him in his reptilian brain. Despite the warmth of her exhalation and the obvious increasing tightness in his pants, he continued driving away from her preferred destination.

"Trust me. This is going to be better than all the other times we've gone to the club put together."

She was unmoved by his hyperbole. "I just bet. So where *are* we going?"

"Tchort's." He turned a corner onto a side street, headed for the highway on-ramp. Em groaned and flopped back into her seat. "What's wrong with Tchort?" he asked.

"You seriously have to ask? His stupid fake name for one.

Second, he's an asshole. Doesn't it bother you that he won't stop staring at my tits?"

He glanced at her pushed up china-white cleavage and said, "Can you blame him? You got nice tits."

She folded her arms across her bosom and sat fuming, waiting for him to slow down, pull over and argue with her. All she'd have to do is whine a little, cuddle some, and he'd see that taking her to the club was his only real option. But first, he had to make the small resignation that would lead to his larger defeat and pull over. Instead, he steered the car onto the highway. He said he was certain that ManRay, or something like it, would reopen somewhere else in a few months. There'd always be clubs to go to. This party was a once-in-a-lifetime event.

"Doesn't Tchort live in JP? You're headed the wrong way, Crankenstein."

His head snapped around and he regarded her with a look approaching contempt before returning to face the road. Clearly, he'd steeled himself for her opposition. "We have to get someone."

"Who?"

"The Lamb," he said.

"Who or what is 'The Lamb'?"

"Dunno. Some friend of Tchort's he asked me pick up. She lives in the sticks."

Em pulled her seatbelt across her lap, riding the rest of the way in pouting silence staring out the window as the city imperceptibly yielded to the suburbs. Twenty minutes later, Jay pulled off the highway and wound through a boring residential neighborhood that, at nine p.m., had rolled up its sidewalks for the night hours ago. He parked the car in front of an unassuming ranch-style house and beeped the horn twice. Em felt like they'd driven out to the country and half-expected the porch light to come on, followed by a wild-eyed guy in a bathrobe holding a shotgun. Instead, out of the house bounded a girl with Manic Panic red hair tied up in pigtails and a candy-goth outfit that made Em's teeth ache with nascent cavities. The girl also made her feel a little tickle below the belt. Then she remembered why they'd made the detour. Picking up Lamb, as hot as she was, was the last nail in her true desire's coffin.

The girl skidded to a stop outside the car, declaring, "I'm Lamb!" as if that introduction was all anyone needed to know about her. Em threw a look at Jay, silently imploring him to abandon this chick and resume the original plan. She wouldn't hold it against him if he turned around now and drove back to Cambridge. Instead, he nodded for her to let the girl in.

She shoved open the car door without mentioning to Lamb that she might want to stand back. The girl skipped away from the swinging steel like she floated on a puff of air. Em crawled out and pulled her seat forward—Jay's was one of the last two-door sedans left in Creation. Grinning, Lamb scrambled in without complaint or comment. Em watched the girl's short skirt slide up revealing the bottom half of her peach-shaped ass as she bent down to duck under low clearance. Em resisted the urge to climb into the back right behind her and instead let the front seat fall into place before plopping in beside Jay. Lamb slid to the center of the back seat, leaned forward, and launched into a peppy monologue about nothing that lasted all the way into Boston.

It took a while, but Jay finally found a berth for his Ford landship near Tchort's apartment. Em noted they could see the Forest Hills T-station from where they parked. She'd already decided that no matter how well the evening went, she wasn't leaving with her boyfriend. He kept stealing glances in the rear view at Lamb, not even trying to hide his fascination with her. She understood why he couldn't keep his eyes off of her, but that didn't lessen the sting. If Lamb was supposed to be Tchort's "date" for the evening, Em figured she'd hijack the girl back to the club when she slipped away herself. It'd be a double score, denying both Jay and Tchort their pleasure for the night. If the girl could fuck, it'd be a hat trick.

On the sidewalk in front of the apartment building, however, Em felt a tinge of curiosity that needed satisfaction. The windows on all three floors were blocked with opaque red blinds that glowed like bloody membranes. She could feel the beat of several different songs throbbing into the night and her heart sped up a touch with the excitement of standing before a building that felt like a living thing. The party apparently spilled onto every floor of the triple-decker. She couldn't imagine how Tchort expected to host a party this big in a neighborhood as "densely settled" as his. That the Boston P.D. would come shut the whole thing down seemed like an inevitability. There was no way a rager this loud and obnoxious could go on uninterrupted. Except the houses on either side of his building were dark. How was it there was no one home to complain on a weeknight? She continued to fantasize about a raid and the look on Tchort's face when the police shut his soiree down as she climbed the steps to the front door. The club could wait for a little while, she told herself.

Lamb ran up ahead of them, pushing through the front doors without waiting for her companions. "There goes your date," Em said to Jay. He screwed up his face with apparent frustration.

"Don't be like that. Let's go in and have some fun." He held the door open for her as though a late show of chivalry made up for hijacking her evening. "Next time we'll go wherever you want." She brushed past, turning her back to him so he couldn't steal another glance at her chest. No matter how she found her way home tonight, there wasn't going to be a next time.

The humid heat in the stairwell was oppressive, and the light rhythm she'd felt outside took her breath away as she stood in the red-hued hall. The door to the first floor apartment hung open. Inside, Em saw people milling around with red Solo cups in their hands, laughing and shouting over the music. The throb of some remixed bland Reggae band shook the walls and a couple inside did some kind of horrendous, rhythmless dance they should have been ashamed to be seen attempting. Most just stood around, however, doing what people did at a party like this—nothing. A trustafarian girl with dreadlocks stared through the door at her and scowled. Em stuck out her tongue.

"Up up up!" Jay shouted as he took her hand and pulled her toward the stairs.

The island beat was soon eclipsed by the sound of some ironic alt-rock band pouring through the open door of the second-floor apartment. The view was similar, but these people were more animated. A novelty disco ball hanging from the ceiling flashed and made everyone sparkle. Still, she wasn't dressed for beer pong and quarters. "It's bullshit," she shouted over the music. "Can we go now?" Jay didn't answer, pulling her up the next flight of stairs instead. She threw a glance over her shoulder as they went and thought she saw the people on the second floor staring out the door at her.

Climbing higher, the music changed again, this time to a darkwave band doing a decent cover of "Paint It Black." Lamb stood at the top of the stairs, waiting with a drink in each hand, declaring, "It's about time." She handed the cups to the couple before disappearing back inside. Jay tipped his cup in a silent toast and smirked.

"Yeah, that totally makes the hour drive to pick her up worth it," Em said. "One drink."

"We're going to have a séance or some shit at midnight and I don't want to miss it."

"Like I care about Tchort's little coven and their spells." She wiggled her fingers in the air like she was swirling around faerie dust.

"It's not a coven. They call it a 'grotto,'" he said.

"I care?"

"Come on. It's going to be fun. Trust me." He sighed and ushered her into the party. Behind them the door slammed and she thought she might have heard a deadbolt snap shut. She glanced over her shoulder but people had filled in the space and she couldn't see the door, let alone whether or not the knob was twisted.

Black Visqueen sheeting covered the walls and the lamps in the apartment were covered with crimson scarves that imbued the space with a smoking, warm glow that matched the temperature. If she squinted, it almost seemed like she was at the club. Deathrockers, punks, and people in BDSM gear filled the space. Some danced while others performed small acts of consensual cruelty upon one another. A couple in the corner were making out so vigorously Em wondered whether they were about to screw or cannibalize each other. Tchort stepped in front of the scene, breaking the spell.

"All nocturnal people are welcome here!" he said, holding out his hands in a mock benediction, sloshing a little of the drink in his right hand on the floor. Em tried to hide her contempt, but failed when he smiled at her tits. At over six feet, he had to look down to make eye contact with almost anyone, but he invariably missed that mark with her, aiming low. His smile was nearly all pink and gray gums, with tiny yellow teeth that were lost in his alligator-sized maw of a mouth. "Always nice to see you, Marianne," he said, using her full name. "Drink?" He extended his cup toward her.

She looked at the golden liquid like it was a glass of piss, or more accurately, a cheap chardonnay swimming with Rohypnol. She tilted the cup she already held to her mouth and gulped at whatever it was Lamb had given her. Finishing, she said, "Where's the bar?" Lamb appeared with another pair of cups, pressing one into her hand.

"Ask, and ye shall—"

"Whatever." She took another long draught, downing half of the drink before realizing it was vodka and ginger ale and something else a little bitter. She daubed at her black lips and smiled a "thank you" at the girl before resting her fist over her cleavage and extending her middle finger. Tchort's expression clouded briefly before splitting again into his fleshy grin.

"I hope you have a good time," he said. "This is a very special night for us all; the Grand Climax is at hand!" He tilted his body in an attempt at a gentlemanly bow, looking Em in the face for the first time that she could remember. The whites of his eyes had a jaundiced cast that matched the crappy wine in his hand. His gaze shifted to Lamb and he licked his lips like a cartoon wolf at a burlesque show. He took the girl's free hand in his and kissed her palm with open lips.

Em grabbed Lamb by the elbow, yanking her away from Tchort and said, "Show me where to refill this." Lamb led her toward the kitchen. Behind them, she thought she heard Tchort say something to Jay that sounded like "delicious." Her stomach turned at the thought of his mouth touching any part of her body, erogenous or not. But then, he hadn't tongued *her* hand.

It seemed everyone wanted a taste of Lamb.

After a couple more drinks, Em enlisted the help of the apartment wall to keep her upright. She closed her eyes, trying to pretend that she didn't feel light-headed. The night was shit and drink wasn't helping her attitude. In fact, it was making it worse. The apartment was getting hotter and more humid and the thumping of the music pressed against her eardrums like the pressure of sliding down into deep water. The way she felt, however, it was too late to cut herself off. She did her best to stay conscious and not slump on the floor like some black balloon low of helium.

"Hey, you okay?" Lamb asked. As the evening had progressed, the girl had been the only bright spot. The party was all right, but the crowd was unfamiliar—despite having thought she knew everyone in the scene in Boston—and she felt isolated in it. Lamb alone kept her company when all of the other partiers ignored her.

"I'm fine," she said. "Just tired." She was also disappointed that her fantasy of the police putting an end to the revels never materialized. She craved Tchort's humiliation almost as much as she wanted to leave and join her friends at ManRay. Still, she hadn't found it in herself to go—she doubted she could remember how to find the front door let alone the subway.

"Drink this!" Lamb pressed a cool drink into her palm. Thirst and sufficiently lowered inhibitions handily defeated her desire to sober up enough to leave. She tipped the cup to her lips. It was good. Cool and strong and sweet. Just what she liked.

"I think I need some fresh air," she said after a sip. "Take me outside?" She'd meant it as a double entendre, but couldn't tell if in her state she'd said it seductively or just slurred the words like some old soak asking for change at a red light. Lamb smiled and slipped an arm around Em's waist, nestling her face near the taller woman's breast. Instead of taking her toward the front door and the sidewalk downstairs, she led her through the back, past the kitchen and the line for the bathroom and the bedrooms. Em wondered what had happened to all of Tchort's furniture as they threaded through the apartment. The place was cleaned out. She glanced to the side as they passed a bedroom. Inside, she thought she saw a twist of writhing bodies on the floor. And then before she could reconcile the image, she was standing in the cool night air on the third floor balcony. Blinking, she tried to clear her head and get her balance so she wouldn't topple over the railing into the brick "yard" below. The image of the bedroom swam behind her eyes. No bed or furniture of any kind—just naked people and a hint of a glimpse of a design painted on the floor.

"Had a little too much?" She opened her eyes and an image of Jay standing at the opposite end of the balcony smoking a cigarette swam in and out of focus. Em shook her head trying to suss out if he'd followed them or been out there already. She couldn't remember seeing him since they'd arrived. How long ago that had been, however, was something she couldn't wrap her head around either.

"I just need . . . some air. It's . . . warm in there."

Jay pushed off the rail. The weather-worn boards beneath their feet trembled at his steps making Em feel for a moment like it had given way and she was falling. She blinked until the multiple images of him shrank to a single approaching form. Despite her plans to remain in control, the evening felt like a defeat. She surrendered. "I don't feel good, Jay. Take me home?" She leaned forward, resting her head on his shoulder.

He pinched her chin between thumb and forefinger, lifting her face so he could look her in the eye and said, "No."

"But I said I don't—"

"No," he repeated. "Tonight is important to Tchort. He's been very generous and you're being rude."

She felt tears welling in her eyes. How had she gotten here? Four drinks? Maybe five. She could hold her liquor and drank more out at the clubs. Someone had to have slipped her something. She tried to remember if she'd ever taken a drink from Tchort or someone else at the party she didn't know well. She could only ever remember Lamb serving her.

"Please? Take me home," she whispered.

Jay kissed her. She tasted whiskey and clove cigarettes as his tongue probed her mouth and felt the world swim off kilter again. She wrapped her arms around him as much for stability as she did out of desire. His hands slipped over her body searching for the places that pleased them. She felt his fingers gliding, squeezing, probing her flesh with insistence. Although, her passion was dampened by the effect of whatever-it-was rushing through her bloodstream, poisoning her brain with confusion and lethargy, she reached for the front of his pants. Another set of hands blocked access to his fly. She opened her eyes and pulled away, seeing Lamb behind him, kissing her boyfriend's shoulder and fondling him. Jay sidled out from between the women. He laid a hand gently on the back of Em's neck and he pushed her toward the girl. Lamb eagerly filled the empty space. Lamb's mouth tasted like rum and sugar; her skin smelled like leather and orchids. Em fell again, this time into a deep wave of lust that left her memory of the balcony feeling unreal and ephemeral.

Hard, smooth boards groaned beneath her as she arched her back, a shivering, electric Jacob's ladder skipping up from the crack of her ass to the base of her skull. Lamb's hot hands and velvet tongue explored her body. She opened her eyes to see a red-shrouded light in the corner, not the moon above them. When had they gone inside? Lamb's crimson hair stuck up from between her thighs and Em forgot about the moon and the night on the balcony, thinking instead of her missing clothes for only an instant before another swell of pleasure upended the room and she drifted on the wave away again, into another time where the voices chanted.

Corpus edimus!

Lamb's hands on her thighs, sliding over goosepimpling flesh.

Sanguinem bibmus!

Lamb's mouth on her pussy and a slender finger in her ass.

Gloria tibi, Domine Lucifere!

Kneeling behind the girl, hands on her china white buttocks, Lamb's elongated coccyx extending out of her body like a tiny tail. Em looked up and gave The Lamb an infernal kiss.

Per omnia saecula saeculorum!

Into the deepening flood again.

Rege Satana!

Em awoke in a corner of the room, slick with sweat and naked. In the center of a red seven-pointed star painted on the floor, a man in a black wolf mask thrust himself into some woman whose eyes rolled like a cow in a slaughterhouse kill box. She felt the arms embracing her tighten reassuringly as she took a startled breath and tried to get to her feet. Behind her, Lamb whispered, "Sit still. He's almost done." The man continued fucking until his flabby butt cheeks clenched and he pulled out and tried to come on the girl like a porn actor, but slipped and ended up spilling his seed on the floorboards. Lamb gave a loud throaty laugh. The man stood up and ripped off his mask, shooting her a nasty look. He yanked a red satin robe out of the hand of another masked figure standing nearby.

"Shut up, bitch!" Tchort said. Em could barely hear him over the music and chanting of the masked men and women standing in the circle around the room. But Lamb's laughter was right in her ear and eased her discomfort. Still, the throb of the house and the heat conspired to steal her breath. Gasping, she tried again to stand. Lamb held on. He slipped the robe over his head, concealing his flagging erection, and stomped toward them.

Em held up a hand to ward him away. "Back off," she choked.

"Think that's funny, cunt?"

Hands fell upon her and Em felt herself yanked up from the floor. Jay twisted her around roughly and restrained her with hands clamped tightly on her upper arms. She struggled, but couldn't slip from his grasp. He shushed her. Tchort leaned down and grabbed Lamb by a wrist, jerking her to her feet.

"Leave her the fuck alone!" Em yelled.

Tchort wrenched Lamb's arm and shoved her into the heptagram, where she fell on her knees. A pair of black clad acolytes parted, revealing an altar adorned with a collection of candles and dime store Halloween props. Tchort strode toward it and plucked a real-enough-looking dagger from the table. He turned toward the star, grinning gums and porcine eyes burning with malevolence.

"What are you doing? Stop!"

Tchort glared at Em, his face filled with stupid hate and said, "She's The Lamb, Marianne. Blood must be spilled."

Em wrenched her body, freeing herself from her boyfriend's grip. She sprinted toward the girl. Her head pounded with hangover, she swooned for a second before the room righted itself and she made it in between them, pulling the sobbing girl to her feet. Tchort took a step forward with his knife. Em pointed a black-nailed finger at him and he stopped. Despite his size, Tchort was a lazy coward. She'd told him off a dozen times in the past and he'd never had the balls to stand up to her. Even naked and surrounded by his "flock" she wasn't about to let him threaten her or anyone else without a fight. "You're not doing a goddamned thing to her. We're getting out of here."

Lamb pulled Em's face around with a hand and kissed her delicately on the mouth. Before Em could argue that it was not the time, the drowning sensation returned for real and she coughed, trying to ask, "why?" as she felt the knife pierce her chest.

The girl smiled madly and pulled the blade from Em's body. Behind her she heard Jay say, "I could bring you to the party against your will, but you had to enter the sigil freely." He said something else she couldn't hear as the sound of the world all around her faded to nothing but a quickening heart throb. She felt his hand in her hair and hot pain as he jerked her head back and dragged a knife along her throat, opening it like a blooming flower. Blood sprayed and splashed Lamb's face and bare chest and the lights dimmed. Em fell to her knees. And to her side. And into the darkness a final time.

Jay held his breath. The CD in the player ended, the black-robed members of Tchort's grotto stopped chanting, and silence descended upon the room. He watched his girlfriend's blood spill onto the floor and listened as she struggled to breathe. Soon, she stopped, and all he could hear was the thump of the music playing at the party downstairs. A cheer went up from below as someone presumably landed their ping pong ball in a glass of beer. The members of the grotto pulled a few strips of Visqueen off the wall and moved in to wrap Em's body. Tchort stood in the corner staring blankly at the dead woman on his bedroom floor.

"I don't understand," Jay whispered.

Lamb absently traced a finger in the blood staining her chest, drawing a down-turned star over her sternum and laughed. She reached out and painted a line from Jay's forehead down his nose and touched his lips. He turned his head and wiped at his mouth with disgust. "What were you waiting for?" she asked. "Thunder and smoke and the fire of the summoned Beast rising up out of the floorboards, come to bestow upon you his infernal blessings? You're cute, but dumb," she said. "Did it ever occur to you that Lucifer is about as interested in your worthless soul as he is in buying the Brooklyn Bridge? Or maybe—just maybe—there's no such thing as the Devil. Either way, you killed a girl for no good reason. Wasted her, literally."

She tasted the tip of her finger and turned to leave. Scooping up her clothes, she sauntered into the hall and turned for the door. Jay thought he saw her vestigial tail wag a little before she turned and said over her shoulder, "I had fun, though."

THE BOY WHO DREAMT HE WAS A BAT

A breeze blew across the water making ripples that sparkled under the blue sky like diamonds, but the boy was still afraid. He stood by the car, away from the sand at the edge of the pond, clinging to a library book and wanting to climb back in to wait for his stepfather to grow tired of fishing. They'd only just gotten to the pond, though, and he knew that would take a while. His grandfather could fish all day long, sitting on the shore, watching the bobber float on the tiny swells, dipping down as the "bait robbers," as he called them, nibbled at the worms speared on his hook. His stepfather had never come with them on even one of those fishing trips. But today, he'd gotten the boy up early, telling him they were going to go and how great it would be. He hoped that Bobby grew tired of it faster than Grandpa did.

It was a long drive to get there, and Bobby had spent the bulk of it telling the boy how excited he was going to be when he saw this secret fishing hole. How full of bass and walleye it was, and how they were going to catch all of them and Mom would be so excited that men had brought home dinner. He emphasized "men" as if including the boy in the word with him was a conspiratorial bond. The boy knew, though, that Bobby didn't think of him as a man. Bobby made fun of him for playing Barbie and Ken dolls with his best friend, Heidi, from up the street. He called him a "puss" and teased him about being a girl. He didn't care. Heidi was nice and shared her toys, even if they were mostly Barbie dolls. More importantly, her parents would always let him stay as long as he wanted. If he was there at lunchtime, they didn't send him home; they made him a sandwich. Bobby never fixed him lunch. He said the boy was six and a half and he could make his own peanut butter sandwich if he was hungry. Sometimes, the boy spent all day with them, pretending out loud that Barbie and Ken were having adventures, while pretending in his head that Heidi was his twin sister and that he lived with her and her parents and would never ever have to go home to Bobby again. Barbies, baby dolls, or makeup, he'd play with anything in the world if he could just stay there.

His stepfather walked to the edge of the water with a single pole in one hand and a tackle box in the other. He set everything down in the sand and motioned for the boy to come closer. "Come on. You can't help me from all the way over there." He opened up the box and started rooting around in it, looking for something.

Grandpa never had to search for anything. He always knew exactly where everything he wanted was.

The boy clutched his book a little tighter and stammered, "Can I . . . Can I . . ."

"Hurry up."

"Can I wear the . . . life preserver?" The boy had seen one in the back of the car. It was there for when his mom wanted to go in the boat when they drove out to the ocean. She couldn't swim, and always wore it. The boy couldn't swim either, and he was scared of the water. They'd tried enrolling him in swim lessons, but his fear overwhelmed him and nothing they tried to teach him took root. His mom eventually gave up sending him.

Bobby looked up with a knitted brow and asked, "Why in hell would you want to wear one of those?"

"In case I fall in."

Bobby laughed at him as walked over to the boy. The boy stepped back and bumped against the car door. It was unexpectedly hot through his thin shirt and the door handle jabbed in between his shoulder blades, making him take an involuntary step toward his stepfather. Bobby grabbed his thin arm and pulled him toward the beach. The boy almost fumbled his book, but he managed to hold on.

"You don't want to wear a life preserver. Don't you know how they work?"

The boy tried to pull his arm out of Bobby's hand, but not too hard. He'd learned what struggling earned him. "Mom wears one. If you fall in with one of those on, then you float on top of the water."

"Well, yes. That's true. But your mom is bigger than you are. With little kids, it depends on how you go in. If you fall in the water head first, your body isn't heavy enough to flip you over and you'll float with your legs sticking up in the air instead of your head. A kid your size'll drown quicker with one than without." The boy wasn't sure if Bobby was teasing, but the idea of his head being *held* under the water was terrifying enough. It put a knot in his throat and he didn't ask again.

Bobby dragged him over to the small beach and let go. The boy sat down reluctantly. Grandpa always brought a big towel for him to sit on. Bobby didn't. The boy didn't want to get his pants dirty; he would get in trouble for that. He remembered how Bobby had shouted the time he'd discovered the grass stains from when the boy and Heidi had gone to the big hill behind the Tildens' barn and tumbled down it over and over. They'd laughed and shouted, "As yooooou wiiiish!" as they rolled and bounced in the tall soft grass. Both of them had come up with dark green stains on their clothes. He didn't know what Heidi's parents had done, but the boy had been made to do his own laundry in his underwear. He had to sit in the chilly basement next to the washer/dryer for the duration of both cycles. At the end, shivering from the damp cold and wheezing from the mold, nothing had ever felt as good as those hot clothes fresh out of the dryer. But they were still stained and Bobby made a big show out of throwing them in the trash, telling him he was lucky to have someone like him in the house. "If your mother saw those, she'd cry and cry."

He brushed a spot as free as possible of leaves and things he thought might stain as he could, and sat carefully in the sand next to the tackle box. He opened his book and picked up where he'd left off. Bobby said, "What stupid thing are you reading now?"

The boy said, "It's not stupid." Bobby's face darkened. Even if it was true that the book wasn't stupid, the boy wasn't allowed to contradict an adult, even when they were wrong. Especially when they were Bobby. He tried to roll over the transgression by rattling on quickly about the book. "It's all about bats. I'm reading the chapter that says how a mom bat can go out to get food and then come back to the colony and still find her one pup out of all the millions of other bats in the cave. It's all about sound and how they smell, and she can remember where she left her baby and—"

Bobby snatched the book out of his hand and flipped the cover over to look at it. The boy heard a page tear and his hands jerked toward the book involuntarily. It was a library book. He'd get in trouble if he ripped it. Bobby read the title aloud. "*Bats, Bats, How Do You Know About That*? Sounds like a baby book. Are you a baby?" The boy shook his head. "We're fishing, not reading before a bottle and naptime." He tossed the book into the dirt out of the boy's reach and opened a Styrofoam cup full of earth and moss. He pulled a long wriggling worm out and shoved it at the boy. "Wanna help me put it on the hook?" The boy shrank away and shook his head. He didn't want to *say* "no" any more than he wanted to get dirty. "Suit yourself, puss."

Bobby speared the thing's pink flesh on the hook and wrapped it over, piercing it again, and then a third time. He pursed his lips, and nodded with satisfaction as he watched the worm struggle against the steel upon which it was impaled. He let go of the hook and let it drop in the sand and dirt.

"Can I . . . can . . . can . . ."

"What!"

"Grampa lets me . . . he lets me cast it."

Bobby frowned and shook his head. "You'll throw the worm off the hook," he said.

"I won't . . . I never . . . I don't do it when . . . Grampa—"

"I'm not George. I said, no!" He picked up his pole and stood. He tried to cast, but he forgot to open the bail and the line didn't feed from the reel. The line snapped and the sinker, hook, and worm flew into the lake. "LITTLE FUCKER!" Bobby hollered. He swung back to throw the pole in after, but didn't. "See what you made me do, goddamn it!" Scowling, he sat down heavily and replaced the hook and sinker on the line. He speared another worm, nicking a finger on the tip of the barbed hook and cursed again. While he didn't blame the boy for *that*, the child winced anyway, waiting for the dark words to batter him. Bobby stood and tried again. This time he did it right, sending the line unfurling in a lazy spiral out over the water. The hook and sinker made a hollow sounding *plonk* as it penetrated the surface. Bobby stood holding the pole, staring quietly out at the rippling surface.

The boy looked over at his book. He didn't want to sit and just stare at the line, waiting. He didn't know anything about this pond, but he knew what fishing was like. And he always brought a book. On the cover was a picture of a bat with its wings outspread and large ears sticking up to hear. Its mouth was closed and the little animal almost looked like it was smiling, happy to be in the air. In the first chapter of the book it discussed how bats were the only mammals that could truly fly. It explained that flying squirrels and the like only glided. It didn't mention people, but the boy knew that airplanes and helicopters didn't count. *Bats* were the only mammals that could fly without something to help them. He so badly wanted to fly. His bedroom window at home looked out at the barn, catty-corner across the road. Every night he'd sit up in his bed and watch as the bats that lived in Clement Tilden's hayloft streamed out at dusk. Hundreds and hundreds of them twisting and swooping around each other in perfectly agile chaos. Old Clem had no animals to live in the barn, and the boy had overheard him saying once that bat guano was excellent fertilizer. *"And damned 'spensive too. I get that fa' free, y'know. S'why m'pumpkins get so big in the autumn."* The boy didn't care about fertilizer or pumpkins, but he was glad that was Old Clem's attitude, because that meant he didn't call the exterminator out to get rid of the bats. And that meant every night in the summer he got to see them fly away. And then he'd go to sleep and dream he was one of them, flying free, lissome and beautiful, with a mother who would always come home and hold him in a warm wing against her body and love him.

He got up on his hands and knees and stretched over to take back his book. His fingers brushed the cover and the next thing he knew the waistband of his jeans was tight and cutting into his belly, and he lost his sense of up and down, disoriented and breathless.

And then he hit the water.

He sank. The coldness of it made him gasp for a breath, and take in a short lungful of water. He kicked like they'd tried to teach him in swim class and he bobbed to the surface, sputtering and choking, getting a half-breath before slipping back under. The brightness of the day was lost. He sank deep into the suffocating depth of the pond. He kicked and thrashed in the water, trying to climb up again, but his vision darkened and he didn't know which way was up. He might be swimming toward the bottom for all he knew. Or he might be doing nothing at all, and treading water below the surface, inches away from life. He tried opening his eyes and the water got in them and he panicked. His heart raced and he wanted to take a breath so badly. Just one breath of air. A last taste of it before dying.

The boy knew he was dying.

Water filled his ears and pressed against his eardrums with a horrible, deep burbling sound all around him that was constant and terrifying. It was in his ears and invaded his head and he couldn't shut it out no matter how hard he tried not to hear it. He wanted to clamp his hands over his ears, but he couldn't stop struggling to move. His body was doing what it wanted, not what he wanted. And still the sound. The overwhelming sound of the pulse of the pond.

A fish materialized out of the dark and swam past him. Its blurry presence confused the boy, and he stopped trying to swim while his mind processed the surreal image of the thing hovering before his eyes before it startled and disappeared. It was upright. He was upright. Not head down like Bobby had teased him. The surface was above. He looked up and saw the sparkle of the sun glinting through the surface. The daylight didn't reach him, though. He was too deep, and slipping farther away.

He wished he could hug his mother one more time. Just a hug, not the feeling of water all around him, making it hard to move, impossible to breathe. Arms around his shoulders and the feeling of her soft belly against his chest and his head on her breast. Her body warm and comforting. But she wasn't there with him, and even if she had been, she couldn't swim any better than he could. They'd die together. So, it was better that he was alone in the deepening dark and getting deeper.

He let go and stopped struggling. A slight feeling of

weightlessness came over him and he imagined that it might be what it felt like to be a bat and fly. He felt contented to die flying.

The surface of the water rushed closer and he became aware of an arm around him as he broke through into the air and bright light and his eyes snapped shut at the blinding brilliance of it. He shivered at a refreshed sensation of freezing and choked on the water in his mouth and lungs keeping him from drawing a deep breath. An unfamiliar voice behind him said, "You can relax, boy. You're gonna be all right!" It was deep and full of soft, long New England "ahs" that made everything sound as comforting as a favorite pillow. *Yah gahnna be ah'right.* The owner of the voice dragged him along the surface and he felt that flying sensation along with the embrace he craved. He was safe in this man's arms, whoever he was.

The man pulled the boy out of the water and laid him on the beach, pressing a hand against the boy's chest. A second later the child coughed and sputtered and water came rushing out of his mouth. It was cold and tasted like dirt and it spilled out through his nostrils and over gaping lips. He panicked again, feeling like he was being killed—drowning on dry land. And then he got a deep breath. And another. Cold and fresh like autumn. All under the reassuring touch of the man who'd saved him. When he finally let go, the boy cried.

"Oh my god!" Bobby shouted. The boy could hear his footsteps as he ran toward them. *Please don't come over here*, he thought. *Please, just leave us alone.*

"How did he end up in the water?" the man said. His voice changed. What had been soft and calming became hard and sharp. He was demanding, no longer comforting. It seemed to rustle in the trees like a strong wind. The boy tried to sit up. The man pressed his hand in the middle of his chest again, not pushing—encouraging him to rest a moment longer. When the man touched him, he felt less like crying. He was happy to lie there. He blinked at the blue sky above. A small dark bird flew overhead, followed by another trailing close, black against the blue sky. He pretended they were bats and imagined himself flying with them.

"He just fell in. I was fishing and . . . he was playing on a log and the next thing I know, in he went. I told him not to get up there."

The man leaned over the boy. He had a reddish beard specked with gray and a long, straight nose. His face was wrinkly around his blue eyes like he was smiling, though he wasn't. The boy blinked and tried to make sense of him; he seemed both there and not there, like a dream outside his head. He blinked again and the man resolved into sharper reality as if he'd become more present at the insistence of the boy's need. The man said, "Izzat true, son? Were ya balancin' on a log?"

The boy wanted to tell the truth, though he knew better. He looked over at Bobby, standing dry on the beach ten feet away, still holding his fishing pole. He stared into the boy's eyes, widening them for a second before letting his face relax. The boy got the message and said, "Yessir. I was . . . I was playing . . . ninja. The . . . stick was my tightrope."

"I told him there was moss on that *log*," Bobby began, "and to be careful, but he's a daredevil, you know. Always pretending to be something stupid." The boy heard his jaws click shut after the word "stupid" as if he was trying to bite off that last word before the man could hear it.

The man turned the boy's face back toward his with a gentle finger. His hand was rough, but warm despite dripping with cold water. He looked the boy in the eyes and asked, "Y'sure about that? Did you slip on the moss?"

He nodded and lied, "Yessir." He wanted to signal him. Make some sign that he wasn't telling the truth, that Bobby had *thrown* him in the water. That he'd brought him here just to do that. He wanted to tell the man that Bobby hated fishing and every time his Grandpa invited him along he'd say, "No, go on without me." He wanted to tell all the other things too, but he didn't say anything. He knew better. He remembered what Bobby had told him.

"You love your mom, right?" he'd ask those nights she worked late. The boy would nod and say "Uh-huh," and Bobby would reply, "Remember Tyler Durrant from school? Remember how God took his mother in that car accident last summer? He must've *told*. But you won't tell, will you? You don't want God to kill *your* mommy, do you?" He did not. It didn't make sense that God would punish him for telling the truth, but he didn't question. And because he didn't want anything to happen to his mom, he never told. Not his grandfather or his teacher or even his best friend up the street, Heidi. He would never tell, and that meant he couldn't say anything to this man either. But how he wanted him to see it in his eyes. *Please* please *know. Just know and don't let him take me back.*

"I fell in," he said.

The man smoothed his wet hair away from his forehead. He helped the boy stand and together they turned to face Bobby, still waiting a few yards away. The bobber and hook dangled from his fishing pole near the end ring at the tip-top. He'd reeled the line in.

The boy saw their car on the opposite side of the pond. "How'd I get all the way over here?" The man kept his hands on the boy's shoulders. They felt so heavy, but right, like gravity.

"You were swimming away from me like a fish," Bobby said. "You got halfway across before I could jump in, and then . . . this guy—"

"You and I both know this boy can't swim a stroke. He didn't get all the way t'the middle of the pond from his own tryin'." The boy looked up at the man. He was staring hard at Bobby, the look on his face darker than anything he'd ever seen. He seemed to waver again. Like he was something else wearing a man mask, and it was slipping. The boy blinked and he was solid again. Just a man. Right?

The boy turned to look up at his rescuer. He said, "I been taking swim lessons. I guess I must've tried to doggy paddle before I got too tired to swim anymore." The man looked down, his mouth pursed the way his teacher did when he told her one of his stories about how he got this bruise, or why he was limping. "I did; I *really really* did. Like this." He pantomimed a dog's paws in the water.

The man shook his head, giving him a sad smile. He wanted the man to take his hand and lead him away to wherever he'd come from. But the boy knew he couldn't go. He wasn't his to take. Bobby's hand fell on his shoulder, tight and painful. He squirmed a little under his grip. He had missed his chance. He'd lied and missed it. And now it was getting ready to walk away. "You need to keep a better eye on this one," the man said. "Little boys can slip right away before you even know they're gone. You need to do better."

Bobby yanked him back, as if he wanted to be far from the man's reach as quickly as he could get away. He nodded so hard the boy could feel it. "I sure do. Especially with this one." He squeezed again and the boy tried not to wince. Bobby tussled his hair too hard and his fingers got caught in a snarl and pulled. "Is there anything I can give you? A little money, maybe?" He wasn't waiting for the man to politely decline as he dragged the boy away with him.

"No reward. Just keep that boy safe." The man stood there with sad eyes and turned to head off in whatever direction he'd originally come. A house, nearby, perhaps. A place close to his favorite fishing hole, *just past that bramble right there*, the boy imagined him telling his friends. *A real quiet spot nobody knows about but me an' the tasty little fishies.*

Bobby yanked hard on his arm, propelling him toward

the car. He opened the driver's side door and the boy clambered inside across the bench seat. He sat, holding his breath, waiting for Bobby to yell at him for getting the seat wet. But he didn't seem to care. He didn't say a thing. Not a single word of worry, or relief, or anything at all. He tossed his fishing pole into the back and climbed in after him, forgetting about the tackle box on the shore. He sat for a moment staring through the windshield at the far shore. The man was gone. The boy assumed he'd disappeared into the trees—he wasn't standing there anymore—but there wasn't anywhere along the entire far shore that looked like the end of a path. The trees were thick as a fairy-tale bramble. Then, his eyes alighted on a flash of movement. A red and gray streak with a fat tail that looked like a fox, maybe, darted into the trees, and was gone.

Bobby put the car in reverse and backed up the dirt path. The boy stared straight ahead at the receding pond. Bobbing up and down on the sparkling wavelets, the bat book floated on the surface of the water, cover open and pages down. It looked like it was flying in nighttime stars. He despaired. The librarian was going to be angry and tell him he had to pay for it. And that was going to make his mom upset. She'd be disappointed and shout at him about how they weren't made of money, even though she worked all day and night. *"What do you mean you don't know what happened to it? It didn't just fly away!"* He didn't need to be reminded either that he couldn't tell her that Bobby had taken him fishing and he dropped it in the pond miles and miles away. Saying Bobby had driven all the way out there to try to drown him would hurt her worst of all because God would kill her to punish him for saying it. Even though he was starting to think there wasn't any God at all. How could there be? Still, he wasn't sure, so to be safe, he wouldn't tell. He'd just stop going to the library so they couldn't ever make him pay. He wouldn't tell about the book, or the fishing trip, or about anything else Bobby did. No. He was going to go home and get into dry pajamas, and put his clothes in the wash, and wait for dusk to come. And when the sun started to set and Old Clem's bats started to fly out of the hayloft, he'd open his window, crawl from his bed out onto the eaves, and join them. And when he did, he wouldn't ever have to worry about keeping any more secrets ever, because when he flew, the only ones who would ever be able to hear him cry aloud would be the bats.

And maybe, just maybe, if he wished hard enough, the man would be waiting to down below to catch him. He'd catch him, and take him into the woods to be foxes and bats together. He was afraid of what would happen if the man wasn't there. But if he wasn't, he wouldn't ever know.

Not as long as he went down head first.

BLOOD MAKES THE GRASS GROW

Sam watched the old man lean over to inspect the deep wound. Despite the severity of the gash in her haunch, the dog was reasonably calm under the veterinarian's hands. She didn't try to scramble off the examination table or even nip or bark. Instead, she sat whining softly as he tended to her. Gina had been a perfect patient ever since Sam and Callie Cooper, her owners, had started bringing her to the clinic as a puppy. By contrast, to say Sam and Callie were agitated was putting it mildly.

"She'll be fine," Pickett reassured them, reaching for a bottle of saline. "This'll be the hardest part 'cause the cut's so deep. Gonna have to get in there. As soon as I'm satisfied we got 'er properly cleaned out, then we'll staple it right up. Before you go, I'll write you a scrip for antibiotics you can have filled over at the Walgreens. Even call it in for you if you want."

Pickett spoke slowly and articulately, enunciating every syllable as carefully as one would expect from a man who'd managed his own rehab after a stroke. Aside from a slightly lazy eye on the right side, he showed no sign. He deliberately chose his words, but he was also showing his age. Sam's father had introduced him to Dr. Pickett maybe twenty-five years ago and he was old back then.

Standing in the low-ceilinged doublewide that served as his veterinary clinic, Pickett looked diminished. Stooped and tired, as though his advancing age was costing him size. He was a tough guy from a family of tough guys. His thick, scarred hands showed it. But every year robbed him of another inch, another five pounds, until eventually, Sam imagined, the man would become so old there would be nothing left of him but a whisper.

Pickett looked Sam in the eyes, his thin mouth upturned slightly in that New England expression of extreme pleasure. Caring for an animal brought him the kind of contentment he'd never found in a bottle, boat, or brothel. And Sam had heard in his youth, Pickett spent considerable time in all three.

"You two make sure she don't move now. I'm gonna give her a local anesthetic. It might sting a little, but not as bad as gettin' the jab in the first place. How'd you say she got this?"

Callie's blushed as she said, "I threw a stick into the pond for her to fetch. She jumped in and yelped and when she came out, she had this. I guess she must have landed on something sharp below the surface."

"Nothing you coulda done about that. Not your fault. Now get ahold of her while I work." Sam leaned in and held Gina's leg while Callie hugged her body and shushed and whispered to the dog. Dr. Pickett went to work. Gina whined louder, but sat still and let the old man do his job. He used to have an assistant—his wife, Joye—but since she'd taken ill, he was left to work on his own.

Despite the stroke that had left his right hand less agile than it had been a decade earlier, Dr. Pickett's hardened hands moved with the practiced ease of a young doctor. His motions looked to Sam like some kind of sleight of hand trick of redirection and dexterity that transformed a bleeding wound into a stapled line of restoration.

"She'll have a scar to show for it," he said. "But don't we all?"

Callie hugged the old man, kissing his cheek with the kind of Midwestern passion that made northern Yankee men blush. "Thank you, Doctor," she said.

"How many times I asked you to call me Garrett, hon?"

Callie dropped her gaze. She stroked her Viszla's muscled golden shoulder and tried to hide her embarrassment behind the few loose dreadlocks that had fallen in front of her face. "How much do we owe you, Garrett?"

"Not sure. I'll have to sit down and figure it out, I reckon. I'll send you a bill when I get around to it."

Sam turned to Callie and said, "Hon, would you fetch me my backpack?"

She smiled, winked, and walked out to their truck cradling Gina in her arms. When she returned, Sam expected her to still be holding the fifty-pound dog like one of those toy breeds skinny ladies from the city carted around in handbags. Instead, she carried only Sam's Army surplus rucksack. He took it from her, undid the canvas fasteners, and withdrew a quart bag of oily green marijuana buds.

"This is for Joye. And a little extra for you too. Send us the *full* bill when you know what we owe."

Garrett Pickett didn't balk or try to do anything but quietly and clearly say "Thank you" as he took the bag. He wasn't the kind of man who shared his problems. He came from that stoic breed of New England men like Sam's grandfather and father. Men who believed dignity was not about breeding or wealth or taste; it was about not trying to lessen your own load by saddling others with your troubles. *People got their own worries*, Sam's father would say. *You got shoulders enough to carry your own without spreading it around.* Few people knew about Joye's pain. The few that did simply gave what help they could and never asked for anything in return. People like Sam and Callie. Good Maine folk.

The way life should be, as the tourist slogan went.

Outside, the heavy crunching of a car skidding to a stop

in the gravel in front of the clinic and the sound of shouting men and slamming car doors cut Sam's next statement off.

"Sounds like something can't wait," Dr. Pickett said, stuffing the quart bag into a cabinet behind him. "Better make some room."

Sam had time to pull Callie away from the door as it slammed open into the wall. Two men carrying a third shoved through the opening.

"Hell, boys! It's open; you don't need to knock the door down."

"Shut the fuck up, old man!" The one with his back turned shuffled toward the table as his partner tried unsuccessfully to kick the door shut while holding on to his friend's legs. He missed the door and knocked over a coat-tree instead. The men hauled their friend up and slammed him down on the table. The young man groaned loudly, clutching at his glistening red gut. Sam thought he couldn't be more than eighteen or nineteen.

"Hey now, fellas," Sam said, "This isn't the E.R. You need to take this kid—"

"I said shut the fuck up," the first man shouted. He reached behind his back and produced a pistol, aiming it at Sam. "Shut the fuckin' door, hippie!" Sam put his hands up involuntarily. Callie tried to pull him away from the gun, but they both backed into a counter that arrested their retreat.

"Let's all just calm down," Dr. Pickett said. "Nobody's done anything they can't take back yet."

The man spun, pointing his pistol in Pickett's face in reply. Pickett kept his hands at his sides, not stepping back. To Sam, he seemed to grow six inches in that moment. He took on the presence of the man he'd met twenty-five years earlier. The kind of man with heavy hands who'd make you regret forcing him to ball them up into fists.

The gunman seemed unimpressed, however. "Mickey! Shut the door." The man's partner shuffled over and slammed the vinyl door closed. He struggled with the lock, but eventually twisted it into place.

"Christ, this guy is ancient," Mickey said.

"S'what Yelp said. A hundred-year-old guy in a trailer. He's the doctor."

"Fuckin' old."

Pickett's eyes narrowed but he didn't protest. "I can only imagine you want me to do something for this young man right here." He said "young" with a mocking undertone, as if there was more life left in him than the man on the table.

"You imagine right, grampa."

"I ain't set up for a gut shot. Don't have the tools or hands to save this boy."

"Bullshit!"

"This trailer look like Maine Medical to you?"

The man pushed forward with the barrel of the gun to emphasize his impatience with the colloquy. "I don't need your sarcasm. I just need you to fix up my friend."

"I don't know what I can do," Pickett said as he snapped into a fresh pair of gloves. He grabbed a few sterile pads and lifted the boy's shirt to get a look. The kid groaned, but he didn't have much fight in him, and lay more or less still. Wiping away the blood that was pooling, Pickett leaned in a little closer and took a deep breath through his nose.

"You smell that? That's the odor of what we in the business call a complication of a diaphragmatic injury. Whoever shot your boy—I'm assuming it weren't you, even though you don't look all that bright—perforated his intestine. You take him somewhere they're equipped to help and he might live. I don't know what else in there is damaged. But if I treat him here, he'll end up dying of fecal peritonitis." When the gunman didn't respond, he added, "You following me, son?"

"You're full of shit," Mickey said from the door.

"No. But your friend's peritoneal cavity has been filling up with it. My professional opinion is his time is short. For however long you geniuses been driving around looking for a country vet on your fancy little phones, his liver maybe—seems to me from eyeballing that wound there and the amount of blood gushing out of it—has been oozing like crazy." Dr. Pickett pulled a box of sterile gauze pads and tape out from under his exam table. He placed a pad over the seeping hole in the kid's stomach. As he pressed it down, however, a fresh circle of blood soaked through, growing in size with alarming speed.

"How the fuck would a vet know?"

"I know exactly what a *vet* knows. I saw my share of gut shot wounds in Korea. I can give him this here battle dressing and then you'd better be on your way to a real hospital. Even if I had something to staunch the bleeding, he needs surgery."

"What fuckin' good are you?"

"You came to *me* for help, son. I didn't invite you. I ain't worked on a human animal since '53. Still, I remember those boys and what done them in. I might need trifocals now but I can still see when something is trouble. Can smell it too."

"Why are you stopping?"

Pickett shook his head slowly. "Can't help him better than tying down the dressing and calling an ambulance. I cut, he dies. Nothin' in life is simpler to understand than that."

The gunman's hand shook as he thumbed back the hammer on his junk gun. "Try!"

Dr. Pickett slowly raised his hands, not in defense of the man holding the gun in his face, but to implore him to use common sense. "You care about this boy, you fellas need to take him up the road to Augusta. I can't help you here anymore than this I'm 'fraid."

"What do we do, Patrick?"

"You shut your mouth, *Mickey*. This old man is gonna help us or else he's gonna die."

"I'm gonna die anyway," Pickett said. "Just like your friend here, you keep wasting time."

"I've got a solution," Sam said. He kept Callie behind him while he drew the gunman's attention. "It's clear you guys can't take him to the hospital without getting in trouble for . . . whatever lead up to this." Sam shrugged. "But *we* can take him. Me and . . ." He didn't want to say Callie's name. It felt like giving them power over her. Of course, the gunman had all the power in the world at the present moment. Instead he said, "Me and my wife. Put him in the back seat of our truck and we'll drive him to the E.R. You guys leave in your own car and no one says a word. We'll make sure they give him the care he needs and you two can go wherever it is you are headed. No one else gets hurt. No one dies if we can help it."

"It's not a bad idea," Mickey said.

"Fuck that! They're just going to take him to the hospital and not tell anyone about us?"

"The writer already called the cops, man!" Patrick's fury distorted his face into a caricature of rage like an ancient Greek theater mask. The sound of Mickey's mouth slamming shut was audible.

"Don't tell me you tried to rob Cutter Pierce," Sam said.

"He wasn't s'posed to be home. Who'd've thought a faggot writer would have a hand-cannon in his desk?"

"Anyone who reads Hunter S. Thompson," Callie said.

"Or Cutter Pierce," Sam finished. "The guy is legendary for taking shots at people." A small smile crept up Sam's face. "Don't tell me you believed that story about him having an attic full of cash."

"I'm supposed to buy he's a violent gun nut, but not that he's squirreling away money like someone waiting for the end of the world?"

"There's a difference between reading the police log and the gossip column, man. Cutter makes the papers up here more often for taking shots at people on his property than he does for releasing a best seller."

"Like it fuckin' matters now," Patrick said.

Sam nodded, understanding what he meant. Patrick and his break-in crew had come north for an urban legend about a retirement score and one of them got retired early instead. Cutter usually shot to scare, not to kill, but they must have left him no choice. Sam wondered how they got off his property at all if they were close enough for the guy to hit the target in the center ring. But then, maybe he hadn't. If Cutter was aiming for the head or the heart, the bullet dropped before it hit the mark. However it played out, it had made the survivors desperate for a getaway.

"We promise we won't tell anyone," Callie said.

"No. This is it. Right here." Patrick turned to Pickett with a look of fury and expectant contempt like he was waiting for more hard truths to dismiss. Pickett offered none. He worked silently to finish the battlefield dressing he'd promised, doing his best to clean and dress the kid's wounds with his meager supplies. He taped down a long piece of gauze holding sterile pads together on either side of the boy's abdomen. Both packs were already crimson, close to turning black with saturation. He wrapped another piece of gauze around and tied this one in a knot.

"Son, these good folk are offering to give you an out. You don't have a choice about trusting people any more. Cutter Pierce took care of that. Take 'yes' for an answer and let them take him up the road."

Patrick turned the gun back on Dr. Garrett Pickett, husband of Joye Pickett, Korean War vet, lifelong resident of New Vineyard, Maine, and friend to animals everywhere.

And pulled the trigger.

The old man's lazy eye collapsed in on itself like a dying star. It erupted with part of his skull and brains out the back of his head. Pickett dropped straight down behind the table, mercifully falling out of sight.

"I am not your son," Patrick said.

Sam stared in mute shock, deafened by the report of the gun in the trailer. He thought he heard Callie behind him screaming for the man to stop, as if she existed a few moments earlier in time than the rest of them.

Patrick shouted, "Let's go," indicating they move for the door with his gun hand while he stuck a finger in an ear with his other. They didn't budge, but continued to stare at the framed portrait of Pickett's Burmese Mountain Dog hanging on the wall behind the table. Pickett's splattered blood ran down the image and dripped off the frame with a soft *plip plip* no one could hear.

Patrick stepped closer to the couple, interrupting their trance. "Get him; we're going."

Sam shook his head. Patrick raised the gun, its barrel still weeping smoke, pressed the muzzle to Sam's forehead and said, "I'm not asking for volunteers."

Callie rubbed her wet eyes against her sleeve and moved around to the boy's legs to grab hold. Sam followed suit without further argument. He glanced behind the table at Dr. Pickett's body slumped on the floor. The sight of it didn't seem enough to confirm what he'd convinced himself in the last few seconds couldn't be true. His mind kept repeating *he's not dead* like a mantra. But there he was.

The old man lay in a heap, black blood pouring out of the hole where his eye once was. Mouth hanging open in dumb silence as his drool mixed with gore on the front of his white coat. One bullet had rendered one of the nicest and most generous men Sam had ever known a drooling piece of cooling meat.

A burning pain bubbled up from his guts, stinging his throat and making his sternum ache. He swallowed his bile and shifted his attention from the dead man to the dying boy. Wrapping his arms under the boy's armpits, he locked his fingers in front of his narrow chest. He looked his wife in the eyes and blinked that he was ready. She gripped behind the knees and together they hauled the body up easily.

As they lurched toward the door, Mickey snapped out of his fugue and struggled again with the lock. He got it undone and wrenched the door open. Patrick pushed past, insisting on going first. "In case you feel like dropping him and running."

"We're taking him to the hospital," Callie said.

The boy's head lolled against Sam's chest. The kid had groaned when the hoods dropped him on the table, but he was limp and silent now because he was slipping out of the world hot on Pickett's trail. In the distance between the trailer door and the truck, he'd be completely gone if he wasn't already. But if it got Patrick to let them go, hell if Sam wouldn't rush that boy to the hospital as quickly as he'd driven anywhere in his life. He said, "We can have him there in twenty minutes."

Patrick's expression darkened. He pointed toward the car with the Massachusetts plates. "Put him in the back."

Sam moved toward the oxidized whatever-it-was they drove. He didn't know a damn thing about cars, but he suspected even if he did, he wouldn't be able to place this one. Some used piece of shit bought or stolen for this occasion only.

Callie opened the door and they lay the boy in the car as gently as the cramped space would allow. Gina barked from Sam and Callie's truck.

"That's our dog," Callie said.

"Like I give a fuck."

"What now?" Sam asked.

"Get in front," Patrick said. "We're going to your place. I need to think."

"What then?"

"I *think*, motherfucker! I think about what to do next. Now get in the car, you hippie assholes!"

Callie nodded at Sam and started to climb in the back. Patrick stopped her. "No. You're riding bitch up front with me. Mickey! Get in back with Pete."

"But he's . . ."

Patrick screamed something unintelligible that might have been "get in the car" or it might have been something else. It didn't matter. Everyone had only one option at the present: whatever Patrick wanted.

Sam nodded at his wife and she crawled in the car through the driver's door. Sam got in after her and waited for the others. Patrick squeezed in next to Callie and slammed his door.

"I don't want to leave Gina in the truck," Callie said. "It's hot."

Patrick opened his mouth to shout something else, but Sam spoke instead, putting his hand on Callie's thigh as he did, to reassure her. His hand shook and he tried not to squeeze too hard, but she gasped at the tightness of his grip and he realized that he was close to coming undone.

"The windows are cracked," he said. "We'll come back for her." Callie nodded and sighed with resignation. They had to go along. For now. Neither of them acknowledged that their chances of coming back for the dog were already slim and growing narrower with each passing minute.

Sam hoped someone would come and rescue their dog. Perhaps someone else needing Garrett's care would find her in the truck . . . and him inside. The clinic was remote, however. There was a town nearby, but the road leading to it was seldom traveled. It didn't lead to anything but the trailer and a house or two a few miles farther. If no one came calling, both Gina and Joye would die of neglect before the weekend.

One bullet could kill so many.

Sam turned the keys dangling from the ignition and put the car in gear, resolving to come back. Not quite sure how, yet, but determined to figure it out on the way. He knew Callie was thinking the same thing.

Sam drove in silence most of the way. His hearing cleared as the miles ticked by, the muddy muffled impact deafness resolving to a low, steady ringing. His head was beginning to ache. As they rounded another corner and Patrick said, "Slow down, Earnhardt." Patrick jammed the handgun in Callie's ribs, making her grunt from the pain.

He looked at the speedometer and saw he was nearing sixty on the winding two-lane highway. Sam forced himself to breathe and ease his foot off the gas, but kept his mouth shut, certain nothing Patrick said was an invitation for a dialogue. Also, not engaging in repartee gave him more time to think. He wanted out of the car as quickly as he could manage it. The kid—Pete—bleeding out in the backseat was bad enough. But the presence of a dead body was far outweighed by the chance that hitting a frost heave in the road would jiggle Patrick's trigger finger too forcefully.

"How much farther?" Patrick asked.

"There," Callie said, pointing.

They approached a striped flag hanging next to a sign that read, *If you have any produce-related puns, lettuce know.*

"What the fuck is that?" Patrick asked.

"Our place," Sam said.

Patrick, for a change, was speechless as Sam pulled onto the dirt ruts leading to their farmhouse. He drove a quarter mile up the driveway from the roadside barn, pulled around behind the house and parked. He turned off the engine and sat.

"What are you waiting for?" Patrick asked.

"Your lead. What do we do with . . . him?" Sam nodded at Pete, whose open, blank eyes stared at the seatbacks.

Despite the wound dressing, Sam could smell the ruptured bowel over the odors of blood and piss. Pickett had been right about the kid's chances. He'd just been on the hopeful side of how long they had.

"Bring him. I don't want him stinking up the car," Patrick said.

Callie said, "You seem pretty okay talking that way about someone who was a friend."

Patrick shoved the muzzle of the gun in her ribcage hard enough to make her gasp. "You don't know a fuckin' thing about me!"

"Let's just go inside and we can take all the time we need to sort things through," Sam suggested.

"You gonna make me some tea, hippie?"

For the second time, Sam decided silence was a better answer than provoking the man with the gun. He opened his door and climbed out. Patrick scrambled out the passenger side door, rushing around the front of the car, desperate to keep his pistol trained on Sam. "You two get Pete and let's go."

Callie and Mickey helped with the body while Patrick let himself into the house. He looked around in a manic state, checking shelves and drawers and small spaces all around. Sam and Callie's home was cluttered, and things toppled over, falling off shelves, breaking or rolling away as he rifled through the place.

"What are you looking for?" Callie asked as she and Sam eased the body onto the hardwood floor.

When Patrick didn't reply, Sam said, "He's looking for something we'd use to defend ourselves."

"Smart man."

"There are no weapons here," Callie said. "We're farmers."

Patrick practically guffawed. "Bullshit! You got knives in the kitchen? A fuckin' meat mallet? Yeah, you're a real pair of hippie peaceniks." Patrick kept searching. Mickey plopped on the sofa, holding his head in his hands. Sam offered to brew the cup of tea that had been joked about in the car.

Patrick closed the distance between them and slammed his fist into Sam's stomach before Sam realized what was happening. The lanky farmer dropped to his knees beside the dead boy. He tried to retrieve the breath that had been knocked out of him and gagged on the smell emanating from the corpse.

"You think I'm stupid? Am I fuckin' stupid?"

"The opposite," Sam choked.

"Fuck, dude!" Mickey said.

"What now?"

"Look!" Mickey held the hinged lid of an ottoman open with one hand while raising a gallon bag of weed for Patrick to see. "The thing is filled with this shit!"

Patrick glanced at his surviving partner, his eyes widening. He walked over and snatched the bag away from Mickey. Opening it, he inhaled deeply. "Farmers, huh?"

"It's a crop," Callie said. "There's a bong in there too if you want to mellow out some. *Please*. That's our personal stash; you're welcome to it."

"You got *more*?"

"We've got a whole field of it outside," she said. "Behind the corn. Leave us alone and you can take as much of it as you want." She looked at her husband with her eyebrows raised. He nodded back at her.

"You two knock that telepathic shit off! I'm not going to go looking for some secret pot field while you call the cops. Where did you really get this stuff?"

"The field is a hundred yards through those doors," Callie said. "Take what you want and go. We won't call the police."

Mickey held open another bag, peering in as if he couldn't decide whether to fill a bowl or stick his head in and motorboat like a teenager with his first thirty-six double Ds.

"Right, you won't. You don't think I know Medical is legal up here?"

Sam sighed. His guts had stopped cramping enough to allow him to sit back on his heels and put some distance between him and Pete. "We look like a dispensary to you? The law says they have to cultivate their own. Plus, there are plenty of people who want to smoke recreationally and don't have a doctor willing to write them a scrip for 'stress.' We don't want the police looking into our business any more than you do."

Callie chimed in. "We'd probably get more time for what's in that ottoman than you would for . . ." She couldn't bring herself to say "killing Garrett." Instead, she clapped a hand over her mouth. She appeared to be growing manic. To Sam she seemed to be almost vibrating with anxiety. If he wasn't fighting nausea and stomach cramps, he'd feel the same way. But Patrick hit hard. A boxer, perhaps. It was all Sam could do to keep from vomiting on the rug—the one they joked really tied the room together but now was covered in a boy's blood.

"We'll take you to the field. You cut as much as you can fit in your car. Take the rest out of the ottoman and leave us alone," Sam said.

Patrick looked ready to rush Sam again as he pushed himself up off the floor. Instead the gunman stayed by his partner, out of swinging range. A comfortable shooting distance away.

"You can have the money from last weekend's market too. It's in the safe in the bedroom. Take it all and leave us alone."

"I look like a drug dealer to you? What am I going to do with a carload of weed?"

"You look like a man who doesn't want to walk away empty-handed," Callie said. "You didn't get what you want at Cutter's place. But you can still win and no one else has to get hurt."

Mickey sidled up to Patrick, the freezer bag still open in his hands. "I know a guy in Pawtucket who'll buy trunkfuls of this shit."

"We'll show you," Callie said. "Make up your mind when you see what we've got."

Patrick waved at the glass doors with his pistol. "After you."

Sam and Callie stepped over Pete's body and opened the doors to the back porch. Patrick and Mickey followed behind. The couple led the way across a big back yard past a bunch of rusting farm equipment and a picnic table. Fifty yards from the house was a row of corn stalks. They pushed their way into the overgrown green mess. The stalks were thick and untended. Patrick kept his hand tight on Callie's elbow in case she or her man decided to make a run for it.

As Sam promised, another fifty yards away, the unmistakable odor of dank began to drift toward him. A combination of pine, sage, and skunk teased his sense of smell. He lifted his head a little to get a deeper whiff.

Callie's arm jerked out of his hand as she and her husband hopped ahead of their guides. Patrick took a quick step forward to catch her arm, but she side-stepped him, disappearing into the green.

Patrick took a lurching step after her. The metal clack sounded a half-second before the dull meaty *thunk* and almost two seconds before the field was filled with his screaming. His wails carried, but never echoed back in the dense vegetation. He dropped to the ground pawing at the bear trap clamped to his shin. Even through his jeans, anyone could see the leg was broken and half torn through. As if the hippies sharpened their traps.

He looked around in a panic for his gun, but couldn't find it. It might as well have vaporized as soon as the trap snapped. He couldn't control anything his arms did for several seconds after it snapped and he figured he'd flung the gun into the stalks. Now he was beginning to shake with shock. His body was refusing to do anything he wanted it to. The dry earth was turning muddy with his life soaking into the earth.

Mickey dropped to his knees next to the trap, looking at it like the device was a living thing that might bite him too. "Fucking shit, dude! What the Christ is that?" After a moment's hesitation, he tried to pry open the jaws, but couldn't. Patrick let out another long yowl as Mickey's efforts to free him only resulted in the steel teeth grinding into his shattered leg, further tearing his flesh and sinew.

Patrick tried to say "bear trap" but couldn't unclench his jaw. He forced out a grunt that sounded like, "Find gun!" but Mickey shook his head, brow furrowed with confusion.

A black shape backlit by the blinding afternoon sun appeared behind Mickey. Patrick's warning was drowned out by the howl Callie let out as she reared back and swung. A *whump* followed her voice and he caught a glimpse of the edge of a short handled military shovel embedded in his brother's neck before she wrenched it free and a hot wet spray splashed Patrick's face like a full glass of hot water. Callie grunted once with effort and began to bellow rage. In his red blindness, Patrick was sprayed and splattered and doused as the dull metal clanging sounded again and again, growing duller, softer with repetition. The dank smell of the cannabis field was overwhelmed by the thick salt and iron taste in his mouth; a fullness in his nostrils made it hard to breathe. He spat and blew crimson snot on his chest, rubbing at his eyes until he could see again.

Callie stood before him holding the red, dripping e-tool shovel. She threw it on the ground next to Mickey's pulped face and squeezed blood from an errant dreadlock. She spat on the body lying at her feet. "Fuck! You know how long it takes these things to dry?"

Patrick retched, vomiting up the blood he'd swallowed. She kicked him in the face with a boot heel, smashing his nose and knocking him onto his back. She screamed unintelligibly at him. Her primal rage penetrating his skull, threatening to burst it like her shovel had done to Mickey's head.

Sam pushed his way out of the stalks and lightly placed a hand on the small of her back. She slumped into him, wrapping her arms around his neck. He kicked at the metal jaws holding the gunman in place. Patrick's eyes fluttered as he struggled to remain conscious. "We don't get many visitors all the way up at the house," he said. "People around here respect our privacy."

"We woulda let you go," Patrick sputtered.

"You believe that, honey?"

Callie turned and sneered, catching her breath. "Not after what he did to poor Garrett." Her voice was edged by palpable hatred.

Sam's face darkened at the mention of their friend. He kissed the top of his wife's head, inadvertently smearing blood on his cheek. "Sorry it took me so long."

"S'okay," she said stepping back, giving him room to pull the gun from a holster nestled in the small of his back.

Unlike Patrick's lost junk gun, Sam's piece was a well-tended Smith and Wesson Governor. It was black and clean and looked like forged death. Sam didn't know shit about cars, but he knew personal firearms. "The writer, Cutter, he shot your boy with a fifty cal Desert Eagle. We talked about our favorite heaters the last time Cutter came around the 'farm stand.' He bragged about the monster he kept in his desk drawer. I'm surprised your kid had any guts at all when you brought him in."

Patrick's face paled.

"What?" Sam flipped his head back whipping his tangled hair away from his eyes. "You see a Bible verse on a burger wrapper and think those people are in it to save souls? It's a brand, man. Would you rather buy your weed from a couple of nice bohemian farmers or some scar-faced biker? Some people—people like you, shitheads from away—see us and think they can sneak into the fields at night to help themselves. Those people never leave the field."

"Blood makes the grass grow," Callie said.

"This isn't how it was supposed to go." Patrick said. "This isn't right."

"This is Maine. This is the way life should be."

SOME OTHER TIME

The percussive blasts coming from the stage stole Miriam's breath as the sound waves broke against her like surf battering a rock at shore. She stood frozen in place on the dance floor, staring through a gap in the crowd at her boyfriend. He was standing at the far end of the club, chatting up some too-young emo girl cinched up in a cheap-looking corset. Miriam's best friend, Sara, had inveigled her to come out to get her mind off of the lab. "You can count cells tomorrow. You're working too hard," she'd said pumping her thumb in a gesture that suggested she needed to put the pipette down for a night and have some fun. It hadn't been hard to convince Erik to get dressed and take her to the club. And she *had* been having fun. Until now. *Erik has always been a flirt*, she rationalized. When he leaned over and placed a lingering, open-mouthed kiss on the girl's neck, Miriam realized that things had suddenly changed. It was an exact mirror image of how she'd come to be with him. Except, this time, she was viewing the scene from the distance of the jilted lover. Her mind was definitely off her enzyme immunoassay results now.

The pressure of the drum-and-bass thump resonated in Miriam's chest. She fought for her breath, inhaling consciously, even though there was plenty of air in the club. The crowd moved back in to fill the space that had emptied long enough for her to watch her relationship die. She turned around to grab Sara, but she was gone also. Standing alone in the crowd, Miriam pretended to laugh, trying to appear in control of herself. Everything was flowing away, leaving her gasping for breath.

The singer groaned and clawed at a wire cage in pained mimicry of a scene from a movie older than almost everyone in the club. A boy dancing next to her accidentally jabbed his elbow into her tit, and the world came rushing back into focus. He didn't turn to apologize. He just danced, oblivious to her pain. She grabbed her aching breast, lifted her other hand to hide her face, and began the long walk off the dance floor. Bodies buffeted her. She pushed through. She emerged from the dance floor and headed straight for the bar. Sara would offer up her sofa, if only Miriam could find her to ask. But first, a drink. Something to settle her nerves.

Jamming in between two towering men, she leaned over the brass rail running the length of the bar and tried to flag down the bartender. He ignored her, set down a glass of something red next to one of the men bookending her, took a twenty left on the bar, and stalked away to make change. Miriam carefully slid the drink away and took a sip through the thin cocktail straw. Something with vodka and Chambord. *Thank God it's not whiskey.* Taking the glass, she slipped out from between the giants to go look for her friend. She despaired as she stared out into the mass of revelers. *And then what?* Whether or not Erik was done with her, she needed to know that she wasn't alone. At that moment she just needed someone who was on her side.

She took a step forward to start swimming through the crowd. An elegant . . . person . . . with slicked, short hair and aquiline features intercepted her. His body and style suggested masculinity, like Tilda Swinton dressed as Bowie's Thin White Duke would—impossibly slender; whitish-blond hair; black, tightly fitted clothes; and a complexion like a China doll in a black and white photograph. But the stranger wore subtle makeup—slightest rouge, dark lips, red eyeliner. And how he . . . she . . . moved, weightless and careful like a Japanese Bunraku puppet. Every gesture was so deliberate. The stranger's fluid sensuality made everyone else look like fumbling pubescents having only just discovered second base. This androgyne knew just how to get under Miriam's skin. But then, they'd never met. The stranger didn't *know* anything about her. It's just that this person was exactly who she pictured when she lay back in her lonely moments. An angel of darkness. A demon of light.

Miriam stared up into a pair of infinitely deep, all-black eyes, and felt her stomach knot and face flush. What if they just kept moving past? What if the stranger wanted to ask her to dance? Anything breaking the trance of being frozen in exactly this moment was terrifying. "That is a lovely hat, dear." *His* voice rumbled in her chest like the band's drumbeat, making her guts twist and loins ache. She felt his compliment more than she heard it. Miriam reached up to touch the black vintage fascinator hat perched in front of a bun of her coiled-up hair. She blinked. Each time she opened her eyes it was like seeing someone different. A male gesture, a female posture, a man's hairstyle, a woman's jawline. He changed like fluid, filling the small spaces around her. He was suffocating water and she wasn't struggling. "How have you attached it?" he asked, reaching out for her with long fingers tipped with silver-polished nails.

"It's . . . I have . . . there's a pin," she stammered.

"May I?" Before Miriam could tell him that her hat and veil would fall off if he removed it, he ran his cool finger up the side of her neck, behind her ear, and slowly pulled the pin. She felt her hat and bun loosen, but didn't care. Her hair unwound and fell down around her shoulders. Holding the long needle up in front of her face, he smiled with half his mouth. She imagined tasting his lipstick, his breath, his tongue. He ran the sharp point lightly down the length of her nose and let the tip rest for a moment on her lips before it disappeared into his vest. "Thank you," he said.

The stranger held out his other hand and summoned a young, black-haired girl with ginger roots. The dim-looking girl giggled as she wrapped her arms around his waist, and he laid a hand on the small of her back. "Perhaps some other time," he said to Miriam before stalking off with the girl. She took an apneatic breath. Her drink slipped from her fingers and smashed on the floor. Someone behind her yelled, "Hey!" but she didn't turn around. Miriam watched the beautiful, genderless creature lead the girl through the club toward the back.

A hand grasped Miriam's shoulder and spun her around. Her hat fell from her head and bounced away into the crowd. "You deaf? I said, did you take my fuckin' drink?" She looked up into the twisted, angry face of one of the giants from the bar. His ugly expression and wavering posture said he'd had more than a few and didn't need the one she'd stolen. It was a moot point anyway, now that it was staining her boots. Unwilling, however, to see how much ethanol had lowered his inhibitions, she bit at his hand and shoved. Clutching his wounded thumb, he stumbled back, tripping over his barstool. The giant banged his back against the metal bar rail and bellowed. Feeling a touch of satisfaction, Miriam pushed into the crowd before the howling drunk could recover and come after her again.

Winding her way through the club, she did her best to track the stranger and his girl. *Some other time? I need this now.* To her right, she heard Sara shout her name. The urgency in her tone suggested she might have run into Erik and the whore he was going to invite home. Unconcerned with where she was going to spend the night, Miriam kept searching, trying to duck away from her friend. But her androgyne Duke was gone. *Out of time.*

Sara caught up to her, pulling some boy along like a glassy-eyed puppy. He tugged impatiently on Sara's hand, looking annoyed that they had taken this detour when he thought they should be headed back to her apartment. She shot him a withering look, assuring that whatever she'd already promised him would be replaced by a crippling case of blue balls if he didn't heel, sit, stay. Miriam knew that, even if he got what he wanted from Sara, he was in for a lot more than he expected. "What the hell is going on, Miri? Have you seen Erik?"

"I saw him," she said, still scanning the crowd.

"Well, what the fuck? Do you want me to castrate him or what?"

Miriam didn't want to admit that her best friend had been right about her boyfriend. She was sure a chorus of *I-told-you-sos* would be sung over more than one bottle of wine in the days to come. All she wanted right now was another glimpse of the stranger—something to take away with her. She dropped her head and wished that she was still wearing her veil so no one could see her cry. "Forget about it." Sara cocked her head in sympathy at her friend's anguish. But she didn't understand what Miriam mourned losing.

"Come on, Clara," the boy said. "Let's go." Sara elbowed him hard in the stomach. He grunted. "I thought we were going to get out of here."

"I told you I needed to find my friend first."

"So? You found her."

"*Now* we need to talk. You can wait." The boy looked Miriam up and down like he was assessing the personal value to him of Sara having found her. He smiled like a boy imagines a wolf would. Miriam narrowed her eyes, shooting him a you're-not-gonna-get-any-from-me look. *In your dreams, ass!*

He turned back to Sara. "Well, I'm not waiting all night. There are hotter chicks than you here."

"Then go find one," Sara said.

"You don't know what you're missing," he said.

"What? Two minutes of heavy breathing in my ear and you staining my sheets? Go fuck yourself. It'll feel the same to me." He glared at Miriam for an uncomfortable few seconds before mouthing "cunt" at her and stomping off.

"I'm sorry, Sara," Miriam said, secretly glad that she'd cock-blocked the guy. "You didn't need to do that."

"What? That? I wasn't going to fuck him anyway. I just wanted someone to pay for my drinks."

Miriam wanted to fake a laugh again, to pretend that she was happy to be having this conversation and not following the stranger into his car, his house, his bed. She couldn't summon the energy to put up the façade. Emotional attrition was getting the better of her. "Is it okay if I sleep on your couch?" she asked instead.

Sara pulled her close in an embrace and gently stroked her hair before tipping her chin up and kissing her tenderly. Her breath smelled like menthol cigarettes and vodka. Miriam thought back to the last time they'd made love. It had been fabulous and hot but in the morning Sara was still Sara, and she wasn't about to be tied down to just one person, no matter how much that person was in love with her. Resigned, Miriam wanted to slip into Sara's bed and lie with her head on her best friend's chest, listen to her breathe, and pretend she was someone else. *Can I make it work? Can I shut my eyes for an entire night, imagine that it's really him and that I'm not just giving up?*

Sara smiled at her and said, "Let me go get my credit card from the bar and we'll go, okay?"

Miriam said, "Okay," and watched Sara disappear back into the crowd, knowing that she wasn't going to go home with her either. She decided to have one more look around before slipping out the back and hitting up Livia at the hostel around the corner for a place to crash. Before that, however, she needed the bathroom.

She sidled up into the line and waited while man after man walked by, smirking at the privilege he enjoyed being able to stand and piss. She looked every one of them up and down as they passed, hoping. . . . Some of the men met her gaze and smiled. Most just ignored her. But none of them were her stranger.

Finally, she made it into the bathroom and took the only empty stall, second to last in the row. Hiking up her skirt, she pushed her panties down to her knees and hovered over the wetly glittering toilet seat. She sighed as her bladder emptied. For the first time that night, she could get a deep breath. As unpleasant as the odor in the room was, it still felt nice to breathe without the music beating at her body.

Miriam pulled a wad of paper off the roll and wiped, careful not to let her dangling satin skirt brush through the trembling amber droplets on the seat. She stood and pulled up her underwear. Outside her stall, a woman shouted, "Oh, come on! You two can't find a better place? It's disgusting!" A few other voices groaned and complained until a high-pitched voice told them to mind their own fucking business. Peeking out through the crack, she saw her stranger and his "date." They passed her door and shoved into the adjacent toilet stall. A few women shouted about safe places and rules, and stomped away, promising to get security to kick them out, but it didn't seem to matter to the couple. The wall to her left banged, and she heard the stupid girl gasp. *That should be me. I should be getting ravished by a beautiful person in a bathroom stall.*

Underneath the divider edge, she watched the girl's panties drop and hang up on her boots. She stomped out of them, kicking them into Miriam's stall. For a moment, she considered kicking them back. Instead, she kept watching. The stranger stepped in between the girl's feet and her legs disappeared upwards. The wall began to bang and shudder, and the girl panted and groaned while he made no noise at all.

Miriam placed her hand on the stall divider and felt the couple's rhythm. Pushing thoughts of Erik and Sara out of her mind, she closed her eyes and pictured the beautiful face of the androgyne who'd complimented her now-missing hat. She turned and leaned back against the divider, feeling the repeated impacts against her back and her ass through the thin wall. Pulling up the front of her skirt, she pushed her hand down into her underwear, caressing and stroking her clit with his imaginary fingers and occasionally plunging them deep inside herself.

She pressed back against the wall, willing herself into the other stall, into another woman's body. She thought of the stranger's mouth tasting her, of his hands feeling her, his cock, firm and soft as velvet in her hand, in her body. She sighed, running the fingers of her other hand through his white hair and looking up into those black eyes that reflected her face. She breathed deeply, smelling him as he pressed into her, kissing her and firmly holding her neck in perfect, soft hands. She pretended to breathe in clove smoke from the stranger's clothes, fresh soap, maybe a bit of breath like juniper from his gin martini. The stranger caressed her sore breast, and he filled her body. The wall pounded harder at her back, and she rubbed faster, trying to finish before they did or someone from the club came in to stop them. She felt him pushing inside of her and she pushed back. Her orgasm swelled up and over her. She shoved herself against the divider, wanting him to know she was there in front of him, that she was his, that she *was*.

The girl between them gasped loudly and then fell silent.

Coming down from the blasts of dopamine and oxytocin saturating her brain, Miriam resolved to follow them back out into the club and have the chance to feel him for real, not just in her mind. She didn't care what his date thought. She wasn't leaving without touching him again. A kiss goodnight. A promise she'd see him again, and he'd be hers.

She heard a loud thump from the next stall. Startled, Miriam tried to adjust her footing and slipped, sitting hard on the filthy floor, a shock of pain jolting up her spine. She knocked her head on the wall, seeing stars. Yanking her hand out of her underwear, she reluctantly planted it on the wet floor and pushed herself back up. The dim light in the bathroom flickered, and a smell like wet pennies stung her nose. Frustrated and embarrassed, she pulled a wad of toilet paper off the roll and wiped at her hands. A feeling of cold wetness seeped through the back of her skirt. *Fucking perfect*, she thought. *You're fingering yourself in a public toilet and you fall in a puddle of piss. Good going. Real sexy.* She was resigned to having to go back to Erik's place—it was now Erik's place, not hers—to get a change of clothes. *Might as well grab your lab ID and laptop while you're up for being humiliated.*

She dropped the toilet paper into the toilet and bent down to flush. Redness spread in the water like a blossom. Miriam looked down at her red-streaked hands and the dark puddle spreading along the floor between her feet in a slow-motion tide. Her breath caught.

A slender line of red metal slipped in the crack between the wall and the door of her stall. It raised and lifted the latch on the door. The stranger pushed the door open and stood there. Hair that had been slicked back fell down across his forehead, curling around a cheekbone and dispelling the illusion of masculinity. His shirt . . . her shirt . . . was unbuttoned, showing a hint of cleavage, and untucked, accentuating feminine hips beneath the vest. The stranger raised a hand, holding Miriam's stained hat pin in front of her face. Without the black contacts, her eyes were the coldest blue. It was him. It was *her*. The stranger smiled broadly, parting stained, crimson lips to show ruddy red teeth. "Thank you," she said, holding out the pin. Her voice was softer than before, like a sigh, but still resounded deep in Miriam's body. She stared at the stranger dumbly, too shocked to move or cry out. The stranger took her hand and turned it up. She leaned down and kissed Miriam's palm, warm, soft lips leaving a red stain severed by her lifeline. White hair tickled Miriam's wrist. Standing up straight, but cocking her head at an angle, the stranger peered out from under her bangs with a smirk. She laid the pin flat in Miriam's hand. "I'm sorry. I have to go. Perhaps some other time." Miriam felt like the words flowed over her, filling her ears, her mouth, her nose.

"Some other time," Miriam whispered. The stranger turned and walked out of the bathroom, hips swaying, leaving Miriam standing in the aftermath next to the girl lying on the floor on the other side of the divider. Careful to step lightly around the spreading red stain on the tile floor, she peeked through the door into the next stall. She held her mouth at the sight of the body lying at her feet. *No one has seen yet. They're all waiting for them to walk out together. They're waiting for the Thin Duke to walk out, not that woman.*

She followed the stranger out of the empty bathroom and watched her walk, head up, out through the front of the club and into the night. No one tried to stop her. She just slipped away.

Sara reappeared. "Hey, there you are. I got your coat. Are you ready to go home?"

Miriam thought about home. She closed her fist around the hat pin, holding tight the stranger's kiss, and realized just what she wanted. What the stranger offered. She leaned up and kissed Sara hard, grabbing a handful of her hair and pulling slightly. Sara moaned a little. "Yeah. You can take me home. But first we need to drop by Erik's place."

"You don't want to do that to yourself. You can borrow some of my clothes for a few days. We'll get your stuff next week."

"I'm not going there for clothes." She said as she wrapped her own hair back up in a loose bun and slid the bloody pin back in. Pulling Sara along behind her, they headed for the front door as the screams from the bathroom began.

MORGENSTERN'S LAST ACT

The smell of caramel popcorn couldn't mask the underlying scents brought to the fairgrounds by the traveling carnival. The elephant ride, spilled beer, engine grease, and the pit toilets all took their turns assaulting Terry Withers' sense of smell. He thanked his lucky stars he wasn't prone to seizures, otherwise the strobing lights assaulting his vision from every direction would have him writhing in the sawdust. He stuffed his hands deep in his pockets despite the temperate climate of the late-September night. Clenching his fists kept him from fidgeting with his collar. Even though it was loose, he felt like he was choking. His problems breathing had nothing to do with the neck size of his shirts.

He walked over to the girl sitting on a stool beside the Rock-O-Plane. She tucked a lock of unnaturally black hair behind an ear. Too young to be dying away gray, he concluded that she was a blonde or a ginger who wanted to be Bettie Page instead of Marilyn. Tattoos covered her bare arms from wrist to shoulder and spread across her chest. He fought conflicting emotions as he looked her over. Despite her best efforts to add hard edges, she had soft curves in all the right places underneath the black and white polka dot dress.

"You know where I can find Sam Morgenstern's act?" he asked. Of course she did. It was her job to know. Still, she blinked at him with wet doe eyes and a dumb, suspicious look like something driven more by instinct than intellect.

He repeated his question, thinking the calliope music from the ride she operated had drowned it out.

"I heardja the first time."

"Well?" he asked. He resisted the urge to pull a hand out of his pocket and fidget with his lip. The woman's cigarette was giving him the jones. He was pretty sure he'd be brushing his teeth in the car and then stopping off for a beer before heading home to his wife and her bloodhound sense of smell. *Belinda'd smell a Lucky Strike before I even got up the driveway.*

The Bettie seemed to sense his craving and exhaled menthol in his face. "I'm thinkin'."

"What's there to think about?"

"I'm thinkin', 'why should I tell you anything?'" she said. "You don't look like a rube. I make you for either a dick or a kneecapper. I don't see a bat; so you must be a dick." She twirled a bit of dyed hair in her fingers and smiled. "And I don't like dick." She pulled her finger free of the curl, frowned, and let it droop in front of his face.

"Everybody's a goddamned smartass," he coughed.

"I don't like coarse language either. Izzat how you talk to a fuckin' lady?"

"Listen, I don't really care what you like or what you don't. You tell me whether you know who I'm talking about or I'll make a call to my friends at the Local 686 and ask how many nuts on this deathtrap *they* tightened." Withers swallowed hard. He really didn't like putting the screws to people— especially people with the right kind of curves, lesbo or not. It offended his sense of chivalry. Then again, her attitude made him want to treat her like a man, if only he could keep his coughing under control.

"Whatever, pal."

"I'm not your pal, gal."

"Helpful hint, guy: you want to threaten a shut-down, do it to the jerk whose take comes out of admissions, not attractions. I could use a night off." She took another deep drag of her cigarette and turned to the control panel on the Rock-O-Plane. Punching a big red button, the ride began to slow and the music wound down. "Another morsel you might chew on is that while shit attracts flies, you *catch* them with honey." She was right. Still, she finally tired of being difficult and sighed again before giving him what he wanted. "Sam's over on the sideshow lane. Check out Dr. Morningstar's tent."

"Dr. Morningstar?"

"Ja, Arschgeige. Morgenstern ist Deutsch für 'morning star.' Now scram, so I can tear my tickets."

Withers reached up toward the brim of his hat but stopped short, making a show of not tipping it. He hadn't gone halfway around the world to kill Krauts to listen to some sideshow freak speak their gibberish at home. The woman at the booth rolled her eyes.

He headed toward the sideshow tent. Up around the bend, he handed a string of red paper tickets to another woman sporting full-sleeve tattoos. He'd expected to find *a* tattooed lady in the freak show, but it looked like they had a full painted burlesque. She ushered him past the gate with a head jerk and a desultory, "Enjoy yourself." He walked up the lane looking at the lurid signs advertising the Freak Show attractions. See the One-Eyed Giant; marvel at the Two-Headed Baby.

There were shrunken heads and the putative World's Tallest Woman, but nothing that looked like what he'd come for. Then, at the very end of the row, he saw it. It was the main-event tent. Outside, a garish painting of a man in a vintage suit, top hat, and a handlebar mustache stood beside a tall sandwich board illuminated with spotlights that cycled from red to blue to white and back.

DR. MORNINGSTAR'S PSYCHIC SURGERY
DEATH DEFIED AND DISEASE DEFEATED DAILY

COME ONE COME ALL
(NO ONE ADMITTED UNDER 18)

He coughed into his handkerchief, not wanting to look at the spot of red inside, but unable to keep himself from it. It wasn't as bad as other nights. Cold comfort when other people didn't cough up blood at all.

Outside the tent, a talker repeated the lines from the sign above giving his own alliterative spin on them. Withers queued up in a long line of people waiting to get in. He tapped the man in front of him on the shoulder and asked, "You seen this act before?"

"I came here last night. The rest of the place is a rip-off, but I had to come see *this* again."

"Worth it?"

"I'd pay twice what they're asking to see the Doctor again. I gotta figure out how he does it."

Withers suppressed a cough and pulled at his collar a little, trying to loosen it without undoing a button. "Can you spare a butt?"

The man grinned at him and shook a cigarette out of a crumpled red pack. "The wife says I'll get lung cancer. She actually believes what they say 'bout that." He laughed. "Suppose if I do, I can just come back a third time."

Withers nodded and smiled back. He wasn't a carnie, but he knew a mark when he saw one. He could tell this guy was going to get taken for everything he had someday. If he hadn't already.

Inside, Withers took a seat far off to the right. Normally, he'd sit near the exit in any place he thought a fire might break out (and the gel covers on the stage lights were already smoldering and throwing up wispy little streams of smoke).

This time, he was headed for the backstage tent flap ten feet in front of him. It was that way out, disaster or not.

A guillotine loomed in front of him, the blade glinting in the sickly yellow light. At the opposite end of the stage stood a coffin with a half-dozen broad-bladed swords shoved through at different angles. But the most compelling prop on the stage was a brushed steel autopsy table with a mirror angled over top like they used in the cooking demonstrations his wife dragged him to at the county fair. *Come see the Treman Electronics Teamco Blend King. It'll revolutionize your kitchen!*

Despite its position behind the torture implements on either side, it was clear the table was the pièce de résistance— the reason anyone would spend hard-earned money to come back to this tetanus trap. Unlike the guillotine and the swords opposite, the table was not gleaming clean. It was stained with dark reddish-brown streaks that credibly resembled dried blood. Very convincing for a sideshow act. It was as convincing as anything he'd seen in the war or his career as a murder cop. He felt a little nervous staring at it. Whoever was in charge of art direction, knew their business. Or, it wasn't paint.

Withers felt his hope grow.

A slender young woman wearing a ruffled, lace-up corset with matching bra and panties, fishnet stockings, stiletto heels, and a black executioner's hood walked out onto the stage. Surprisingly, she had no tattoos. The crowd immediately quieted down even though she didn't say a word. A couple of men in the back let out weak wolf calls, but the hood was a boner-killer. She made a slight curtsy and sashayed over to the coffin. Wheeling it into the center of the stage, she slid a sword out and set it in a rack behind. She walked around the box shaking her skinny ass, removing swords and stacking them in the rear rack, until only one remained. Spinning around with her back to the audience, she unlatched the front and swung open the lid revealing a pale man in a black mortician's suit, run through by the wide blade. The assistant slowly drew the sword from the box. From Withers' angle it looked like the thing was going right through the man's body. He was impressed by the quality of the illusion. He was no expert, but the blade sure didn't look collapsible.

As the tip slipped free of the man's body, he stepped out of the box and held out his hand. His assistant handed him the sword and he held it up in front of his face in a salute before dropping the tip and driving it into the wooden floorboards, where it stuck most solidly, wobbling a bit. The crowd erupted in enthusiastic cheers and applause. The man bowed deeply and held up hands with long, spidery fingers imploring the assembled spectators to save some of their energy. He smiled with a look that said *I'm just getting started.*

"Thank you for coming," he said. "I am Dr. Samael Morningstar and *this* . . . is my psychic surgery!" The crowd began clapping again. Not the polite kind of applause you give when someone has done nothing to earn it. They seemed ready to leap to their feet. Withers wondered how many, like the man ahead of him in line, had seen this show before.

"Although I do see some familiar faces in the audience, it is incumbent upon me to repeat that this display is for adults only. And even then, if you find that you are easily shocked, have a weak constitution, or any infirmity of the heart, the acceleration of which would endanger your life, I beseech you to go and find other entertainments along our midway to fill your evening. The good people at the front of the tent will be happy to refund the price of admission if you leave now." Morgenstern . . . Morningstar waited a beat. No one moved. He closed his eyes slowly and bowed his head. "Then let us begin."

Withers sat quietly while Morningstar ran through the paces of several pedestrian sleight of hand illusions and fakir's tricks with needles, broken glass, and razor blades. The audience kept its rapt attention, but seemed to be waiting out these minor miracles for the sake of the large props behind the performer. Eventually, he wrapped up the small part of the act and reintroduced his assistant. Withers couldn't take his eyes off of her as she wheeled the guillotine out into the center of the stage. *That's the point of having a beautiful assistant: redirection. Every second I'm looking at her, I'm missing him doing something he doesn't want me to see.* Withers looked back at the tall man to find him standing still, staring at the girl with a momentary look of confusion. He regained his composure and launched into the next part of the act.

"Previously reserved for 'criminals of noble birth,' decapitation was perfected by Joseph-Ignace Guillotin in 1789, and during The Terror in revolutionary France, the National Razor claimed the lives of over sixteen thousand." The assistant walked around the front of the device and started to crank a winch, raising the gleaming blade. Morgenstern placed a melon in the bottom half of the circle where a neck would rest—the "lunette" as he called it. "Although its use has decreased since the war, Madame Guillotine is still in use today, having just kissed Jacques Fesch, the murderer of a French policeman not even a year ago." Morgenstern glanced at Withers in the front row, winked, and pulled a small handle he called a *"déclic"* sending the angled blade slamming down with a terrible ferocity that made the audience gasp and sent a shiver up Withers' spine.

As Morningstar's baritone boomed through the tent discussing the finer points of death by beheading, his assistant bound his arms behind him. When she finished with his arms, she tied a blindfold around his eyes. The magician continued his soliloquy blindly as she rewound the winch, raising the blade to the crossbar again: "And now, to satisfy any representatives of *law enforcement* in the audience tonight, I submit to you that this demonstration is presented for scientific and educational purposes exclusively. If you bring any prurient, ill intentions with you to this theater, they are yours alone and the management and performers are not responsible." The girl led Morningstar around to the rear of the device where she strapped him to a teeterboard before tilting his body down and pushing him forward so his head emerged through the lunette. She closed the trap over Morningstar's neck and moved a basket underneath his face. Withers thought he saw Morningstar's forehead wrinkle in confusion.

With no more ceremony, the black-hooded assistant pulled the *déclic*, sending the blade crashing down. Despite his certain knowledge that it was another illusion, Withers could barely keep his hands from flying up to shield his eyes. Although it was subtle, unlike with the fruit, the blade seemed to bog down at the last second as it slammed into place. Morningstar's head fell into the wicker basket below. A gush of convincing stage blood jetted from behind the blade and coated the rolling platform upon which the device stood. The assistant walked over to the basket. Withers expected her to withdraw from it a badly rendered rubber likeness of the magician's head in deathly repose. Instead, she draped a small black shroud over it and left the stage.

The crowd murmured discontent and Withers heard one woman begin to sob. At the back of the audience, the talker pulled open the tent flaps and announced, "That's it folks. Next show is at noon tomorrow. You don't wanna miss Dr. Morningstar's miraculous resurrection!" Withers' agitated mind raced. *Next show? He didn't finish* this *show.* The crowd collectively grumbled as it filed out into the night to spend more money on rigged games and rickety rides. Withers slipped the opposite direction, toward the back of the tent where the assistant had fled. He paused beside the guillotine. Noting the lack of a body on the teeterboard, he was tempted to pull the black shroud off the basket and satisfy himself fully that it was only an illusion. *Of course it's an illusion, you fucking mook. Now go do what you came for.* Withers sneaked through the backstage curtain. Behind the stage was a narrow area where the magician stored his trays of needles and glass and other props. Behind that, another tent flap led the way outside. Withers slipped out into the night. He paused, coughing into his fist, trying to catch a breath in the cool air.

"Hey, you can't be back here!" said a carnie in an unseasonable white undershirt stretched across improbably large muscles. Withers' frayed nerves had him reaching behind his back, under his sport coat for the comfortable feel of his piece before he realized what he was doing. He slowly removed his hand from inside his coat. The gesture was not lost on the carnie.

"I was just looking for Morgen—Morningstar. I want an autograph," he said.

"You're a fan, huh?"

"Yeah. His biggest. You know where I can find him?"

"Next show's tomorrow." The muscled man jerked his thumb back over his shoulder toward the midway.

"You sure I can't get an autograph right now? My kids would just love it."

"Look pal, you don't want Sam gettin' his hands on you. Whatever it is you really want, better just take it on the heels and pretend you never saw him."

"You're doing me a favor, huh?"

The strongman folded his massive arms. Ropey muscle bulged and flexed, but the gesture looked more like a freezing man trying to protect his organs than a tough guy puffing up. "If you're looking for trouble, you found it, brother."

"I ain't your brother."

The strongman gave him another long, hard look before deciding that if Withers wanted to go running toward disaster, who was he to stand in his way. "Suit yourself, cuz." The man nodded his head toward the gate in the movable fence a few yards behind him. "Trailers're back there. Sam lives in the gypsy one."

"Was that so hard?"

"Not on me," the man chuckled. He stalked off leaving Withers alone in the dark. Withers patted the gun in his waistband for reassurance as he pushed through the gate. Ahead, he saw a row of pull-along trailers ranging from silver streamlines to Winnebago campers. In the middle was an ornate vintage Romani vardo wagon. Withers climbed the first carved wooden step and knocked on the gilt door, keeping his other hand on the pistol grip in the small of his back. A girl opened the top half of the Dutch door. "Hello," he said, putting his foot up onto the next caravan step. "You must be . . . the assistant. I'm looking for—" Before he could climb higher, he found the world swimming around him. And then it went away.

The voices were faint, as if miles away, drifting on the fog that obscured Withers' mind and blurred his vision. "What about him?" one asked. "He's a cop."

"By the time they figure out what's left of him ain't me, we'll be in Mexico. Let's dust out."

Withers tried to blink away the haze. His head ached. Every movement made him feel vertiginous and sick. He cautiously opened an eye. The blinding light sent a convulsion of sharp pain arcing from the back of his skull down into his stomach. He felt sick.

"I think he's awake."

"So what," the girl said. "I thought you were my big strong

man. You tied him down. Do you think he can slip your knots?"

"Not one I tied."

"Then leave him. They'll burn away too."

Withers smelled it then. Kerosene. He opened his other eye and made an effort to focus his vision. Ahead of him the doll was splashing the shit around the small trailer. The inside of the place looked like the outside: antiquey. Like a transplant from another time—another continent.

She doused the velvet curtains, the chair cushions, and the bed at the far end. Behind him, he felt someone tugging on the ropes that held his arms and legs tight to the chair. "Sorry about this," the man said. Withers tilted his head back carefully and peeked. The strongman. "I told you to take it on the heels."

"Don't talk to him," the girl shouted.

"I'm looking for Morgenstern," Withers said through the pain. "I don't give a shit about anything else."

The girl stood up straight and looked at her hulking partner. Although it was plenty big enough, he still looked confined in the space. Unable to stand up to his full height or square his shoulders as though the caravan were shrinking around him, pushing him down. "Well, you can tell Sam what I think of him when he meets you in Hell," she said. Her voice was nothing like Withers had expected. It was rough and gravelly like she'd been the one doing the razor-eating act instead of her boss . . . and it'd gone wrong.

"My inside coat pocket. Look there." The couple stared at him as though opening his coat might trigger a bomb or a gas canister. The strongman crept over and pulled open Withers' sport coat. "Other side," he directed. The meathead did as he was told. Withers assumed that was the whole reason he was along for this ride: indomitable physical presence—didn't ask questions. He felt like telling the goon that as soon as she got clear of the midway, she'd need to be clear of him too. She looked like she was getting ready for a vanishing act and a body like his was going to draw attention wherever they went. The key to a magic trick like disappearing was to have the audience looking in the other direction as you slipped out of sight. *Nobody* took their eyes off a gorilla if it was out of its cage.

The man dug in Withers' pocket with clumsy, short fingers, pulling out the thick envelope. He held it up to the girl who asked, "What is it?"

"Dunno," he said.

"It's from my doctor," Withers explained. "Open it." He nodded at them to let them know it was okay to look. The small gesture hurt. He wondered if the ape had hit him with a lead sap or a brick wall. Either way, lung cancer didn't look like it would be what killed him after all. If the swelling in his brain didn't do it, being burned alive would. He'd never smoked a velvet curtain before. He hoped that he got a good couple of satisfying last drags before the smoke suffocated him.

He was racked by a coughing fit, but couldn't cover his mouth with his hands tied behind his back. A spray of red mist billowed out of his mouth, and blood-tinged saliva dripped down his chin.

"You're really sick."

"I told you. I came to see Morgenstern. Dr. Morningstar."

"The *psychic surgery* bit? You think he can really pull tumors out of your fuckin' lungs and cure you?"

"If he can do the tumors, then radiation will do the rest. They say they can't operate."

"I don't get it," the meathead said.

"Psychic surgery. It's a swindle," she explained. "A shyster like Sam tells people he can pull tumors and shit out of their bodies without even making a cut. He folds a bunch of their flabby skin over—and they're *all* flabby—pinching so it feels like he's doing something, and then he palms a chicken liver or some blob of meat out on to their stomach. 'Voila! I have removed your wicked tumor!'" She mocked Morgenstern's stage presence, throwing back her head and then sharply bowing. "Desperate rubes eat it up and then shit greenbacks. Best part of the grift is they all die, so nobody comes back looking for a refund."

"Morgenstern beat cancer," Withers said.

"That's what he tells suckers like you. Right before they give up their life savings. 'I stared death in the face,'" she mocked, "'and spat in his eye! I am—'"

"I am constant as the northern star!" The booming voice rattled the caravan like a cannon blast.

The caravan door came off its hinges and flew away into the night, replaced by the tall magician, stooping to enter his home. His white shirt was stained a brownish red and the collar had been hewn off. A ragged, weeping line encircled the man's neck. "Lili, this has been very dispiriting."

"But, I—"

"You jammed the trap, so it didn't open in time. I dropped *after* the blade hit. Clever girl. I can imagine the write-up in the papers now. 'Dr. Morningstar died in an accident owing to an occupational hazard of the death defier.' And then, what? You were so distraught you *self-immolated*?" Morgenstern shook his head with disappointment. "My dear. I thought you believed in me."

The strongman fired Withers' pilfered gun at the figure in the doorway. The bullets made Morgenstern's black suit puff and ripple, like firing into smoke. He smirked and stepped fully into the caravan. "And you, Karl." The magician held up a finger, cocked his thumb, and aimed. "Well, you can hardly blame an ass for pulling against a harness." He dropped his thumb. The man dropped to the floor.

Morgenstern walked past Withers' chair toward his assistant. She held up a can of kerosene and a Zippo. "Don't come any closer!" she shouted.

"Fire?" Morgenstern's black suit fluttered, though the air in the caravan was still. "Didn't you know I was baptized in fire?" He snapped his delicate fingers and the can in Lili's hands burst, soaking her with the clear fluid. With a sleight of hand gesture, a match appeared between the great man's fingers. "I love you," he whispered.

"I. Never. Loved. You!" She stood shivering. Defiant.

Morgenstern smiled. "It's your rebelliousness I loved most." He turned his back and she burst into flame. Morgenstern walked back toward the door as flame began to overtake the small space, tossing the unused match in the corner.

"Wait!" Withers cried out. "Please don't leave me!"

Morgenstern turned and appraised the man. The magician looked at him with sad eyes that looked as dry as glass. "You were in the audience tonight. You are dying." He smiled again.

"I don't want to die."

"That's not the first time I've heard that." Thick black smoke began to pool and eddy along the ceiling of the caravan spreading out behind the magician like a broad set of black wings. "Why should I listen *now*?"

Withers coughed. He couldn't catch his breath to plead.

Morgenstern bent down close, holding a finger to his lips to quiet him. His touch was pleasantly warm and soft. "I could feel your cancer when you first sat down in my audience. It's inoperable."

Withers blinked against the rising heat and wished that the thing in front of him would untie his hands at least so he could rub at his stinging eyes. "I'll give you anything," he choked.

"Anything?" The black angel beat his wings, swirling the smoke around him in dark, suffocating eddies.

Withers breath caught. And then he said, "Anything. Everything!"

Morgenstern laughed in his face. Withers felt the ropes loosen and fall away. He staggered up from the chair and the room pitched as he swooned from the sudden pain in his head. The beast caught him and held him up.

Withers cried out as Morgenstern's hand plunged into his abdomen. The dark man pushed his flesh aside and slid his hands up under Withers' ribs. The thinning air in the room was overtaken by thickening smoke. He was suffocating. His vision dimmed. His hearing lessened. From far away he heard a voice that said, "Never repent."

Withers felt a ripping in his body that eclipsed every other sensation of pain he'd experienced, in war, on the force, in sickness. Every hard thing in his life was a joy compared to what Morgenstern did with his hand. And as much as he wanted to black out, to fall out of the world into blissful oblivion, he was held right there, in his body, feeling every searing tug and jerk and tear. Until Morgenstern pulled his hand free and held it up, showing Withers a wetly shining mass of meat—the meat that had once been killing him.

The magician tore at it with white teeth until a piece the size of a plum came off and the thing swallowed it like a pelican eating a fish: chin up, tissue sliding down.

"Want a taste?" he asked.

Withers squinted his eyes shut as hard as he could and shook his head like a child being offered ipecac.

"You don't know what you're missing. None of you have any taste, really." Two more bites and the ball of rebellious flesh was gone. Morgenstern picked Withers up in his arms and carried him outside the trailer. He set the man down in the grass by the fence. People rushed around them with buckets and hoses trying to put out the fire. None of them paid the men any mind.

"What did you just do? Did I just sell you my soul?"

Morgenstern laughed again. "Of all the things you have— this planet, your time on it, a comfortable life in a universe hostile to *everything* . . . and still, you want a soul. Don't be so greedy. You already got more than you deserve."

The magician left to get a bucket to help put out the fire. Withers heard him shout, "My God, Lili's in there!" as though he meant it.

Withers rolled over in the grass and pushed himself up off the ground. He took a deep breath in the night air and relished it.

ALL DREAMS DIE IN THE MORNING

Everything was disorienting. Rifles popped in a constant dull crackle competing with mortar bombs and grenades to still his ears. The rain fell in heavy sheets, obscuring the men behind the tree line shooting at him, making their muzzle flashes sparkle in the dark like the starry sky above Ripton, back home, on the Fourth of July. Thunder boomed softer than bombs, and men screamed and splashed as they ran and fell in the maelstrom. And he tried to make sense of a tiny spot in the chaos of it all, and find one of them to kill. Everything worked in bombastic concert to prevent Jake from seeing the enemy. Focusing on a shadow, he aimed and fired. A shadow fell. He fired. Nothing changed. He fired, and a grenade exploded in front of him, peppering his face with hot sand that felt like a thousand little stings. He fell back behind his fortification, gasping in panic and pawing at his eyes, desperate to assure himself he still had them.

He choked and sputtered as the rain beat down on his stinging face. A pair of hands gripped him. He panicked, not knowing whose they were. With his M1 firmly in his grasp, he tensed, ready to fire or swing the stock around. What he couldn't do was see whether it was another Marine grabbing him, or the enemy. A voice called through the din. "Blackmun! Jake! Are you all right?" He shook his head and wiped at his eyes. The rain blurred them again the second he brushed them clear. A flare lit up overhead, lighting the rain like falling embers. The face above him was a backlit silhouette, indistinguishable from all the others rushing back and forth behind it, but he recognized the voice. Jim from Georgia—who gave him a raft of shit about being a New England Yankee but always held out a hand when Jake needed one—was looming over him pulling him out of the dark. "Up, Jake. On your fuckin' feet!" he cried out over the sounds of war. Jake pawed at his head feeling for his helmet before sitting up, and felt only the damp hair that had grown out long past regulation length since they'd landed on the island. Jim shoved his lost helmet at him and pulled him upright. He heard a bullet cut through the air right next to his head before he saw the tracer round rip into Jim's chest and send the big man sprawling on his back.

He slapped his helmet on, dumping filthy water over his head, and jumped on top of Jim, trying to find the wound, trying to see if he would be okay. The rain pattered against Jim's fixed, open eyes. The ragged black hole above his heart stained the Marine green fabric of his shirt black. He would never be okay again.

Jake pivoted on his knee and swung his rifle around at the line of muzzle flashes in the bushes across the creek, firing blindly at the lights. Movement to his left drew his attention and he saw a row of their soldiers splashing in the water, trying to advance on their flank. Sergeant Hull shouted at the men on the line to redirect fire, but he didn't need to be told. He advanced, turned his aim on them, squeezed the trigger, and a man fell. Two more behind that one crumpled before he had a chance to get a bead on either one. One after another, the enemy collapsed into the water, dead. Jake fired until he heard his clip ping as it ejected from his rifle. He jammed another clip in and kept firing until he heard the Sergeant scream, "Cease fire, cease fire," his words almost lost in the thunder and rain. The men obeyed. Their guns and mortars silenced, only the weather disobeyed his command.

Every peal of thunder made him flinch. He returned to his part of the entrenchment to find Sterling and Stone squatting next to Jim. They weren't working to rescue him. Neither applied pressure or tried to beat life back into his body. They sat, staring into the face of their friend who used to tell jokes and share his rations though he complained of being hungry. When they'd kidded him that his size made him a bigger target than the rest of them, Jim beat a fist against his chest, and said, "Stay behind me, boys!"

Jake clenched his jaw and looked at the bodies of the enemy on the far shore, lying still in shallow water. One of them was responsible for that hole in Jim's chest. One of them had killed him. And though dead, in Jake's mind, that account wasn't square. Not by a long shot. Whoever he was, he might've died for his Emperor, but the rat bastard deserved to die again for killing his friend. He scanned the line looking for someone who could take the guilty man's punishment and deliver it to him in Jap Hell. Not a single one, dead or alive, volunteered to courier his punishment. So, Jake sat in the hot dark, soaking wet. For the first time since landing on the island, he was thankful for the rain. Thankful it concealed his tears.

He awoke with a start, gasping and crying out. His feet caught in the sheets and he kicked, struggling to free himself before they could get him, hold him down and bayonet him. A cool hand on his chest preceded a light "Shhh. You're all right. You're here with me." He gripped her wrist and blinked away the dream lingering behind in his eyes. The island jungle retreated, leaving him in their bedroom lit in the blue hue of early morning, not the cold white fire of an enemy flare. The sheers Dene had sewn the winter before moved slightly with the gentle air pushing through the gaps in the window frame. He'd rather sleep with the windows open, but he didn't want the neighbors to hear his screams. Though he felt fairly certain they could anyway.

"Was it the same one?" she asked. He nodded. He never told her what the dream was about, but she knew the same one had been haunting him for more than a decade. Though it didn't visit him every night, it came often enough he dreaded sleep, especially in summer when the heat and humidity settled in and reminded him of the islands. That morning was cool, though. The temperature had finally dropped overnight and their bedroom was almost chilly. It was nice under the covers with her.

He fell back onto his pillow and she lay down beside him with her head on his shoulder, tracing a finger up and down the center of his undershirt. Her touch was electric and made him stir under the covers. He turned his head and she looked up and kissed him with dry lips that tasted like salt and sleep. She smiled and the lines around her dark eyes deepened, giving him a peek at her face as it would be in another twenty or thirty years when those lines were permanent. He loved the future of her as much as the present and the past all in that single moment.

Cupping her breast in his hand, Jake craned his neck forward for another kiss. She caressed his stomach, slipping her fingers under the bottom of his shirt to tickle the hair around his navel, then walked them down and pulled at the drawstring at the front of his pajama bottoms. He drew her closer and her hand came out of his pants and pushed lightly against his chest. She got up on an elbow and turned her head away, coughing. She took a deep, dry-sounding breath before coughing again, harder, with a rattle in her lungs he could feel through the mattress. He tried waiting for the spell to pass, but she rolled away from him and sat upright on the edge of the bed. Her back convulsed with each painful sounding hack and wheeze.

"You call the doctor yesterday, like I asked you to?" he asked, timing his words in between her explosions.

She looked over her shoulder at him, one hand covering her mouth and shook her head, no. While she liked her doctor fine, she disliked doctors in general and avoided calling on them on principle. Shy of needing stitches or a cast, she'd say they had more important things to do than worry about her. "It's just this damn cold," she said. Her voice was a rasp. "I'll get over it. Doc Haringa has real sick people to look after."

"You *are* sick. Been a month you since first caught that cold. How much longer you going to hold out?"

With a hand on her sternum, she rolled her eyes and sighed. "If it's not better by tomorrow, I'll call on him."

"Promise?"

"I promise, Punkin. I'll do it." She leaned back on one hand and he got up on an elbow, craning his neck forward for a kiss. Instead, she tussled his hair and stood. He knew her cough wouldn't be better tomorrow or the next day. He knew that it wouldn't ever be better unless someone looked at it and maybe gave her something to fight the infection. But there was no arguing with Dene. She was convinced it was just a cold that she couldn't shake and there'd be no telling her otherwise—no matter how many letters came after your name. He resolved to call Dr. Haringa after breakfast. He reckoned he'd done harder things than drag her to the doctor's office kicking and screaming.

She pulled her robe around her shoulders. "I'll go fix us up some coffee," she said. "You want eggs?" He wanted to say all he desired was her getting back into bed with him. But their attempt at affection had kicked off another coughing spell. A second try would just start that rattling motor running even harder. He sat up, trying to hide the last of his erection by bunching up the covers in his lap. The sad look on her face told him she noticed as much as he did that both of them were getting out of bed unsatisfied. She picked a pack of cigarettes up off the nightstand and lit one before holding the pack out to him.

He slid one out even though he preferred Lucky Strikes to her menthols, struck a match and said, "Eggs'd be aces, Swee'Pea."

She walked out of the bedroom leaving him alone with his memories of intimacy and killing. The breeze stole through the gaps like a low breath and the smell of rosemary from the garden rode in on it. His stomach rumbled. He took a drag of her menthol.

The stink of cigarettes and body odor woke Jake from already fitful sleep. Not one of them had enjoyed a shower in weeks, but Private Foster smelled riper than anyone else on the island. As if his body was producing a protective cocoon of musk strong enough to block out everyone else's B.O. He sure as shit didn't smell like rosemary. That was it, right? He'd dreamed about smelling rosemary. And about her again. Whoever she was. Like all his dreams, her face faded from his mind until he was left only with an idea of who his Swee'Pea might be.

"Jesus wept, Foster. You could make a vulture puke." Foster smiled, stuck up a middle finger and walked on, seeming proud of his reek.

Jake stuck a leg out of his rack and tried to stand without dumping himself out of the hammock onto the ground. The sun was barely up but it was already oppressively hot and humid. The sensation recalled the memory of the steam towel shave his father had treated him to the day before he left for Camp Lejeune. His mother had balked and said, "Willya look at his chin? There aren't enough hairs on it to pluck, let alone shave." She wanted to protect her boy—or the idea of him still being a boy, anyway. The old man had insisted, telling her that "the boy" was a man, and goddamn it, he needed a proper shave before he sailed halfway around the world to fight a war. He marched Jake out of the house and they loaded into the truck and his Pop drove him to Frank's Tonsorial Parlor. Pop didn't much care for the name—he didn't like to put on "airs"—but Frank was a buddy from the First War and he wouldn't go anywhere else to get his hair cut, no matter how high-toned the sign above his barbershop door might be. Not if his life depended on it.

Frank welcomed Jake inside, standing in his white, side-buttoned barber's jacket and holding a pair of silver shears as if he been interrupted cutting a phantom's hair. Pop told him they were there for his son's first steam shave, and Frank sat him down and didn't say a single word about how little soft red stubble there actually was on his chin. The barber reclined the chair, wrapped his smooth face in that steaming, moist towel, and talked to him about ladies and politics like he was a regular old friend, instead of some seventeen-year-old kid who had as much need for a straight razor to be drawn across his skin as he had an idea what awaited him under a skirt or in the Solomon Islands.

Standing in front of his hammock felt like being under that towel, except it was wrapped around his entire body instead of only his face, and no matter what he did, he couldn't get untangled from it. Sterling and Stone waved to him from the chow line.

He shambled over and wished them a good morning. "Breakfast that bad, or do you always look like that?"

Passing by with a freshly filled tin cup, Jim from Georgia said, "Say what you will, but Uncle Sam only provides the finest meals for his boys overseas." He pulled something out of his cup that looked like a long grain of rice . . . until it squirmed between his fingers. He popped it in his mouth and the others groaned. Jim pounded his fist against his chest.

"Protein, Marines! It's the fuel that'll take us to Tokyo!" He wandered off, fingers searching for another maggot.

Jake said, "Something seem . . . off about Jim today?"

His friends shrugged. "No more'n any day, I guess," Sterling replied. "Why?" Jake couldn't put his finger on it. He shrugged and joined the line to wait his turn for a ladle full of something tan and flavorless and hopefully devoid of bugs. He got half of what he wished for.

He found the others sitting in the tall grass on a rise near their camp, laughing and smoking Lucky Strikes. Jake settled in near them and wiped the last of his meager portion of breakfast out of his cup with a filthy finger. He stuck it in his mouth and sucked it clean before wiping his hands on his equally filthy dungarees.

Chris Sterling pulled a picture out of his breast pocket and passed it over to Stone. "That's her," he said. "Connie. She's waiting for me back home. Smart as a whip. She's a teacher." Stone made a wolf whistle and passed the picture on to Pearl who said something about wanting her to teach him something. Sterling shot him a glare with no promise behind it. Stone pulled a picture out of his wallet and handed it over. Sterling said, "Ooh, she's a destroyer all right."

"Don't you know it! Her name's Roberta." Stone held his hands out in front of his chest and said, "She's smart too." They laughed and kept passing pictures around, talking about the one back home, re-reading the last letters they'd gotten from them. They all listened to the same tales of life in the States, about picnics and paper drives and how proud everyone was of what they were doing, as if someone told all the girls not to mention anything that might sour the mood of the boys. They declared that they wanted them home safe and soon and made unwritten promises in between the innocent words of their letters.

"Hey, Blackmun. Show us yours. Who's waiting for you?"

Jake stared into his empty mug, brows furrowed and lips

tightly pressed together. There was no picture in his pocket or wallet. The only girls waiting for him to come back home were his mom and a nun from St. Mary's school who wept before he left, even though she used to threaten him with Hell for shooting spit wads at the chalkboard. He glanced over at Rod Freeman sitting next to him and snatched a picture out of his wallet. Freeman demanded the photograph back, saying that was his sister, but Jake held him off with a hand and said, "That's her. That's the girl I'm gonna marry when I get home." He looked at his friend and said, "What's her name?" The Marines laughed at the absurdity of it. Freeman's eyes narrowed and his jaw flexed. But his face relaxed when he seemed to realize that no harm could come to his sister through her picture.

"Hildene. 'Cept she goes by Dene." He quickly added, "If you're going to write her, you better ask first if you can call her that. And if you put any racy shit in your letters, I'll drown your freckled ass in a dugout. You hip to what I'm telling you?" Jake nodded and put his hand over his heart. Jake passed the picture to Stone who nodded and wolf whistled to Freeman's consternation. Sterling said she was a real blackout girl, and Pearl agreed. He handed the picture back to Jake, who reluctantly held it out to Freeman to put back in his wallet. He shook his head and said, "Yeah, I guess you can keep it for a while. I mean if you're gonna get *married* and all."

"Thanks, Rod." Jake put the picture in his breast pocket, above his heart. He looked around. "Where's Jim? I want to show him too."

The men looked down into the grass and stopped laughing about the girls back home. Sterling stood, put his helmet on, and excused himself. The others pocketed their photographs and one by one wandered off to clean their rifles or report for watch or try to find a card game. And when Jake was left alone with his only thoughts and the mosquitoes for company, he pulled Dene's picture out of his pocket, and went to scrounge up a pencil and some paper to write her a letter.

Jake stood with his hat in hand as people filed past, mumbling their condolences. He did his best to say "thank you" to each of them for coming, but he didn't feel gratitude. He didn't feel much of anything. Except longing. He longed for the hand on his chest every time he had a nightmare and the soft voice whispering in his ear that he was not in danger. Her sweet breath pulling him out of the jungle into their bedroom, into their bed and her arms and the world he wanted to live in, not that other one. And not this one. He longed for the space in between then and now, when he had someone to see him through those early morning moments where he didn't know who or where he was. But all he had left were the nightmares and an empty bed and the goddamned breeze through the gaps in the windows.

His Pop stepped in front of him with a face full of sadness and said, "I'm sorry, my son." For the first time in knowing him thirty years, Jake saw his father cry. The old man was overwhelmed and dropped his face so his boy, taller than he and sturdier too, wouldn't see him weep, wouldn't see what he was reduced to. His mother took Pop by the shoulders and tried to lead him off so Jake could be alone in his grief, but the man refused and stood fast. Jake reached out a hand to shake. Pop took a halting step forward and embraced him instead. Jake wrapped his arms around his father and held him while the elder man cried. His mother put one hand on her husband's back, and with her other grasped her son's wrist. They stood like that for a long time while the bright daylight sun shone on Dene's coffin, mocking it, and her inside. Telling Jake so clearly what he already knew:

the sun would shine on all their graves and make the grass grow green to hide their remains. Only the stones preserved their names. And not forever. He looked aside to one of the ancient headstones a few yards away, worn by time and the weather until it couldn't be read. No one came to lay flowers on that grave. No one knelt at it and whispered their sorrowful longing. It stood alone, remembered only as a place where someone once had been lowered to the sound of tears and shovels of dirt raining down.

His mother finally pulled the old man away, and Jake said, "Thanks, Pop." His parents walked off, leaving him the last man standing at the grave except the mortician and the preacher. Jake thanked the mortician for everything he'd done for Dene. He said nothing to the preacher. That man hadn't done jack shit in all his life and he knew it. Jake stared hotly at him until the funeral director offered to take him back to the hearse that had brought them. Jake refused, telling him not to wait. He'd be along in his own time. The funeral director led the preacher off instead and Jake stayed behind to watch the workmen lower his bride into the ground under the noonday sun.

He pulled the envelope with his last letter to Dene out of his breast pocket, dropped it in the hole after her pine box, turned, and walked home alone to fix himself lunch in an empty house. The mortician stood by the side of the car watching him go. He didn't need the ride home; he was used to long walks in all kinds of weather.

He ran with abandon, like a child gripping a kite string, trying to make a diamond of color lift and fly behind him like a paper soul at the end of fate's string. He skidded in the mud to the left to avoid another explosion, though the destruction was wrought and over before he even saw it flower. He gripped the ammunition belts over his shoulders tighter and scrambled for the fortification where his friends held on to hope that this was not the hole in which they'd die. The mud pulled at his feet, slowing him. He worked to stay upright and find the earthen pit in which there was safety from the flying bullets. He ran furiously and unhindered by impediments of vanity or inhibition. Though he knew fear. He knew it better than he knew himself, because it was always with him. Except when it stepped behind its siblings, fury and grief, for a rest.

A root jutted up from the earth and reached for his foot, uncoiling and whipping at him, trying to pull him down into the mud. Lightning lit up the night and thunder followed immediately upon it. A tree splintered and he couldn't tell if it was the bolt or a bomb that did it. The world clawed at his clothes and screamed at him to slow down and stop. Give in to inertia and give up. Lie down. Let go of the string and let the kite fall. Jake sprinted on, counting time only in pounding footsteps and heartbeats. He refused the false comforts of stillness and rest, staggered and pushed himself ahead. He ran because not running meant to die. And Jake would be damned if he would die without ever meeting the woman who'd agreed to marry him. The woman he only knew in her letters and his dreams. He'd be damned and tear down Hell before he'd stop for anything or anyone but her.

A flash of yellow and red in the dark erupted in front of him, cascading up with embers and down with rain. And the hole toward which he'd propelled himself was black and quiet as it smoked. Jake stopped, staring into it with wide eyes and a gaping mouth. The fortified position lay torn open in smoldering ruin. Sterling, Pearl, and Stone were all inside it, a tangle of terrible familiarity. Bodies broken and rent in ways he'd seen often, but never with this kind of intimacy. Rain pummeled his friends' bodies, mingling their blood with earth and washing them clean as headstones. Silence descended on him. The kite drooped.

A hand gripped the back of his shirt and pulled. "Blackmun! Move!" He turned and the dark giant pulled again, shouting his name and raising an arm to point the way, away from this death, toward a different hole in the earth. Toward one that barked gunfire and shouts of defiance. He followed and they fled toward a different gun position—a different band of men trying to survive the night and fire. A flash of light and he saw Jim from Georgia leading him to a new grave. He leaped in. Throwing the belt ammunition at the gunner, and turned back to pull Jim in after him.

Only, he was gone.

Of course, Jim was weeks dead and but a dream. Jake told himself it had to be someone else. Hart or Pluck. They too were big men like Jim; it was one of them who saved him. He looked around and found them steady in their own positions on the line.

And then the rain fell harder. He looked up and watched the sparkling sky falling around him.

He toweled off his wet hair. The southern hemisphere sun had turned it bright red as it tanned his skin a golden brown he'd never enjoyed before. He looked in the mirror and felt transformed from who he'd been when he left home more than two years ago. Deprivation had made his face gaunt and hardship toned his thin muscles. The boy his mother had been desperate to preserve was long gone. Though he still couldn't grow a beard.

"He's not decent; you can't go back there," he heard his auntie shout from the front room. Jake wrapped the towel around his head and peeked out of the bathroom. The woman strode down the hall toward him, her face aglow. He recognized her from the picture she'd sent so he could give the other one back to Rod. He'd stared long and hard at the image of her sitting on the wooden rail fence, leaning back on her arms with a knee cocked up like a nosecone pin-up painting—a pose just for Jake—wondering what it would be like to see her in the real world, full and flesh and alive. And here she was. She skipped to him with a smile like a lightning strike and almost jumped into his arms. They were the same height and she might've outweighed him, but he caught her and held her and they kissed like they were already married, though they weren't headed to see the Justice of the Peace for another few hours yet.

The towel fell from his head and she leaned back in his arms to get a good look at him. "Saaaay!" she cried. "You said you were bald." Her eyes narrowed and she added, "It's so . . . so red."

He laughed. He'd written in a letter that he was prematurely bald and hoped that when they finally met, his appearance wouldn't matter. She'd replied that she loved him, so he could look like a troll from under a bridge and she'd still marry him. His lie wasn't a test as much as a tease, and the look on her face was worth it. "I hope you're not disappointed. I figured saying I was bald might be less upsetting than telling you I was a carrot top."

Dene ran her fingers through his hair and giggled. She looked at her future husband and the smile grew wider and she held him tighter. "You are a scoundrel."

"Tell you what, I'll buy you breakfast to make up for it."

"It's almost lunchtime, Punkinhead."

He looked at his watch. He'd been indulging himself in the comforts of a home, not a hole, and had lost track of time. "Punkinhead, huh?"

"How 'bout Punkin' for short?"

His auntie stood at the end of the hallway, arms folded across her chest. While she didn't condone the two of them, him dressed only in a pair of boxer shorts and an A-shirt, unmarried and holding each other in the hall, she didn't say anything—only stared disapprovingly. When it was clear they weren't going to pay her any mind, she turned and disappeared into the living room, stomping along the way as if they needed reminding she was there.

"I s'pose I ought to get spiffy for our date with the J.P.," he said.

She shook her head and whispered in his ear, "I'm never letting you get dressed."

"I imagine they might not truck with that at City Hall, but whatever you want. I'll report for our nuptials in my privies if it makes you happy."

"*You* make me happy, mister."

"Glad to hear it, missus."

From the living room, his auntie called out, "Close only counts in horseshoes and hand grenades! You two aren't mister and missus yet."

His face clouded at the thought of hand grenades, as if the word came with the concussion of one spitting fire, blood, and sand in his eyes. Dene pressed her palm against his cheek and kissed him once more, lightly, on the mouth. His darkness drained and his head felt light and a little dizzy, like he had been drowning until she pulled him out of the dark water.

"Get dressed, Marine. We've got a date to get hitched."

He stepped back and saluted. "Yes ma'am."

She started toward the living room, but paused at the end of the hall, looking at him over her shoulder, doing something she couldn't in a letter or a photo. Jake's mouth hung open. He thought he could watch her walk away all day long, but he never wanted to see her leave again. She smiled and said, "It's nice to meet you, Jacob Blackmun."

"The pleasure's all mine, Hildene Freeman."

He started awake with a stab of pain in his back that made him want to call out. A cough cut off his cry, and he tried to sit up to get a breath. A cool hand pressed to his chest and a soft voice in his ear told him, "Relax, it was only a dream." His throat was dry and he couldn't get the words out, "No, not the dream. The pain." Instead, he coughed. The hand retreated from his chest and returned with a small salmon-colored plastic jug with a white straw jutting out. He lifted a thin, pale hand to help guide the straw toward his lips, to wet his mouth and throat and try again to speak. The needle in the back of his hand ached dully when the tube connected to it pulled against the part of his bed it had become hung up on.

The soft voice returned. "Here, let me." She leaned in, pointing the end of the straw at his lips, and he suckled at it. Cold water filled his mouth. He could only swallow half of what he drew out before another round of coughing made him sputter and spit the rest down his chin. "Oh no. I'm sorry, Mr. Blackmun." The cup disappeared, replaced by a cloth. She wiped the water from his chin like a mother tending an infant learning how to drink from a cup. "You need to slow down, okay?" He nodded and tried again.

"How are you feeling, Mr. Blackmun?" the nurse asked.

The question was so cruel. How could she ask it? Once, he'd been a strong man—a Marine, tall and imposing. A man who fought with intention. Who laughed and loved with abandon. Looking now at his diminished legs under the thin white blankets, he was no longer that man, except in dreams. If he tried to laugh, he coughed. If he tried to stand, he fell. He was lost. Confined in a home of weakened flesh and brittle bone. His body hurt so much they had to pump him full of painkillers, when all he wanted was to run and jump and kiss and fuck and laugh and tell stories and drink whiskey and be alive. And most of all, he wanted to be with *her* and not here, alone in this place, unable to get out of bed. And if he couldn't do any of that, then he wanted to dream.

If he couldn't dream, what remained?

Underneath the astringent antiseptic scent that filled the room, he could smell the unpleasant odor of his body. He smelled like a man who hadn't had a shower in an age. While the nurses washed him with sponges and changed his gown and bedclothes regularly, he could still smell himself. Despite their efforts, he smelled like a man dying in bed.

She leaned close to look into his eyes, searching for the spark of lucidity that would tell her he was fully present and his pain wasn't overwhelming. That he wasn't delirious with the cancer that had been eating him from the prostate up since he first ignored his symptoms. Toughing it out. The nurse was beautiful and young and undoubtedly made someone very happy. A lover, husband, parent or child who couldn't imagine the world without her in it, and sought every conscious moment near her shine. And she, he hoped, knew that feeling too. But then, she was here with him and not that person. She was here and Dene was twenty years gone, and this was his first waking moment in he didn't know how long. Jake knew he only had so many moments left in his life, and while she was lovely, she wasn't his and he wasn't hers, and he didn't want to spend this time awake, no matter how caring and kind and beautiful she was. He wanted to dream. Even if, half the time, he was in a hell of fighting and pain. Because the rest of the time, he was there with her, and a dream felt like a present moment while you were in it. Awake, he had only his memories and the room where no more memories worth preserving were made. Every moment he lived, his memories fell farther behind him. He could think of Dene—remember her hazel eyes and chestnut hair and her breath that smelled like the menthols that took her from him. But none of it was here, now. It was all so long ago.

He blinked at the nurse and opened his mouth as if to say sure, you bet he was feeling all right, but instead, he winced and let out a wheezing, whining sigh that it shamed him to make. Still, it earned him the response he wanted. Her forehead wrinkled with concern, and she made a noise that sounded like pity. She put her cool hand on his chest again and said, "It's early, Mr. Blackmun, but I'll see if the doctor will let me give you something."

She left the room. He exhaled a shuddering breath and let his head drop back on his pillow. The pain in his spine *was* terrible and he could barely breathe. But it was discomfort he could endure. He'd known so much already. He could take a little more, if it meant she came back with the bottle in her pocket and the sleep inside it. But the ache in his back grew and spread. It became a cramp in his guts and a feeling like his brain was pushing against the inside of his skull, and he wasn't sure how much more he could take. He tried to push back. He tried to stay on top of it. That's what they said when they spoke about him like he wasn't even there: "Stay on top of it." If they gave him the drugs on schedule, they could stay on top of his pain and he would sleep peacefully . . . and dream. But if they let it get too bad, then they'd have to give him more and more and he knew he wouldn't sleep as much as he would be sedated, and then he'd go down deeper, to where there was nothing. When he was first diagnosed and they tried surgery, they'd sent him down that hole. A doctor told him to count backward from a hundred and put a mask over his face. Next thing he knew he was waking up in recovery with no memory of hours of surgery—and no dreams. Just the blank oblivion of heavy sedation. He'd happily deal with a measure of suffering and nightmares to have his dreams. Anyone would. Good dreams were worth the pain. Good dreams were all he had now that everything else was gone.

His breath hitched and the pain in his back and stomach spread into his chest. He attempted a deep breath and began to cough again. He couldn't call out. He couldn't breathe. It hurt. Behind his head, he heard an alarm begin to sound. An insistent beeping that kept pace with his accelerating fear. He took tiny breaths trying to feel a fullness of air, but his lungs wouldn't cooperate. He chest was so heavy, like someone standing on him.

After an endless moment, the door to his room burst open and people dressed in white flooded in with urgency, dragging something behind them he couldn't see through the blur of tears and panic. Their urgent voices were so far away as they came near. A man said something, but Jake couldn't hear over the thrum of blood in his ears and the damned beeping behind his head, now joined by another machine alarm. He reached with a shaking hand for the one who looked like the nurse who'd gone to fetch him sleep. He reached for her jacket. Dene was in the bottle she kept there. The bottle in her pocket. The needle in the bottle. The drug in the IV line. Rest in his blood. And in his dreams, the woman he loved. The woman so long gone, leaving him with only sleep and memory to live for.

Though the world was just about finished with him, he wasn't done. He had more to dream.

He tried to speak. There was something over his face, forcing air in his mouth, into his lungs. He didn't want it. Hands on his body and voices all around. And everything hurt. And he was so afraid. He wanted to call for his mother the way he'd done when it seemed like the world was too big a place to be in and all he needed was her arms around him—a small embrace of comfort and security. The nurse and her bottle. Mother's nourishing morphine.

Then the hands were gone and there was a new beeping, so distant. And the flash like a nighttime storm on

Guadalcanal. And afterward, everything was softer, more distant and dimmer. *Just one more, please. One more dream and then I'll go. Let me run in the rain with my brothers. Let me make love to my wife one last time before leaving. Just one more dream. Please.*

Jacob Blackmun turned his head and another flash blossomed behind his eyes. And when it cleared, he saw the rising sun outside his window, and he said goodbye to no one because there wasn't anyone he loved left to hear him say it. Mom and Pop. Jim from Georgia, Sterling, Pearl, Rod and Stone. And Dene. Most of all, Dene. All gone.

Only he remained, along with the memory of a dream a moment ago.

And then nothing else in the early morning light but the dark and silence.

The dream of a man was done.

MINE, NOT YOURS

Some of the kids next to me laugh as the girl on the hospital bed screams about killing her baby. Fake blood coats the inside of her thighs and the bedspread between them. A couple of kids dressed as a doctor and nurse say something I can't hear because the hyperventilating girl behind me keeps repeating "ohmygodohmygodohmygod" and sobbing. She's been like that since the second room on the tour of The Hallows House. Peter Stott—"Pastor Pete" to the kids—pops up again from behind the bed wearing a ridiculous rubber devil mask and begins preaching. "You thought that you were going to find love in cyberspace, but instead you were raped! And now you've killed! Your! Baby!" He's shouting much louder than he needs to in the enclosed space. Maybe he thinks we can't hear him through the mask. He steps around the bed with a flourishing gesture to redirect our attention between the teenager's legs, just in case any of us thought there was anything more interesting to look at than a young girl's thighs. The boy playing the doctor continues the morality play.

"Nurse. This bleeding isn't normal. I don't think we can stop it."

"Oh my God, Doctor. What do we do?"

"It's too late; this one's gone. Come on. We have other abortions to perform."

Pete laughs again from behind the mask and shouts at

the bleeding girl. "You're going to Hell! But it's okay because it was your *choice!*" The girl on the bed pretends to die while the doctor shrugs like that sort of thing happens to him all the time and walks out of the room.

Not one of them has ever actually been in this situation and it plays like a politician talking about hard work. Even though this is my third time through the house, I still haven't gotten over my urge to howl for these kids to stop pretending they know what pain is.

I unclench my fists and stuff them back in my jacket. I have to consciously fight to keep from wrapping my fingers around the butt of the gun in my right pocket.

The girl behind me sobs again. Her friends are dragging her through the house despite the fact that she's clearly wanted to leave since the drunk-driving skit in the first room. The girls on either side of her whisper reassuringly, "It's okay," and "It's not real," in between giggles and groans of excited disgust.

The Devil laughs again, sounding like a Bela Lugosi impression done by someone who's never actually seen Dracula. "We'll be seeing her again real soon," he shouts, hinting at the penultimate room in which we're treated to the pleasure of watching the sinners from all the previous skits suffering in Hell.

The teenager dressed up like an angel who has been our guide apologizes again for the sights she must subject us to. Her smug look belies any real regret. She loves every minute of trying to send us running in a panic into the arms of her lord. She motions for everyone to proceed. Awaiting us in the next room is a semi-racist gangbanger party that'll devolve into an argument over a "ho" and a shooting. While everyone else files past, I lag behind, slipping into the shadow of black plastic stapled to the wall. The last of the kids leave and the angel shuts the plywood door behind her. I hear the latch of the slide bolt on the other side.

No one gets to backtrack; no one escapes Hell.

I step out of the darkness and over the cheap rope separating the performance area from the spectator path. Walking up to the Devil, I say, "Pastor? Excuse me, Pastor Stott." He lifts up his mask to reveal black-ringed raccoon eyes and a confused expression.

"I'm sorry sir, but you need to stay with the group."

I know he recognizes me. He pretends not to and gives me that Cheshire smile he wore the first day I saw him. He was standing up in a pulpit and my daughter sitting next to me on the pew was on the edge of her seat like she was at a rock concert. He kept looking down at her from that perch of his and I remember thinking at the time, *Damn, this guy knows how to work a room.* Even my wife seemed moved and she grew up around Evangelicals and Charismatics.

"I'm Andrew Matheson," I say, like we haven't met after sermons, church barbecues, bake sales, Easter passion plays. My wife and daughter were always the vanguard at those events. I was the quiet guy who hung back trying to give my daughter the room to be herself without her old man intruding and embarrassing her. How I wish I had ever stepped forward to stand beside her. To be seen along with her. "I'm Mattie Matheson's father."

"Mattie? Oh, *Amanda.*"

She hated being called Amanda. She was christened "Amanda Hugginkiss" in the fourth grade and was mortified. We told her she could be called anything she liked and my wife suggested Mattie. I hated it. I sounded to me like some blue-haired Indian Bingo player down by my mom's place in Florida, but for her it was like being born again. Taking control of her name had allowed her to take control of her life. She took the name and wore it like armor.

"We haven't seen Amanda in a long time," he said.

I want to pistol whip him for his feigned ignorance. "I'm sure you haven't," I say instead. My hands are shaking and

I'm afraid the gun might slip out of my pocket. I grab hold of it and a soothing calm like morphine flows through my body, the weapon's cool grip pressing into my palm, warming, taking my heat and becoming a part of me.

"You tell her we miss her at Loving Heart. She should come back to service on Sunday. In the meantime, you should head on into the next room. You're missing the show." He points toward the locked door. "I'll radio and get Sheila to let you through."

I grab his pudgy arm and pull him closer. "I've *seen* the show. I want you to know that I'm Mattie Matheson's father." I look into his eyes searching for a hint of guilt. If there is any, either the black grease paint hides it or he's a much better actor without the mask.

"Got it," he says, shaking me off. I get the first real glimpse at the devil beneath the disguise. He's got a moon-shaped face with bright blue eyes that peer through that greasepaint like pools of ice. I can see that he knows me but won't admit it. Not given what else he knows.

"Pastor Pete?" The girl from the bed appears out of the gloom at the back of the stage. Fuck! I was too anxious to corner my target and I didn't make sure the room was clear first. The other two times I cased the show I was paying attention to the live act, not looking behind the scenes. I take a step back. Not with a witness. Not with a child in the room.

She approaches us timidly, her hospital gown fallen back down covering the red Karo syrup staining her thighs. Her hands are bright red from pawing at the gore. She and the other kids were supposed to be moving on to take their places under the Lexan glass in the floor of the "Hell Room" where the teenagers who "died in their sins" throughout the house will writhe in eternal agony.

"Laylah. Would you please take Mr. Matheson to meet his friends in Hell?" He looks at me with the Sunday morning smile. "Or maybe you'd just rather go right to the prayer room, since you've already been through it."

"It's funny you'd put it like that."

"Pastor Pete?" the girl repeats. She looks afraid to come near me. I can't tell if it's how I look or who I am. Either way, her instincts are good.

"What is it, Laylah?" Pete asks.

"Amanda Matheson . . . Mattie . . . she . . ."

"My daughter killed herself last month," I finish for her.

My wife says she "passed away" or "she left us." But that's bullshit. Our only child killed herself. No euphemism exists that can soften the truth of it.

Pastor Pete stands quietly, trying to look shocked to hear the news. It must not be a look he tries on often, because I can see the muscles in his face twitching at the unfamiliarity of this expression. He knows what she did as well as why she did it. He took everything we built up and broke it down, taking everything from her—even her name—until all she had to lean on was him. "Mr. Matheson," he says, "I am sorry to hear we've lost Amanda, but—"

"*We* haven't lost shit."

"I understand you must be upset, but—"

I slap him. The Devil mask pushed back up on his head goes flying and he steps back a couple of feet, holding his face. *That* expression is real. Laylah gives a shocked squeak. I close the distance, hitting him again, this time with a closed fist. He drops the walkie-talkie. It chirps as it clatters away. Laylah shrieks. I really wish she wasn't here to see this, but she is and I won't get another opportunity to be alone with Pete again. Not after this.

I hold a finger up to my mouth encouraging her to be quiet. With all the shouting coming from the next room, there's really no need. She could start screaming her head off and it'd all sound like part of the act. It's why I want to do this here. Gunshots and screams are what you get for the price of admission. Still, I want Pete to hear me without having to shout. I don't like raised voices.

"What do you want?" he slurs. Blood dribbles out of his mouth as he paws at the floor looking for the radio in the dark.

"Mattie's dead because of you."

"You said she killed herself. If she chose to sin, I only ever tried to keep her on the right—" I'm not even close to getting tired of hitting Pete, but we don't have all night so I pull the gun and shove it in his face as encouragement to be judicious with his words. I really want him to be conscious when I pull the trigger but everything he says makes me want to beat him to death instead of shoot him.

He opens his mouth to say something. I slip my finger inside the trigger guard and he thinks better of verbalizing whatever it was that occurred to him. Instead, he paws at his split lip and stands back up to face me.

"She left a note," I say. "Do you want to know what she wrote?"

"I don't think it's anything I want to hear, Andy."

No one calls me Andy. The way he's making me feel, I can barely keep to the plan. He took Mattie's name and now he's messing with mine, trying to use it against me.

"Before you do anything you'll regret," he continues, "why don't you just hand me the pistol?" He holds out his hand. It's soft and white and I imagine it touching my girl. I want to break his fucking fingers.

Laylah hesitantly moves closer. I watch his eyes tracking her, trying to give her subtle directions with them. I don't know what she can see through the dim light and his makeup, but I pay attention to her in my peripheral vision anyway. Despite the gloom, she's easy to see in the white gown. She's almost glowing.

"Mattie wrote that she hoped that her baby in Heaven would never be able to look down and see its mother burning in Hell. She hoped it wasn't really like The Hallows House." Saying the words is harder than I thought it would be. I don't want to utter them. I hid the note from the police so they wouldn't see her final confession. I didn't want them to know what he had done to my little girl. But then the medical examiner found the fetus and I had to give the police my DNA to prove it wasn't my baby. That's when my wife moved out. I was cleared, but she's stayed away anyway.

Pete's caring-preacher look falls away and his expression goes blank. He saw it then. Laylah being in the room wasn't going to stop me. "I d-don't know what this has to do with me," he stammers, lying. "Can we pray together?" The tremor in his voice getting worse. "Matthew 6:14 says—"

"She mentioned you by name in her note. Her last words were that she hoped you would forgive her for killing your baby when she died. *Your* baby."

His stupid round face is covered in sweat despite the chill in the house. I can see in his eyes he's thinking hard about how to get out of this. He's making a plan and playing it out in his head. Struggle with me for the gun? Run for the door? Call out for help? But I've been planning longer. I'm stronger than he is. The doors are locked and we're alone. The overacted fight in the room next door will soon erupt in hysterics and shooting. And that's all I'm waiting for. He's running out of time.

I check my watch. The tour is staggered every twenty minutes. I've kept Pastor Pete for five, maybe seven. I don't know; I lost count. The first time I saw his face the only thing that occurred to me was blowing a hole in it. I can't wait much longer. If I do, they'll notice the Lord of Hell is missing. "Pray," I say.

"What?"

My hand is shaking, but I'm pretty sure at this range I won't miss. Pastor Pete has to see that as well. "Pray! Pray that I'll let you live. Get on your fucking knees and ask *Him* to move me."

Pete drops to the floor, blank look in place, and begins performing like it's a Sunday morning tent revival. "Dear Lord, Jesus Christ, I pray in your name that you deliver us from the influence of the . . . of the Devil and that you move dear brother Andrew's heart—"

I clock him in the forehead with the butt of the gun. The dull thud of metal on bone sounds like a hosanna to me. "Don't pray for deliverance. Pray for *forgiveness*," I say.

Struggling to get back up to his knees he says, "I have nothing to ask forg—"

"I dare you to say that again. Say it again with a straight face so I can feel even better about killing you."

Slowly, so I don't startle and accidentally pull the trigger, Laylah places her hand on my forearm. Her skin is sticky from the fake blood, but her touch is still tender and soft, like the down of her white wings. I don't remember her having angel's wings in the scene. I guess she was getting ready for her next part in the play when I interrupted her. I try to remember whether at the end she's saved or one of the damned, but all I can think of is Pastor Pete. His eyes narrow as he judges whether her distraction would be enough for him to make a dash for it. It isn't. I'm focused on him kneeling there looking like a dog that doesn't know whether to jump or roll over.

"Can I have the gun, Mr. Matheson?" she asks.

"Sorry, kid. I need it. I need it until I feel the hand of God move me. Do you think we've got his attention?" My anger is turning into sorrow as I try to keep the hitch out of my voice. Everything has gone wrong and the plan doesn't make sense to me anymore. I know that this won't bring my Mattie back. Nothing will. Not prayer, not faith, not hope— all things I've given up. The girl is sapping my resolve. She's not part of the plan. I don't want to hurt her.

She looks so much like my daughter.

"Our Father, who art in Heaven, Hallowed be thy name," Pete says.

"Not feeling it." I bluff, holding back my tears. "Try harder."

"Forgive us our trespasses as we forgive those who trespass against us."

"You're running out of time."

Laylah's hand slides down my arm, lightly squeezing my wrist. She's gentle, but there's something else there: the strength I'm losing. She whispers to me, "You don't have to do this. It's not your fault."

"You're right. It's his," I insist.

"What does your heart tell you?" She places her other hand flat on my chest—those slender hands like Mattie's.

". . . and the glory. Forever and ever."

I lower the gun.

"God has touched your heart," he says. "Amen."

"Laylah changed my mind. *She* touched me."

"Forgiveness is the first—"

"I don't forgive you!" For a moment the look on his face turns from satisfaction to fear as he expects me to raise the gun again and fire. Without the girl there, I might have done just that. Instead, I feel calmness wash over me. Someone cares about me even though I don't. Feeling clean for the first time since I put the flesh of my flesh in the earth, I let the girl in the angel costume take the gun from me. I shouldn't let her have it—it's irresponsible—but I can't stand the weight of it in my hand any more. I'll make sure she gives it to the police when they get here. She lets her other hand linger on my chest. The coldness of her fingers pierces through my coat.

"I'm sorry, Mr. Matheson," she says.

"Don't be."

With a voice that sounds like a velvet bow pulling gently across cello strings, she says, "Vengeance is *mine*, not yours." The sound of the shot makes my ears pop and ring. Pete falls forward choking and grasping at his guts as his life splashes out through his fingers.

"What did you do?" My words are muted and far away, like I'm standing at the far end of a tunnel shouting at myself. If Laylah answers me, I can't hear it. She fires again into the top of his head and he crumples. The second shot is just a dull thud. Smoke drifts into my eyes. Pete chokes his bloody last breath onto the plywood floor.

The girl with the terrible, shining face turns around. She's a horrifying vision that fills me with despair. All light and no warmth. And she looks like my daughter. She extends her great wings and beats them once, buffeting me with a frigid wind that stings my eyes. Embracing me, she holds me tightly and whispers in that sonorous string quartet voice, "Blessed are those who mourn, for they shall be comforted." Her body leeches my heat and I'm not comforted.

I feel cheated.

I push back and try to look in her face. "Where were you when Mattie needed comforting?"

She looks at me with blank, all-black eyes. "I was with her. She was heavy laden and I gave her rest." Her face is an expressionless nightmare of frigid detachment and brilliant light like reflecting silver. Tears sting my eyes. I try not to see my daughter staring at me, cold and dead, a vicious shining thing with wings and no soul. I try not to see Pete behind her, on his knees bowing down like a supplicant.

Her voice grows louder and thicker and painful. "Come. Take comfort in your faith. Let me give you rest."

"Like you gave it to Pete? To my daughter?"

It steps back. "Who are you to question me?" it asks, raising the gun to my face. I lurch forward grabbing for the pistol. The angel resists. "Where were you when the foundations of the Earth were laid?" The thickness of its voice is pounding in my head like a hangover or a concussion. I try to twist the gun out of its hand, but it's stronger than I am. I shove with the last bit of force I can muster and its howls deaden the shot. The gleaming white thing falls in a sudden heap to the floor. I look down at the angel as it blows away like smoke on a breezy hilltop leaving behind only Laylah in her stained hospital gown. The right side of her skull is a ruin of torn tissue and black wetness under the red lights. Kneeling down, I pull the wingless corpse up onto my lap. She's warm.

But getting colder.

A kid in a shitty silver lamé angel costume unlatches the door and peeks in looking for Pete, ready to lead the next group through. He looks at us, silent and mouth agape, trying to contextualize this fresh Hell out of place among all of the other scenes. I look up at him, imagining what he sees: a sobbing man embracing a girl with half a face and his church leader crumpled and ruined in front of us—a mockery of the *Pietà* or Caravaggio's *Entombment*. The boy sprints back out the door screaming for help.

His cries sound like part of the act. Just like I planned.

I think about the angel and pull Laylah closer. I think about faith. Without hope, what's that really worth? I put the gun to my temple. "This is mine, not yours."

THIRTEEN VIEWS OF THE SUICIDE WOODS

1

Skip sat on the tree branch letting his feet dangle as he looked up through the leaves toward the peak of Mt. Schoenborn, hidden in the ever-present clouds. He smiled thinking about the time work paid for him to take a tiny single-propeller plane home from Port Atwood and he got to see the summit of the mountain pushing through the white blanket permanently pulled over the city. Looking at the mountain from the co-pilot's seat, he'd vowed to one day climb it and stand on the summit to watch the misty sea below roil and drift. But like all dreams, it was ethereal. The highest he'd ever climb was twelve feet up into this tree.

Half a billion years, he thought. *In half a billion years there'll be no mountain. Wind and rain are beating away at the peak, eroding it—wearing it down to nothing.* Little by little, he knew the mountain would succumb to entropy. *But by then who'll be left to care? No one will be around to even know there once was anything but a plain.*

He pushed forward with his hips and slipped off the branch, bracing himself for the shock of the rope that would snap his neck.

2

Mandy held the note in her hand. She couldn't read it through the blur of tears welling in her eyes, but after a dozen or more times through already, the words were seared in her brain like a brand. *My dearest Amanda, I've gone to Schoenborn. Please don't come to find me. Let's just have last night. I love you. Your Skipper, always.*

She looked at the phone in her hand to be sure the call was still connected. The police had put her on hold. *Hold!* There wasn't any music or even an occasional beep to let you know your call hadn't been dropped. She sat listening to silence on the line as the minutes ticked away, waiting for her chance to tell the dispatcher, "You've got to stop him! You've got to go find him."

Outside, the sounds of her neighborhood carried on. People passed by on the sidewalk shouting into cell phones as their dogs barked at passing cars and each other. In the distance, an ambulance siren wound up and wailed off into the city, the crew rushing to save someone. Not Skip. Of course it wasn't Skip. She hadn't gotten through to a dispatcher yet. For all anyone else knew, he'd gone out for muffins and coffee.

A voice squawked out of the telephone, jarring Mandy from her trance. "Brattle Police Department. This call is being recorded. What's your emergency?" Mandy sat up straight in shock at the sudden, welcome intrusion. Although she'd been practicing them, she found herself struggling to find the right words.

"He's gone. You . . . have to go. He's in the woods."

"Who's gone, ma'am? Who's gone to the woods?" The dispatcher didn't ask "What woods?" or "What is he planning to do in the woods?" Everyone in the Brattle Basin Area knew what "going to the woods" meant. They were as well known as The Crossing Tower or Compass Fells or even

Schoenborn Mountain. You just said, the Tower, the Fells, the Mountain.

The Suicide Woods.

"My father. My father, Skip Clover. He left me a note to say—"

"How long ago did he leave, Ma'am?"

She didn't know. She knew how long it'd take to get there—*an hour to drive out of town and make it up to the State Park. Ten minutes to park the car and walk to the trail head and who knows how much longer to . . . find the right spot*—but she had no idea when to start the clock ticking. He could have written the note last night after she went to bed or early this morning. Who knew how long it would take him to actually do whatever it was he had planned? Maybe she'd catch a break and he'd just take a hike and change his mind and come home. How long before she had to cross that off as an option?

All she knew for sure was that it had taken his whole life to write the note. How much time he had left to live after that was left to him.

3

The call crackled over the radio, interrupting Rick and Kate's game of Bicycle Tag. They sat in their car, watching bicyclists run red lights, taking bets on which one was going to get "tagged" by a car in cross-traffic. "Unit 19. Proceed to the west entrance of Mt. Schoenborn State Park for a possible 10-56. Skip Clover. Caucasian male, five ten, forty-nine. Thinning brown and blue. Red down parka."

Kate sighed and pulled the transmitter up to her mouth. "10-56. Copy that. Unit 19 en route." Her partner flipped the switch on the lightbar and siren. He shrugged.

"Hey, the family needs to know whether to put his name in for the gift exchange, right?" Kate didn't laugh. She didn't like the idea of another hike through The Woods. Looking for one always meant finding a couple or more, whether or not the original subject was located. It was depressing and she had been doing her best to get in the holiday spirit. But then, that's when they started to really head to the forest. It didn't matter how many lights you hung in the windows, it was impossible to break through the crepuscular gloom of autumn in Brattle. As they pulled out into traffic, she zipped up her jacket in anticipation of a long hike.

"The annual body hunt is starting early," she said. Kate remembered her first hunt better than her first kiss. She'd been on the force less than a year and the town council had decided that it was important to clear the rotters out of the woods as soon as the thaw began. Before an unsuspecting hiker—who was unsuspecting anymore?—stumbled across some scene of horror. Her training officer back then was a guy with a bleak gallows sense of humor named Jesse. He'd blanched at the thought of a thorough sweep of the woods. Since he'd started on the force ten years earlier, he told her, it had just kept getting worse until things were the way they are now. "Some asshole did a story on the news on that place in Chiner or Japan or whateva whereva those people went to scrag themselves. 'The Sea of Trees,' or some shit. And that was that. Every sad sack from three counties made for the Schoenborn that year. Yep, it was a record. Twenty-seven stiffs in twelve months. Since then, the record just keeps gettin' broke, you know. Always anotha one. Sometimes *couples* go in there together. I say we cut the whole place down. Turn it into a shopping mall or bouncy house playground. Someplace nobody can get hurt. You know?"

She hadn't known. Not until she found her first body. Most of the women who went to the woods used poison, but that one chose a razor. And Jesse explained that meant this girl got *extra* attention from the Homicide detectives. "There are plenty a bodies in the forest," he explained, "and that makes it a great place to bring a murder victim and stage a suicide." He called it in and left his rookie to secure the scene. "Don't let her leave," he said, as he stumbled away to find a private place to have a sip—or ten—from his flask. Kate had to stick around for hours to guard the body before the lazy murder dicks showed up, the medical examiner trailing behind. They poked around, careful not to spill their coffee, until one found a straight razor near her body and the M.E. declared her wound consistent with a left-handed, self-inflicted cut. Kate asked how down-in-the-dumps you had to be to slash your own throat. The dicks didn't say anything and the M.E. just looked at her and walked off, replying, "She's all yours, officer." And she was. Forever. Some nights Kate would wake up from a nightmare convinced that the girl was standing in the corner of her bedroom, holding the razor, smiling redly from under her chin and waiting for the cop to do something. What was there to do? She couldn't stop her. She couldn't stop any of them.

And yet, here she was. On her way to find another one.

4

Danny pulled his hood over his head to keep the freezing drizzle from running down the back of his neck into his shirt. He kept to the trail, for now. The trees grew close to one another on either side, fighting to survive in a climate with ample moisture but insufficient light. Around them, the corpses of the fallen lay, soggy and rotten, their bark peeling and falling off into the brown needle bed. He forged ahead for maybe another quarter of a mile before venturing off on a barely visible path of desire worn by other infrequent off-trail hikers. Those paths never became well-worn. Too few followed them back out. He kept his hands stuffed deep into his pockets for warmth.

Clambering over a fallen tree that was slowly breaking

down in the rain, he steadied himself with a hand that slipped and pushed through the decaying trunk up to his wrist. Soft slick pieces of rotting wood slid up into the sleeve of his jacket. He heaved himself over, pulled his hand out of the compost, shaking off the moldy slime, and checked the gun in his pocket again. Still there. He was shivering. His boots and socks were soaked. The legs of his jeans stuck to his shins and calves and his legs were slowly going numb below the knees. *Not much farther. You don't need to go much farther. There's a good spot up ahead.*

He could see it. There was a break in the evergreens where you could get a good view of the mountain. Really see it and feel its fullness. Feel your own emptiness and insignificance and the pull to lie down and slowly crumble into the earth. There was a compulsion to be part of the mountain that tugged at Danny's guts. Like when he was driving on the interstate, sometimes he'd get the urge to jerk the wheel hard to the left or the right and feel the truck go up onto two wheels and flip over into the air. He imagined what it would be like as it came crashing down on the roof. Sometimes at night he'd climb onto the fire escape and look five flights down and think about what it would feel like to jump out into the darkness—just sail away and down. The French called it *L'appel du vide.*

It pulled at him.

A few feet farther into the brush he looked up and saw a flash of red—a down jacket worn by a man perched on a low branch. The man pushed forward and slipped off into space. Answering the call of the void.

5

Rick and Kate parked their cruiser at the head of the trail, leaving the lightbar flashing. They walked past the strobing blue beacon and shined their flashlights into the growing darkness up the path. "After you," Rick said.

"Why me?"

He didn't answer. They were here and there were no more jokes to tell. Not until they were on their way back out, with or without Skip Clover. But then, Kate knew Rick wasn't the kind to walk out of the woods without him.

They walked at a brisk pace, glancing from side to side, looking for a red parka, but all Kate could see were the same dun shades of late autumn. Everyone in Brattle was outdoorsy and wore the same neon brands of R.E.I. and The North Face clothing. Cheerful bright colors meant to combat the perpetual gloom of the cloud canopy or stand out against the blinding white snow when it fell. No camouflage. It wasn't that kind of town. Every spring, the department sent everyone but a skeleton crew into the woods to look for those bright yellows and blues peeking up after the thaw—before the weather became too warm and decay could begin again. It was the worst Easter hunt imaginable because every egg was rotten.

They paused when they came to the first fork in the path. Blazes of paint on nearby trees indicated the green trail leading off to the right, the blue to the left, and another thousand yards up, the "strenuous" red trail broke off on a long, challenging hike up the base of the mountain. Kate didn't bother to ask "Which way?" Most people who walked into the woods without any intention of walking back out eventually left the paths. Green didn't get you deep enough into the woods and only the most elite jumped from the high rocks on red. The blue trail had a reasonable amount of deadfall and debris to find a measure of privacy in the peaceful calm of the forest, and the views of Schoenborn were just as good. She wondered if the person at the Forest Service responsible for marking the trails had a reason in mind for choosing blue. *I'd have picked black.*

She paused in front of a sign post and drop box that the

department had installed the year before. The sign read, *Take a moment! If you are hurting, don't hold it in. Counselors are waiting to listen to you. Please call for help.* She flipped open the lid of the box to see how many of the Suicide Hotline flyers remained. They were all gone, replaced by something else. She pulled one out. Bold orange text declaring, *IT'S NOT YOUR CHOICE!* bordered an anguished cartoon face surrounded by flames. Kate crumpled the religious tract up in her fist and took a deep breath, managing her anger.

"Come on, let's go," Rick said as he forged up the blue trail. Kate looked at the mirror installed on the post above the sign. Her image in the fogged glass was a ghostly blue and white blur. Was it a reflection or a promise? She promised herself she'd mention the post to the chief later as she trotted to catch up to her partner before he disappeared into the mist.

6

Skip dangled at the end of his rope. The fall felt like it took ages. His jacket caught the branch as he pushed off, preventing him from dropping hard. He'd slumped down a few inches and then slowly broke free in a jerky descent that eventually constricted his windpipe and tightened the noose around his throat, but didn't snap his neck. When he felt the rope go taut and the loop tighten it reminded him of a snake slowly crushing its prey instead of the quick cinch it should have been. His perception of reality was slowing down the way it did when things went wrong. And he was at the center of time's distortion, hanging like a black hole in space, as light changed, gravity changed, everything that approached him elongated and became drawn out, ghostly and indistinct. He'd read somewhere it took six minutes for a person whose neck didn't break to strangle in a noose. What had it been already? Five seconds? Ten? He wondered how many lifetimes six minutes would take.

He didn't see his life flash before his eyes—just a single still moment of someone else's. He saw his daughter sitting at their dinner table where he'd left the note. He saw her reading and weeping. Her head dropped into her hands, hope slipping away as his had done over the years, gently sliding into the black hole he'd become.

For the first time since Audrey walked out, he felt like trying to live.

Skip tried to reach for the branch above him. He was pretty sure he couldn't do a pull up if he tried. But he felt like giving it a go. The way the rope pulled up and under his chin, he could barely raise his hands over his head.

Living or dying, whatever he felt like now was irrelevant. The him of a few distorted æons ago had left the new him with nothing to do but wait out the rest of his life.

7

Although it seemed to Rick like she never looked down at the path, Kate never tripped. She'd told him, "Keep your eyes on what's coming ahead instead of on your feet. That way you can keep your head up and maybe see our guy." It didn't help. Rick stumbled over a rock half-buried in the middle of the path. He raised his arms to ward off a low branch that threatened to tear at his eyes as he careened into it. No matter where he kept his focus, the forest sent roots and branches clutching at his clothes and grasping at his feet. The obstacles she ducked around and stepped lightly over no more than a second before him threatened to trip him up, tie him down, drag him under. He staggered another step before regaining his balance and pride. He righted his plastic-covered hat and pulled at the bottom of his jacket, trying not to look so disheveled, although he felt like it was a losing battle.

Kate turned to face her partner. On any other occasion she'd be smiling at his awkwardness, or at least putting on the pretense of holding back a smile. Not today. Today, she looked pale and half gone. Glancing over her shoulder, he spied a flash of weather-muted yellow. It was a jacket that used to be Day-Glo. The weather had brought it low and dulled its vibrance. For a moment it looked as though someone had hung it on a tree as if to dry it or at least just keep it up off the damp forest floor. A blink and another look showed him differently. The figure in the distance was propped up by the tree, arms and branches entwined like lovers embracing. There was probably also a rope helping keep the corpse erect, but Rick couldn't see it. No matter how many times he saw a scene like that—and he'd seen it a few times—he never understood how someone could hang themselves to death with their feet on the ground. *I think I'd stand up. I'd just . . . have to stand up.*

There wasn't time to stop and log it and call it in. They had to keep moving. The longer they delayed, the less likely they were to find the man they'd been sent to rescue. He made a mental note to return here once their primary goal was achieved. He didn't want to, but that was someone's son or husband or father. It was someone who deserved to be taken home. It was someone.

"Should we be shouting his name or something?" he asked.

"I don't know." Neither of them had ever been summoned to look for a *living* person in the woods. Rick was sure that there was some kind of procedure for searching for a suicide in progress that would make the process safer and more effective, but if it existed, Brattle PD didn't want to discuss it or teach it or even acknowledge it. Instituting a protocol meant acknowledging that this was a regular occurrence, and that meant admitting that there was a problem, which no elected official from mayor on down to dog catcher wanted to do. He needed the win, though. After fifteen years, Brattle was getting to him. He was hearing the call.

"Let's just push on," Kate said. "If he hasn't already pulled the trigger, I'd rather not give him a reason to speed things up."

"Copy that."

8

Pocket . . . knife. Pocketknife. Skip fumbled with weakening fingers at his right pants pocket. Since his father had given him a Buck Knife for his eighth birthday, he'd never been without a blade in that pocket. Friends counted on him to have it. A misbehaving string on a blouse at dinner was like a show. "Hey, Skip. You got that knife?" they'd ask with a smile and hold up an elbow to let the loose thread dangle. He'd produce the knife with a flourish and perform as requested. His newest one was a C.K.R.T. Ripple. It was lightweight and opened easily and had a lovely black handle with an elegant gray blade that gently arced up into a point. One year Mandy had gotten him a Japanese tanto-style knife as a gift, but he just felt too silly pulling it out with its odd angles and non-reflective black blade. He wasn't a ninja; he was just a guy who liked to be dependable. He was the person who was able to easily open that box, cut the twine used to tie down the hatchback door, to trim an errant branch on the rosebush.

The rope. Cut the rope.

He pawed at his hip. His hands were numbing as his vision narrowed and the world got a little grayer. Pulling up the bottom of his parka, he slipped the knife from his pocket and brought it up in front of his face. Carefully unfolding it, he reached behind his head to find the rope. A light breeze blew through the trees and his body swayed and disoriented him more. His dulled fingers found the line—strong sport rope designed for shock and to hold several times the body weight of a climber scaling a cliff face . . . or a mountain. It was built for safety, but it suited this other purpose just fine. Even though that purpose no longer suited him, the rope was doing a workmanlike job indeed.

The fog of the woods infected him—clouded his mind and muddied his thoughts.

Cut. The. Rope.

He reached up with his knife hand and began to saw through the line. The knife slipped several times and he never felt it bite. Not until it bit into his hand and he instinctively let go. He felt it bounce off his shoulder as it fell to the ground.

Useless.

9

Danny carefully stepped around and looked up into the face of the man hanging from the branch. The man's purpling tongue protruded from between white lips and his eyes rolled wildly as he kicked and struggled with the knot at the back of his head. Danny bent down and picked up the knife the man had dropped in the spongy needles carpeting the forest floor. It was nice. Sharp and well cared for. He looked up and the man's eyes rolled around one last time before fixing on him. They welled with tears. His lips moved. "Help me," the hanging man mouthed.

Following the rope up over the branch and back down with his eyes, Danny climbed the tree and found where the man had tied it off. He clearly knew how to tie a good knot that wouldn't come loose. Not while there was tension on the line anyway. He also knew enough to tie the end low to the ground. He didn't want to slip while tying it to a branch, and break his arm or leg instead of his neck. All he had to do when he got up into the tree was pull the loop end over his head and jump.

Danny cut the line. The man fell the last five feet, crashing down in a heap in the cold mud. Rain made a quiet *pat pat pat pat* noise on their jackets. The man loosened his noose and tried to speak, but his crushed larynx wouldn't allow words. Instead he took in a long, rasping breath. And another. And another. Danny had saved his life. He had pulled a man back from the void, back into the world.

10

Kate was the one who caught the flash of red in her peripheral vision before it dropped out of sight. She grabbed the back of Rick's jacket and pulled.

"Hey what's—"

"Mr. Clover," she shouted at the memory of the streak. "Skip Clover! Is that you?" She jumped off the trail and began bounding through the woods as fast as she could, scrambling and slipping over sodden deadfall and slick underbrush.

"Brattle Police, Mr. Clover! Your daughter sent us to find you. Mr. Clover?"

They ran ahead heedless of roots that jutted up, threatening to trip them, break their ankles, dash their heads against hidden stones. They felt the pull of need. *Oh, please, just a few seconds. Hang in there for a few seconds more, Skip*, Kate thought. No matter how hard it was to pull a body out of the woods, it was nothing compared to having to sit down with a wife, or a child, or a parent, and explain that someone they loved was never coming home again. Every time she did it, she felt like a piece of her died. It was a death of inches, each grieving family bringing her closer to her own day in the woods. She pushed harder, ran faster, jumped farther, closing the distance between her and the red. Her own voice became a distant echo as her ears went dull and began to ring at the sound of the shot.

11

Danny stared at the man lying face down, bleeding into the earth. From behind the trees he heard them coming. They shouted. Their feet pounded. But nothing they did or said could bring down the mountain. Nothing could wear it away. There was no answer to its summons but one.

"What have you done?" shouted a man with a shining badge on his chest.

Danny tilted his head at the cop, trying to understand why he couldn't see. "I gave him to the mountain. The mountain wanted him and I give him to it."

"Put down the weapon!" The woman pointed her own gun at him. She wasn't ready to do what needed to be done. Not yet.

Danny raised his pistol to show her how.

12

"I.A. is going to call it a clean shoot, Kate," Captain Wright said, holding out his hand. "But I'm still going to need your piece." She unclipped the holster from her belt and handed it to him before resting her forehead back on her palms, pressing the heels of her hands into her eyes. The posture eased her headache, but more than that, it blinded her to the scene around them.

Still, she couldn't help but hear when they zipped up Rick's bag.

13

While she waited for the call, Mandy thought about the night before with her father. Although he looked the same as he always did, somehow he seemed heavier, as if gravity was pulling at him harder than it did anyone else. His normally square shoulders slumped and he stared at his plate, never making eye contact. She thought of asking him what was wrong, but she already knew. He struggled daily to pull himself out of the hole her mother had dug. Some days he got up over the edge of it and the sunlight shone on his face and he was the man he'd been before. Before it all came apart. And then some days she could see, he just lay down, deep in the pit, and prayed for the rain to come and fill it.

She'd made small talk about her classes and professors, about her plans for the summer, and all the places she'd love to see. She talked about spending a semester abroad in Spain or maybe southern Italy—somewhere warm. Somewhere they grew lemon trees on apartment balconies and she could tour vineyards and taste wine out of the barrel. She told him she was changing her major to Agricultural Sciences. "You know, since U. Brattle doesn't have a Viticulture and Enology department like UC Davis does down in California." He'd encouraged her to transfer to a school with a wine program, but she'd refused, saying that U. Brattle was good enough for her undergrad. She'd get a summer job on a vineyard and then do her masters at one of the big wine schools after that.

"Why don't you go now?" he'd asked. "Why put it off?" She told him she wanted to stay close to home for a while—another couple of semesters at least.

"I'd miss you too much, Daddy," she said, squeezing his hand. He'd smiled and squeezed back. His shoulders straightened a little and he looked her in the eyes as she told him something else meaningless while they finished up dinner.

That night, he hugged and kissed her goodnight before she went to bed in the room where she'd grown up. She lay there in the dark wishing he'd come to tuck her in like he had when she was little. He used to pull the covers as tight as he could. Her mom would complain and say that he was going to suffocate her, but Mandy always giggled and lay flat, letting the covers get tighter and tighter like a hug. And he would bend down and kiss her forehead and say "Sleep *tight*," and they would both laugh.

She clutched her phone now, afraid that she'd miss the call from the police saying that they'd found him and that he was all right. That he was just out for a hike and got lost and it was all a big misunderstanding. *You knew all the time that you were going to write that fucking note and leave. Just like Mom.* She looked out her window at the mountain. It called and people answered, leaving everyone they loved—that loved them—behind. She hoped that what Skip had told her so long ago about entropy was true. That the wind and the rain would wear it down and leave it flat someday. *I hope it never stops raining here. Not for a billion years.*

She walked back into her bedroom and slipped under the loose covers. Waiting.

THE TEXAS CHAINSAW BREAKFAST CLUB
OR
I DON'T LIKE MONDAYS

She dreamed.

Shopping malls and parties at Blair's house with that boy she liked—Sean from the wrestling team—blended together the way one's surroundings changed in a dream, seamless and natural in shifting absurdity. Allison glided from a neon setting to pastel to a muted room down a passage that reminded her of the time her parents had taken her on a tour of the Paris catacombs. How could she have gone from Ralph Lauren to the underworld without noticing? Why was it getting so dark? Nobody would be able to see how cute her blouse was if the lights were out. It smelled like her grandpa's cellar. Mold and rust and rotting wooden boxes.

Why are we going downstairs? Your parents don't mind if we toke up in your room. Blair? Blair, can you hear me? Can anyone hear me?

No one answered.

⌒

He dreamed.

The shield on his arm weighed him down, but penetrating the underworld required armor, no matter how burdensome.

Slaying dragons, saving damsels, fulfilling the quest, these things weren't for the faint of heart or weak of limb. They required fortitude and drive. The kind of heroic attributes Reginald the White brought to the campaign. A paladin's heart beat under his cuirasse.

Hey, queer ass! Make a saving throw.

It's a cuirass. You know, a breast plate.

Whatever. Roll, queer ass.

The lights in the library rec-room dimmed as the twenty-sided die tumbled away from his hand, bouncing from eleven to nine to fifteen, coming to rest beyond his reach, beyond his ability to alter the outcome of chance. No matter the number of plusses on his blade and his gauntlets, there it was pointing at him like the arrow loosed from a goblin's bow.

You rolled a one, loser. You failed your saving throw.

Reginald the White's world went black.

She didn't dream.

Neither did she sleep. Leslie scooted as far back as she could. The sharp stones jutting from the uneven rock wall jabbed into her back as she scuttled away from the dim circle of light in the middle of the room. A lone bulb in an aluminum cone shone down on the iron ring bolted to the floor. The metal cuff bit painfully into her ankle as she reached the end of her chain. Her gauze skirt pulled and the rough floor caught at her tights. She didn't care about her clothes or her back. If she didn't get out of the shackle she'd end up like the guy hanging from the hook at the opposite end of the cellar.

With his head slumped down, the boy's blond bangs hung in his face, but Leslie could still tell that it was John Wilden at the end of the hook. He was the one who'd cut the sleeves off his letterman's jacket so everyone could see his stee-roided arms better. His body didn't twitch or sway or do anything but hang there, still. Although she couldn't see it, she imagined the hook piercing through his back into his ribs, through a lung, drowning him in his own blood. He dangled at the end of a short chain, a long line of crimson slobber hanging from his lips like a drooling dead idiot.

She looked around, imagining her escape. Even if she got out of the cuff, where would she go? No bulkhead opening led out into the back yard. There was no low, slender window to break and yell at some passerby on the sidewalk. The only way out of the basement was through the locked door at the top of the stairs. The way she presumed she'd been brought in. She couldn't remember, but it was the only way that made sense.

To her left, the dweeb was stirring. He snuffled like a baby, blowing up a puff of dirt from the floor that made him gag when he tried to take another breath. Rolling onto his back, the boy rubbed at his eyes with balled fists while he coughed the rest of the cellar dust out of his throat. Leslie wanted to hiss at him to shut up. *Be quiet or he'll come back!* Instead, she waited for him to fully come around before trying to communicate.

She tried to shrink deeper into the shadows, to be invisible, but the cuff and taut chain kept her leg straight. Four other chains extended away in compass directions from the center ring: one to the dweeb, one to the sleeping princess opposite him, and two more yet to be attached. Leslie figured one of those might have been meant for the jock. She'd been awake for a while though and he'd always been hanging from the hook. If he ever had a place in the circle, it was before she'd come to.

"Where the hell—"

"Shh!" Leslie hissed, leaning forward, hoping it'd seem more insistent. The dweeb stared at her with a look of stupid disbelief on his face as he carefully sat up. His mouth hung open the way it always did. She'd seen him walking down the halls of Shermerville High, mouth gaping like he was trying to catch flies—as her grandfather would say—occasionally sighing as he tried to catch his breath from the exertion of being upright. *Except he probably has asthma. He breathes through his mouth because it's hard for him to get enough air in his lungs. He's gasping, not sighing. He'll probably die from all the mold and dust down here way before it's his turn on a hook.*

The boy began panting and looking around frantically for the pack that always seemed to be growing out of his back like some space parasite—the evil intelligence that controlled his brain and made him obsess over knights and wizards and fantasy shit instead of being normal like everybody else. Well, normal like the princess and Wilden. People like Leslie and the dweeb . . . they were something else. Not normal.

Leslie snapped her fingers twice. The dweeb turned his panicked face toward her. She hunched her shoulders and with a hand up by her cheek pointed toward the workbench at the end of the basement. Sitting on it, below the jock's Chuck Taylors was the dweeb's bag. All of his shit was spread out, gaming books and pencils and a couple of little felt bags she figured had dice and maybe those little pewter figures, and—there it was!—his inhaler sitting in a puddle of drooled-out blood and spit.

"My Albuterol!"

He scrambled toward the table, but his chain snapped tight, stopping him long before he got close enough to reach it. He tugged at the restraint a couple of times before letting out a long wheezing sob. Leslie wrapped her arms around the leg she could pull up and hid her face, waiting for the sound of steps overhead.

"Shit! I need that," the dweeb said. His rasping breath punctuated his statement better than a line of desperately drawn exclamation points. "I can't breathe."

If you can talk, you can breathe, dork.

Finally, the princess began to wake up. She held her head like she had a hangover. She probably did. Leslie's own skull pounded like she'd killed a bottle of vodka. Of course, she hadn't. Whatever their captor used to knock them out didn't leave a person feeling fresh and well-rested. *Try CHLOROFORM! All the hangover and none of the fun.* At least the princess wasn't hyperventilating and freaking out. Yet.

The princess muttered something that Leslie couldn't make out. She thought she heard the words "thirsty" and "Coke." The girl in the pastel outfit shifted her legs and the shackle clanked loudly against the floor. Her mouth dropped open and then closed. Open. Closed. Like she was trying to formulate a question but couldn't wrap her head around the situation well enough to sufficiently form the right one. Open. Closed.

She looks like a fish. He sounds like one and she looks like one. It's a people-aquarium!

Leslie stifled a grin, shoving her face down into her arms. Their situation wasn't funny. Still, she couldn't seem to help but want to laugh. *Maybe I'm crazy and all of this is just going on in my head. I'm sitting in a padded room somewhere and this is just what I think I'm seeing instead of all the people who are actually trying to help me.* Except she knew she wasn't nuts.

She was fucked.

There was a world of difference.

"What's happening?" the princess whispered.

Leslie hunched her shoulders up tighter. Her neck cramped. She wanted to say, "What does it look like?" Instead, she pointed at the door at the top of the stairs with one hand while holding a finger in front of her lips with the other.

"Where are we?"

The princess wasn't any good at charades, apparently.

"It's a basement," Leslie said. Her throat was dry and hurt when she tried to talk. She couldn't remember the last time she'd said anything to anyone. It was long before she'd been abducted and woke up in chains, anyway.

"Whose basement? Where the frick are we?"

Really? You've been kidnapped and locked in a cellar and you still can't swear? Leslie pointed again, this time toward Wilden. She had to stifle another smile as the princess tried to scream, but instead vomited down the front of her clothes.

"I don't get it," the dweeb said. "Why us? What did we do? I didn't do anything, I shouldn't be here."

"And I should?" Princess answered, wiping her face. She turned away from the jock and refused to look back. She sat smoothing out her pink and teal skirt like it wasn't covered in grime and puke. Futilely trying to make herself as presentable and perfect as she always looked.

Whatever helps you keep it together.

"I'm not saying that. I'm just saying that I've never, like, done anything that would, you know," he held up a portion of his chain before dropping it with a loud rattle, "justify this."

Leslie shushed them again, louder.

"Shush, yourself, weirdo. I didn't do anything to deserve being down here either."

"You sure about that, Princess?" Leslie asked.

"My name is Allison."

"Everybody knows who you are," the dweeb said. "I'm Reginald. Some people call me Reggie but I prefer Reginald, you know? My grandfather's name is Reggie and it's confusing if someone calls the house and my—"

"Like anyone cares, Reggie."

Reginald tried to get his wheezing under control. He seemed to be growing more alarmed and twitchy with each increasingly difficult breath.

"What about you?" Allison asked. "Do you *deserve* to be here?"

Leslie shrugged. She briefly considered the repercussions of trying to gnaw off her foot. If it meant being able to get away from these two it might be worth it. Still, they were in this together; she wasn't coming up with an escape plan on her own. Princess Allison wasn't likely to have any bright ideas unless she knew how to pick a padlock with a hair clip. Reggie, on the other hand . . . he probably wasn't a Houdini, but he was a brain and maybe he knew something about something.

"Leslie."

"What?" Reggie leaned in, cupping a hand to his ear.

"My name's Leslie," she said a little louder.

"I know your name. You're Lezzie Leslie," Allison said. She might not have ever noticed Reginald, but she had P.E. with Leslie three times a week. Sometimes Allison and her friends did horrible things like putting Leslie's gym shorts in a pissed-in toilet or hanging a couple dozen tampons on the outside of her locker. Being taken captive was bad enough, but chaining Leslie in a cellar with the princess was a special kind of torture.

"I'm not a lesbian."

"But you *are* Lezzie Leslie." Allison scooted away from the puddle of her vomit and pulled her feet under her to try to find a more comfortable way to sit; she fidgeted with the chain and shackle for a second before giving up with a sigh.

"I'm not gay."

"The all-black mumble-mouth thing. Totally gaaay."

"I think she means it figuratively, Leslie," Reginald said. "You know, more like 'that's gay' instead of 'that's homose—'"

"Shut up, nerd. She knows what I mean."

"I'm just saying, if her objection is that she's not actually a lesbian—"

"Shut up!" both girls shouted.

Leslie stared up at the ceiling, knowing for certain that outburst would get a rise out of their captor. When nothing happened, she began to feel a faint glimmer of hope. *Maybe he killed himself. Maybe he realized that what he's doing is totally fucked and he committed suicide instead of letting himself be taken alive by the cops. And now all we have to do is escape. All I have to do.*

"I said, do you deserve to be here, Leslie?"

"Does it matter? I could disappear and nobody would even notice."

Reginald coughed and cleared his throat. "You did disappear."

He's right. We all have.

"So what do we do about it?" Leslie asked.

"We have to figure out a way out of—"

"No shit, Sherlock! How?" Allison shouted. Leslie watched the flash of pain and disorientation unfocus the girl's eyes as she swooned. The princess let out a long sob and buried her face in her hands. Whatever their abductor had used to knock them out was hitting the skinny girl a lot harder than Leslie and the dweeb.

Upstairs, a door slammed. Heavy steps moved slowly from the distant end of the house toward the cellar door. The sound of something being dragged across the floor above them accompanied the pounding foot falls. Leslie tried to listen but Allison's sobbing was too loud, too near. A shaft of light grew and shone down from the open doorway before a shadow blocked it out. A body crashed down the stairs, tumbling part way, coming to rest in a twisted heap halfway down. Behind it, Leslie heard a gravelly voice say, "Goddamn it!" A few plodding footsteps followed and then the body lurched and fell the rest of the way to the cellar floor.

Leslie renewed her attempt to shrink from the light, stopped once again by the length of chain and the rock wall at her back. Reginald skittered away from the staircase like a beaten dog. And Allison just sat. Crying.

The shape walked the rest of the way down the stairs. At the bottom, it grabbed the body's ankles and dragged it toward the table. Leslie recognized the unconscious boy. His liberty fin mohawk was wilted, but unmistakable. There were plenty of punks in Shermerville, but Freddie was the only one with hair as white as that. At least it had been white. Now it was stained pinkish red and was growing increasingly brown as their captor dragged him though the dirt. The shape bent down and hoisted Freddie up on his shoulder like a fireman. It crouched low and lifted the gangly boy on his shoulders like the jocks did when doing squats in the weight room.

Is he a coach?

It slammed Freddie's body down on the table with a loud thump. His head made a hollow sound as it hit the wood like the gourd Leslie's hippie band teacher made her play. Reginald's atomizer cracked and skipped off the table, bouncing into the center of the room. The dweeb lunged for it. Grasping the dented tube in both hands, he took a hit. The quick hiss of the medicine sounded like a librarian's warning. *Shh!* The shape slipped into the light and kicked the boy in the face with a brown wingtip shoe, audibly crushing the dweeb's nose. Reginald gagged and fell on his back, clawing at his face, the small canister of medicated aerosol wedged up into his mouth. The heel of the wingtip came down on the boy's stomach. The atomizer popped up like a stomp-rocket and the shape caught it in mid-air. The shape held it between thumb and forefinger as he bent over the gasping boy.

"Do you have a doctor's note for this? We have a no-tolerance policy for drugs," it said before stuffing the medicine in his suit pocket.

Mr. Brendan!

She'd only officially met with her guidance counselor once, but he remembered her name and said it every time he ran into her in the halls. He was one of the only people who used her name without appending "Lezzie" to it. She was sure even some of the teachers called her that when they sat smoking in their special lounge. Mr. Brendan never used the lounge—not that she saw. He roamed the halls in between classes. He said "hi" to her like she wasn't invisible. Leslie almost ran toward him looking for comfort and freedom.

She stayed in the shadows when he stomped on Reginald again. Leslie thought she heard some of the kid's ribs break. She wasn't sure. Allison barked fearful yips at every hit. *Like she gives a shit what happens to Reginald.*

"Stop!" Leslie shouted.

Mr. Brendan straightened his back and looked at her. Fading into the shadows was worthless if you couldn't keep yourself from screaming.

"Do you have something to say, Leslie?"

She shook her head. Her hair dropped into her eyes. For an instant Mr. Brendan was the shape again, obscured and dark. Something you could turn your back on and hope it was just a shade dispelled by turning on the light or waking up. Her eyes focused and he was the guidance counselor once more. Firm and distinct. Unbanishable. He stared with hot malice. He pointed at her with his forefinger and pinky and said, "I didn't think so."

"Please let us go," Allison said. "We didn't do anything."

Brendan turned to the princess and pointed the cornuto at her. "You want to add something, missy? You think your time could be better spent somewhere else? Let me tell you . . . let me tell *all* of you, you're not going anywhere. You should take this time to reflect on what you really are. Not who you think you are or what you want to be when you're trying to impress people, but what kind of little monsters you really are beneath all of this superficial bullshit.

"I hear you in the halls. Making jokes about the guidance counselor. How useless my job is; how useless I am. I work and I have the respect of my colleagues. Nothing's coming to me from dear old daddy and his Wall Street larceny. *I* help you punks get into college. *I* help you fill out applications and schedule tours and arrange your class schedules so you can make something out of your lives and then you laugh at me? At how little I matter?"

"I don't laugh," Leslie said.

"Yes you do. I see you, Ms. Lasseter. You don't have any friends to mock me in front of, but I see the way you look at me." Brendan adjusted his suit coat and popped his cuffs. He stood for a silent moment composing himself before returning his gaze to the boy lying at his feet. He gave Reginald one last kick in the face before heading back to the stairs.

"I'm going to be right on the other side of this door. If I hear another sound out of any of you, I'm coming back down."

"Let us go," Allison said. "My father will pay you whatever you want."

"Pay? For *all* of you?"

Allison looked taken aback by the question. She nodded. Brendan chuckled. "No. I'm not going to let you go. I'm gonna come back and kick the living shit out of each one of you. But first, I want you to do some thinking." He pointed at Wilden's body. "Then I'm going to hang you all up like that."

"Because we make fun of you?" Leslie asked.

"Because I don't like Mondays," he said, climbing the stairs. The door slamming behind him echoed through the basement. No amount of sobbing or choking could out-compete its gunshot finality.

Reginald lay doubled up like a pill bug. His sparse breathing more labored than ever. Leslie supposed he was dying in front of them. He was suffocating in open air and there was nothing anyone could do.

She looked at Freddie's body lying on the table. She'd

made out with him a couple of times, even let him feel her up. One time she'd even been ready to go down on him, but he was too distracted by some other something she couldn't remember—a band, probably—and had killed the mood. Still, she kind of liked him, even if he only ever treated her like a back-up piece of ass when he couldn't find one of his regular punker chicks. Maybe, like everyone else, he thought she was a basket case. Nevertheless, every once in a while he squeezed her tits and said nice things to her.

Brendan killed the kids who could have taken him out, she realized. Freddie and John Wilden. The rest of them—the princess, the dweeb, and her, the maladapt—he didn't fear them. He was as bad as all the bitches who took Leslie's notebooks and laughed at her poetry or the jocks who slapped Reginald's game manuals out of his hands and kicked them down the hall. Spencer Brendan was as bad as the punks and goths who laughed behind the backs of the popular girls and joked about how much their knee-pad allowances had to be. As bad as calling the wrestlers, "mat-fags." Everybody was shitty to each other. Everyone relentlessly bagged on everyone else like high school was some Hobbsian state of nature where life was brutish, ugly, and short. *And for some of us, it is.*

Freddie's arm slipped away from his body and dangled off the edge of the table, startling her out of her reverie. A glint of light sparked off his hand. He still wore all of his rings. Brendan had taken their things away, but he'd not removed Freddie's jewelry. Leslie rose to her haunches and clenched her fists. She squinted and held her breath and pushed down her fear until she had enough resolve to open her eyes and stand. She took a halting step forward. And then another. And a third. Eventually, she made it to the ring in the center of the room. It was welded to a big square plate bolted to the floor. She pulled at her chain. It held fast. The plate wasn't coming up without Reginald and Allison's help and maybe not even then.

"What are you doing?" Allison said.

"I need to get to Freddie."

"What for?"

"He has a ring."

Allison raised her eyebrows to silently ask the question, "So what?"

Leslie just looked at her and said, "Give me a hand?"

Allison crawled over to the center ring and together they tried to loosen it. No luck. Leslie figured that Brendan had used extra-long bolts or something that went way down into the concrete.

She sat down and stripped off her boot. The shackle had bitten into the flesh around her ankle, but only irritated it. She hadn't tugged at it enough to break the skin. She spit on her hands with what little saliva she could work up and rubbed at her foot and ankle trying to slicken her skin. It didn't help.

Reginald groaned a little half-croak and a high-pitched wheeze of air whistled through his throat.

Leslie crawled to him and rubbed her hands over his face. She could feel where his skull was broken. Soft places that should have been hard and rough, grainy-feeling spots that should have been smooth. His skin was hot and tight with swelling. He groaned in pain as she smeared his blood on her hands, getting then as wet as she could. She sat beside the boy and wiped his gore on her foot, saying, "Sorry."

She shoved and pushed and pulled at the cuff. It was tight, but she wore oversize shoes and her foot was smaller than it appeared. She got the thing halfway over her heel before the hinge pinched a nerve in the top of her foot and pain lanced to the tips of her toes. She fell on her back, biting at a hand to stifle the scream.

"You almost got it," Allison whispered. "Keep trying."

"I can't. It hurts."

"You have to do it. He's going to kill us."

Allison lurched toward her, grabbed the shackle cuff and yanked. Leslie thought her ankle was going to break. She stifled a scream, biting down hard on her thumb. It felt like a knife slashing her foot wide open. Still, the other girl pulled until she fell away, the chain clattering across the floor. The cuff thunked hollowly on the concrete. Empty.

Leslie rolled onto her side, clutching her shredded foot. It was hot and throbbing in time with her heart and hurt so badly she couldn't take a breath. She thought she might suffocate right next to Reginald if she didn't get a taste of clean air. Wiping away the tears with a black sweater sleeve, she opened her eyes and looked at her blurry foot through the tears. A ragged, shallow gash opened from where the cuff had once sat, extending to her middle toe. It bled. A lot. She pulled her sock out of the shackle, tearing it as it snagged on the hinge that had done her flesh such damage, and slipped it back on, trying to pretend that the pain didn't make her want to throw up and pass out.

"Okay, now what?" Allison said.

Leslie didn't answer. She collected herself, stood, taking a moment to find her balance, and hobbled over to Freddie's body. She pulled up one of his hands and looked for the right ring. It wasn't there. Just a bunch of rocker bullshit, horned skulls and iron crosses. *The other hand!* She reached over his body, bumping against Wilden's feet. He swayed away, twisting and bumping back into her. A drop of crimson drool spattered warmly on her shoulder. She held her breath and ignored it. *Don'tfuckinlookdon'tfuckinlookdon'tfuckinlook!* Allison let out a strained squeak from across the room. Leslie heard the sound of the girl's hands slapping over her mouth. She went back to work, pushing herself. Everything took effort: leaving the house, going to class, not collapsing in on herself like a black hole. She was always pushing against that thing that told her to stay home, stay alone, live in her head. She pushed harder. This time she thought she might break.

Getting up on tiptoe, she reached across and dragged Freddie's left arm out from under his body. The ring she wanted was on his third finger. She pulled but it wouldn't come free. Reginald's blood on her hands was drying and tacky and wouldn't be any use. She stuck his cold finger in her mouth and pulled it out slowly trying to slick it. His skin tasted like cigarettes and engine oil, like he'd been working on his scooter when Brendan took him. She closed her lips around his cold digit and sucked, suppressing her gag reflex as his fingernail tickled the back of her throat. Her mouth was dry but the effort was rewarded when the ring eventually slipped off.

"Why do you want that so bad?" Allison asked.

Leslie hobbled over and held up the prize. "It's a magician's ring. It has a handcuff lock pick." Poking a finger inside the steel circle she pushed out the thin, inch long wand of metal curled inside. She began trying to jimmy Allison's padlock. She had no idea what she was doing, however. It wasn't working. She'd imagined the bolt popping open and them walking out, holding each other around the shoulders and the waist, emboldened by their escape to stand up to the judgmental eyes of the world outside. They'd walk off, arm in arm, unafraid of what they left behind.

Except, the lock held.

She dropped the ring.

Allison sobbed and said, "No. Keep trying."

"I can go get help."

"You can't leave me. I'll scream."

"He'll come and kill us both if you do."

"Don't leave me here. I'll do it."

"You'd rather we both die than I get help?"

"You won't come back. If you go without me," Allison looked her in the eye and said, "I'll scream."

Leslie sat back, astonished at Allison's declaration. She couldn't think of anything to say in response. It was so amazingly short-sighted and selfish. *I can bring help. I can bring the police and an ambulance and maybe they can save Reginald and you both. What the fuck is wrong with you?*

"How did you get to be like this?" she asked instead.

"What do you mean?"

She stood and backed away from the princess, daring her to raise her voice. Leslie grabbed her boot, wincing as she slipped it carefully over her torn foot. "I'll send help."

"Don't go. Please, don't leave me here." Tears streamed down the princess's face. Leslie tried to imagine herself tomorrow or the day after saying "hi" to Allison in the halls. Calling her "Alli" like her friends did. Alli smiling back and introducing Leslie to all the other popular girls, explaining that she had saved everyone from creepy Mr. Brendan and his torture basement. Thanking her and apologizing for all the mean things they'd ever done to her, one of them—Blair—invited Leslie to a party, saying she could bring anyone she wanted. Any friend of Leslie's was a friend of theirs, she assured her. Leslie imagined herself standing in the living room of a big house on the hill with a picture window looking out over the city. Gazing at the view of the night as grand as standing on a mesa cliff with only sky for a ceiling: starlight above, city lights below. Freddie holding her hand and telling her how happy he was she hadn't abandoned them. How much it meant to him that she'd risked everything to get help.

Behind her, Reginald wheezed feebly. And then he was silent.

She dreamed.

"I'll send help."

Allison's face fell. "Don't forget about me."

Leslie staggered to the table and picked up Reginald's backpack. She began stuffing books inside, trying to give it enough weight to use as a weapon. A weird flap on the side caught her eye and she folded it over, exposing the hidden zipper. Pulling it open, she found the snub-nosed revolver Brendan had missed. *Was this for the dweeb's protection? Or something else?*

It didn't matter.

She cocked the hammer. Turning back to the princess, she said, "Go ahead and do it."

"Do what?"

"Scream."

"I don't—"

Leslie pointed the gun at the princess. "Scream."

Allie did.

The footsteps above them were heavy and hurried. Brendan sounded ready to stomp another one of them to death. Leslie hobbled away, almost tripping over the iron ring as she passed it on her way toward the darkness beneath the stairs. The locks above her clacked and the door slammed open. The guidance counselor's footfalls on the stairs boomed and echoed through the basement like the thunderclaps of an angry god.

"What the hell is going on in here?" he shouted, staring dumbly at Allison, processing the scene.

Leslie leveled the gun at the back of his head. She hesitated, glancing around him at Allison. The princess's eyes were as wide as an owl's and were trained on her instead of Brendan. He turned, swinging an arm.

"You mess with the bu—"

She pulled the trigger.

～

He didn't dream.

Neither did he sleep.

IN THE BONES

Carol was stable, but still unconscious. She had tubes going into her arms and mouth, bandages around her head covering the portion they'd shaved in order to operate, and a large contraption that looked like an inquisitor's device holding together what was left of her leg. Large metal circles with wires leading to screws and pins invaded pink and red inflamed flesh, torn and cut and loosely stapled back together. All for the sake of holding together a single bone which had been made several.

Although it wasn't permitted, the night staff bent the rules and moved one of the fold-out chairs from Maternity into Carol's room for her husband, Paul Goddard, to sleep on. It was uncomfortable, but after two nights in the hard visitor's chair leaning over to rest with his head propped at the end of the bed, it felt like a feather mattress. The doctor who came in the following morning to check on Carol seemed to tut-tut softly when he saw what they'd done, but had nothing else to say about it. Paul doubted that the doctor kept quiet purely out of sympathy for his plight. It was likely just a matter below his pay grade. Come in. Check the patient's condition. Move on to the next one.

He looked at his wife's butchered thigh and thought about the things coating the floors and floating through the air in any hospital that might take up residence in her. Tiny invisible things cast off from one person, infecting another, passed from mouth to hand to wound. Everyone directly caring for Carol washed their hands compulsively. For the other staff and lighter-contact visits, there were alcohol hand-sanitizer dispensers hanging on the walls in every single doorway and hallway in the place. Hospital protocols bred obsession. A dose on the way in and a dose on the way out. The drip leading into Carol's arm fed her an antibiotic to keep infection at bay.

Still. You had to be vigilant.

Paul had read about MRSA, Methicillin-resistant Staphylococcus aureus. It was natural selection at work—a strain of bacteria resistant to antibiotics that, while not any more virulent than normal staph, was much more difficult to treat once infection set in, thus making it deadly in certain cases. Cases like hers.

Paul sat up in the chair to look out the window at the Charles River. The water sparkled under the light of the rising sun. On the surface of the calm water, a young man pulled on long thin oars, his narrow boat lacing delicately across the surface leaving a pattern like the water-skippers he used to stare at as a child when his parents took him to the woods.

Beyond the river, the city skyline rose up like distant, jagged spires stabbing at the white and blue sky. The Hancock Tower, 111 Huntington, the Pru. The city was once a peninsula connected to the mainland by only a slender isthmus until they built up the Back Bay and other parts of the city using landfill. They displaced the bay with the shattered fragments of earth and forest, old docks and tons and tons of gravel transported there by truck, arriving every forty-five minutes, day and night, for fifty years. It was all buried to build a bigger city, a stronger city. But it was never strong enough. The fill is weak. The gleaming towers that rise above the Back Bay are built with supports that pierce down through it, right down to the bedrock. Man's reach for the sky rooted to the bones of the earth.

He looked at the windows of the tall buildings that had been checkerboard lit and dark in the night. Now, in the light of the morning, they were all uniform squares of reflective anonymity. People moved behind them invisibly, carrying on as if nothing had changed in the world, always looking forward in time as though they would see no end of it.

Somewhere in the glittering skyline was a single window that looked into his Back Bay apartment. *Their* apartment. He thought of the bare walls beyond the window. Carol had taken the art, leaving behind blank white squares where the time hadn't been allowed to dim the walls' luster. They were a faint reminder of the purity of the first time they'd stepped foot into their home. She'd taken the paintings down and placed them, along with her half of the closet and the clothes in the drawers, along with her books and CDs, and everything of hers that could be packed into boxes, by the door. There they sat waiting for the men to take them. Strangers who take lives away to other places.

He'd asked her to stay. Asked her to remember all the wonderful times they'd had. He reminded her of their days together in college, of their wedding in Vermont, their tenth anniversary spent in Capestrano, and a dozen other memories immortalized in digital photographs never printed out. Ephemeral images that only existed in ones and zeros. He tried to move her not to leave. "Don't you remember how good it used to be?" he'd asked.

She reminded him of the hard times—of law school and endless billable hours as an associate at the firm, the miscarriage, the second miscarriage, not making partner, the fights and broken dishes, all the moments that had left her feeling alone in a house full of things while he was gone. All the things that made her feel like a thing. "I remember our life," she said. "That's why I'm leaving."

And he understood.

Sitting in a bare living room, he stared for hours at a television broadcasting one program after another empty of meaning or relevance. He listened to her music, digitized on his iPod—more ones and zeros—hearing the sounds that had moved her but never him. He read the same paragraph in a forgotten book a dozen times never seeing the words, instead seeing her reading it on the sofa, in the bathtub, in bed. And he understood. There was a profound emptiness in the house. His life was outside of it. And he'd left her there in the middle of all the nothing he'd amassed, desperately looking for something to make the days stand out from one another.

And so she had.

Thinking of the empty squares on the wall reminded him of her face every time she brought home a new painting. Some scrawl of chiaroscuro paint more texture and passion than technique. A half-illuminated face of smears and drips that had stared back at him from above the television. She'd thought it was funny to have the portrait above the set, watching them watch it. The joke wasn't all that amusing to him, but he got it. He stared at that face, not seeing it, for years. Pale shoulders beside breasts that emerged like bare islands from a dark sea. A long neck stretched above them in the gloom beneath a shrouded face, darkened and sad. The model's eyes were lost in twin pools of gloom, framed by gaunt cheeks that hinted at the figure's skull hidden just beneath the skin.

That painted woman had watched him, grimly anonymous and unrelenting in her gaze. He'd never realized it was a portrait of his wife; not until she took that face from the wall.

He turned away from the city view to look at Carol lying in her hospital bed. Her face now was a mottled mess of bruises and cuts and smashed and reconstructed bone and swollen flesh. Maroon deposits of dried blood inhabited the cracks of taped-together incisions, lacerations, and scrapes.

Her eyes darted left and right under trembling, thin eyelids. Her chest rose and fell softly to the hiss of the machine beside the bed.

"It'll work out. She'll wake up," the doctor had said. "She will open her eyes. And you'll be the first thing she sees." He'd smiled while he said it, expecting that the promise she would behold him before all other things would bring Paul a measure of comfort and satisfaction. The surgeon assumed that Paul was the loving center of Carol's world. Their relationship the bedrock upon which they built their lives.

The ambulance had brought them to the hospital together: her lying on a gurney, him sitting beside her on the bench, trying not to topple over as the driver snaked through traffic. It had been late, but there was always traffic in Cambridge. There was always someone sitting in a car, annoyed at the siren that broke through the bubble, forcing him to detour off to the side of the road while another life was carried forward. Given priority. In all the years he'd driven in the city, Paul had never thought about the fate of any occupant of an ambulance passing him. It was always a nuisance. A distraction from real life as he tried to get from point A to point B with a minimum of delay. At the sound of the keening wail, he would begrudgingly pull over to make way and then immediately dart back out into the emergency vehicle's wake, trying to take advantage of the swath they cut through traffic, indifferent to the sick and dying leading the way.

Then he rode in one and it all came into focus. These men and women drove through the city, siren screaming, trying to keep people together, keep death at bay, save lives, save families. The wailing was the sound of people hurtling toward the team waiting to pull souls back from oblivion—hurtling toward people dedicated to keeping a mother, father, son . . . or your wife from leaving before you were ready.

And who was ever ready?

Staring at her lying in the bed, he thought back to before the ride. He recalled standing in the dim light spilling out onto the third-floor deck, speaking to Carol in hushed tones, both of them trying not to make more of a spectacle of themselves at the party than they already were. She was on her fourth glass of wine. For a change, she wasn't driving. When the party wound down, and the last guests left, she'd remain. With Glenn. The artist.

Paul hadn't been invited to the party. But he'd heard about it from a friend who had been asked to attend. One of *their* friends. He found Glenn's name and address on an old receipt for a different painting—the one Carol had bought him for his office at the firm—stuffed in a file cabinet back in his study. The piece still hung above his office chair. He faced it every day when he entered, but never saw it again as he always kept his back turned to it. The painting had cost her two thousand dollars, and since he hung it up at work he wrote it off their taxes as a business expense. A double gift.

Her face as she first opened the door to Glenn's apartment studio was astounding to him. She stood shaded, lit from above and slightly behind, the living embodiment of the painting she'd taken from above the television. The mole on her collarbone stood out, casting a small shadow and he wondered how he'd ever missed it in the portrait. For years he'd asked her to have the blemish removed. She reacted as if that imperfection made her unique and asking her to slice it off was like asking her to become a faceless Stepford wife.

In the doorway, she didn't ask what he was doing there. Neither did she ask him to leave, however. She simply said, "Paul?" As if that single syllable communicated everything else that needed to be said. *This is not where you are meant to be. This is not our life. It's mine.*

She wore a lightweight, peasanty-looking dress that hung loosely over her pronounced bones. It looked vaguely Indian and reminded him of the outfits that the waitresses at their favorite restaurant wore. Somehow, though, it also looked right on her. With her kinky hair up in a bun, errant strands poking out here and there, she looked loose and relaxed, like when he'd first seen her in college. She certainly looked nothing like the woman in the form-fitting Little Black Dress he took to the various firm functions when they were together.

"Carol," he said. She stood in the doorway staring at him sadly, waiting for Paul to say something else. When he didn't speak, she filled the empty space.

"I'm surprised to see you." She gave him a peck on the cheek, bending at the waist, keeping as much space between their bodies as she could while still making contact. Tenderness at a distant remove. Her warm lips brushed against his smooth-shaven cheek. He smelled wine on her breath. She inquired of him how he'd come to know about the party, but he didn't sell out their friend. Paul figured she'd put it together eventually. Pamela was the only one who'd refused to take sides. Their last living connection.

"I was hoping to see you," he said. "I just wanted to . . . see how you're doing."

"I'm good. I'm happy."

"Are you?" he asked. She stepped back from the door into the light and changed from the sad woman in the painting to a fresh new Carol. Not the Carol he'd married. An older, experienced Carol. One who smiled.

She raised her eyebrows in that way she did before saying something she expected might upset him and said, "If I invite you in, will I regret it?"

He grinned. "Of course not. We're adults, right? No reason we can't be friends." Although he knew she disagreed with that last statement, she gestured for him to come inside anyway. A crash and a tinkle of glass sounded from deep in the room behind her. She excused herself and hurried off. Paul closed the door behind him.

The space was a built-out studio on the third floor of a triple-decker near Harvard Square. Low tables struggled under the weight of books. On top of them rested glasses half-filled with white or red wine. More books were stacked on the floor in front of shelves covered in seemingly endless and dusty bric-a-brac and objets d'art. When they'd been together, she insisted on hiring a cleaning service to come once a week to dust and polish the empty surfaces of their condo. He wondered how she lived with such clutter in this apartment.

The walls were covered with paintings similar to the ones she'd been buying all those years. Although they maintained a thematic style, they showed a progression—growth as an artist. Half of them were portraits. Many of those were recognizably of the same model.

Carol.

His estranged wife.

Someone else's muse.

As guests drifted around the space looking at the art on display, he shuffled off to a black and brushed aluminum IKEA kitchen island that had been moved into the living room to serve as a bar. He set about fixing himself a gin and tonic while he waited for Carol to come back. Taking a sip, he turned to face the room, scanning for anyone he recognized. Although their friends had divided themselves after the split, he saw none of the ones who'd taken up with Carol's camp. *This is Glenn's show, after all.*

And then he saw them, huddled in the far corner. Reva and Andrew, Jean and Willa, Julia and Ryan. Julia cast a glance over her shoulder at him before turning away when she saw Paul looking back. Her husband, Ryan, said something and a couple of the others chuckled. The rest just stood, lips pursed, and nodded at whatever sage bon mot he'd dropped. Whatever he'd uttered, it fell on them with more gravity than levity.

Emerging from the kitchen, Carol went to stand with their

friends. She upturned the dregs of her glass of wine before holding it out for one of the assembled tribe to fill. Julia picked up a bottle of something red from a nearby bookshelf and filled the glass practically to the rim. Carol took another big slug off it and excused herself from the group. As she broke away, Ryan laid a hand on her shoulder. Paul read his lips as he said, "We're here for you." Carol moved away, weaving slightly as she glided through the space.

Paul put on his best I'm-happy-for-you face and held out his hands, palms up. Carol laid her empty hand in one of his and he gave it a reassuring squeeze. She withdrew from his grip as soon as he let up the pressure. "It's good to see you," he said. "You look well." She flashed a small smile and looked down at her feet and said something about feeling well. He was unconvinced. She took another drink.

"The place is . . . nice."

"Why are you here?" she asked.

Paul looked over her shoulder at the pack of friends whose houses they used to go to for brunch and cocktails and dinner parties. They all stared at him. He nodded. The two men nodded back. The women just stared. The artist, Glenn, wandered over to them and cocked his head. Jean pointed her weirdly long finger in Paul's direction. Glenn turned around. From across the room Paul could still see his eyes narrow and his thin, pale lips purse underneath the oh-so-boho hipster beard.

"I just wanted to see you, Carol," Paul said. "Ironically, I figured the party was my only chance to actually get you alone for a second to talk." He didn't add, *because I know you'd do anything to avoid me making a scene in front of our friends.* He was sure she had gathered that already.

"We don't have anything to talk about," she said. And she was right. He'd come to the party with a hundred things on his mind. More entreaties to come home, more reminisces about the early, bright days of their courtship. But when he saw her, he knew that it was over. There was nothing he could say that she couldn't counter with "No."

Glenn appeared and slid an arm around Carol's waist in a practiced way like he'd been doing it for years. He had a painterly look, like he spent more time indoors than out, but there was something else beneath it. Paul's own carefully crafted appearance was meant to belie the indoor softness of his profession—he worked hard to make himself look strong and sun-kissed and vital. But where Paul had cultivated gym muscles and sun-bed tan, there was something primal and savage in Glenn. His eyes were wild like a French fur trapper from a history book. He was pale, but hard-looking. Like stone. He made Paul feel like a pretender.

"How are we doing?" Glenn asked. "Is everything okay?" Although he addressed them both, it was clear he was inquiring only of Carol's well-being.

She nodded and awkwardly introduced her lover to her husband. Paul held out his hand for Glenn to shake. "Pleased to meet you finally." The wildman took it and gave a firm, but not overbearing single pump before letting go.

He shakes hands like a lawyer.

Glenn smiled with half his mouth and gestured at the apartment/gallery. "So what do you think?" Paul was uncertain how to respond until Glenn glanced left and right at the paintings on the walls.

"Oh! The show? Very nice. I've admired your work for a long time."

"Glad you could make it then," Glenn said. "Now, if you don't mind, I need to introduce Carol to someone. You can find your own way out, I'm sure." Paul marveled at how well the artist controlled the situation. He'd appeared courteous, but was firm and gave an order in a way that sounded like small talk. Paul was certain that before the man became a hippie layabout, he'd been in his tribe: a litigator.

"If I could just have one more minute of Carol's time, I'll

be on my way. I don't want to overstay my welcome."

The look in the wildman's eyes said, *too late.* But after silently consulting Carol he said, "I'm sure you won't," instead. He bent down and gave her a lingering kiss on the lips before saying, "Don't keep us waiting too long."

Marking his territory.

Carol squeezed Glenn's hand and let go, allowing him to return to the huddle to observe and whisper with the others. She turned back to Paul and asked what it was he wanted to discuss that couldn't wait. He tilted his head toward the deck and asked if she'd step outside with him. It was a warm spring, but the nights were cold. No one was standing outside, not even to smoke. She rolled her eyes and led the way.

The sliding glass door jammed halfway and she had to put her shoulder into getting it open enough for them to step through. Paul followed her out and pulled the door shut behind him. The thump of the jamb sliding home pleased him.

"So what is it? What do you want?" she asked.

He reached for her hand but she pulled away. He sighed loudly and said, "I'll sign the papers. Have your lawyer send them to my office."

She gave him another expression he recognized—the squint-eyed what's-your-angle look—and said, "You're kidding, right?"

"No bullshit. No fights." He made another grab for her hand. This time she let him take it. "I can see you have something here. I won't stand in the way."

She hugged him, carelessly dribbling wine from her glass down the back of his sport coat. He held her tightly, feeling the softness of her body against him, her breathing, her breasts pressed against his chest.

"I'm sorry. We just grew in different directions," she said. "It's not you or me, it's just . . . us, I guess."

"Oh no. It's definitely you," he breathed into her ear.

She pulled back to look into his eyes, screwing up her face in frustration at his need to have the last stab at whatever piercing game of emotional pain they played. Like always. She let go and backed up to the wooden railing of the deck, wavering slightly. "You should go. I'll make sure you get the papers." The wine in her hand seemed to have an equal chance of slipping from her fingers and toppling over the edge as it did being raised to her lips.

He thought about what it would be like to fall over the side—the sensation of slipping through the cool night air. That last moment of quiet, pure panic right before hard ruin on the concrete below.

He nodded and reached for the door. Struggling with it, he banged and clattered the door in its track.

"Ugh! Let me get that. There's a trick." She balanced her wine glass on the edge of the rail and staggered over to him.

"I got it," he said, yanking hard. The door jerked open to the sticking point. His hand slipped off the handle and he jammed his elbow into her. She gasped and staggered backward clutching at her breast. He cried out, lurching at her. She slammed up against the rail and toppled over. He snatched at her, catching her wrist. Her weight jerked him down and he thought for a second that she might pull him off the platform after her. But they both hung there suspended in air for a moment, the rail between them folding him in half, holding him in place. The wine glass shattered on the concrete below in a soft tinkle of devastation.

He barely registered the sound of people behind him screaming and rushing for the deck.

Carol looked up, pleading with him to haul her back up. She looked at him with shadowed eyes and said, "Paul?" Her face was a distorted mask of panic and need. And then wide-eyed fear. "Paul!"

He reached down with his other hand and firmly grasped

her gauzy sleeve before letting go of her wrist. The cheap peasant frock tore, leaving him holding a length of rent cloth. He watched as she disappeared into the darkness below. The sound of her landing with a *whump* and the snap of breaking bones against denting steel, more shattering glass, and then a hollow crack against the pavement like a gunshot carried up and over the screams of the other guests as they arrived behind him on the deck. He turned, holding up the sleeve by way of explanation.

"I had her. I had her!" he said.

The rest of the evening was a blur. Shrieks and shouts, threats and recriminations, the police and paramedics . . . the ambulance ride.

And then the hospital.

Paul informed the staff that he was Carol's husband—a lawyer at Tinder, Gibson and Parry LLC. They led him right past the velvet rope. All access. Glenn arrived directly behind, but since he was only a "friend," the responsibility to make decisions fell to Paul. He still held her power of attorney. Glenn was exiled.

She moved from emergency into surgery and then recovery. Once she stabilized, Paul was allowed into the room to see her. And from that moment on, he never left her side. Watching. Waiting for the movements of her eyes beneath the lids to develop into a flutter. And then wakefulness. And he'd be the first person she saw. Not Glenn. Him.

And then what? She'd realize that she still loved him, have a change of heart? She'd feel let down and betrayed that her artist wildman wasn't waiting to immortalize her in yet another half-formed series of haphazard paint streaks?

No.

She'd ask where Glenn was. Paul would explain about hospital policy and the power of attorney and that she needed someone to care for her and that it had been him. It had always been him. He'd pour his heart out and still she'd be unmoved. Because that was Carol. She couldn't remember the good times.

He stood up from the chair beside the bed and stretched his back. It was stiff from that damned new-father's chair. He grabbed his wallet from the radiator sill below the window and looked out again at his beloved city. The city *across* the river. The home she'd not returned to since betraying him and moving across the Charles like it was some clear line demarking one life traded for another. An impassible barrier between the past and her future.

But he'd crossed it. For her.

It was all for her.

Paul pulled the sheer curtains closed and walked out of the room into the hall to buy a bottle of water from the vending machine in the lobby. "Mr. Goddard," a nurse called out to him. "Mr. Goddard, stop!" He turned to face her, hands on hips. She stared at him with a look of mild annoyance. "Mr. Goddard, you have to put your shoes on. We're allowing you to sleep here, but this is still a *hospital*." He looked down at his stocking feet. Thin black work socks that he hadn't changed since Carol had been admitted forty-eight hours ago stood in stark contrast to the white tile beneath them.

"Oh my god, I didn't even realize."

The nurse huffed and grabbed his elbow to lead him back to the room like *he* was the patient who needed her healing touch. "It's okay, Mr. Goddard." She patted his hand. "She'll come through it. But when she does wake up, you need to be strong enough for the both of you." She spoke as if his shoelessness was physical a symptom of the psychological trauma that a good husband *must* be feeling in such circumstances. Of course, he'd forgotten to slip into his shoes due to worry over his wife.

The woman turned him toward her and looked soulfully into his eyes as if stage positioning enhanced the sincerity of her delivery. "She's lucky to be alive. Carol is going to need a lot of help adjusting to her new life after the surgeons are through. She's lucky to have a husband as devoted as you."

"And I'm lucky to still have her."

"Yes you are." She smiled at him. The nurse wasn't ugly. Just not quite pretty either. Nothing that would inspire anyone to paint.

Not like his wife.

His wife, who when she awoke would tell what had really happened out in the cold night on the deck.

He walked into the room and shut the door behind him. Running the tap in the sink at the far end of the suite, he let the water fall over his finger until it felt lukewarm. He filled the pink plastic pitcher another friendly nurse had brought in the night before. Returning to his side of the bed he sat and stripped off his socks and dunked them in the water. After a minute or two of swirling them around, he pulled them out and wrung the cloudy water back into the pitcher. He repeated the process. When he was satisfied with his tea, he stood and peeled back the dressing covering the wounds she'd received in the fall and then in the operating theater. He tilted the pitcher, drizzling warm water along the length her wounds, soaking the points of penetration of the pins and screws and wires holding Carol's legs together. When the wounds were glistening wet, and dried blood in between folds of cut flesh looked newly tacky and soft, he replaced the gauze as well as he could so the stains of pus and blood lined up with her wounds. He daubed the scrapes on her face and wiped around her ventilation tube before taking the damp socks into the bathroom to wring out thoroughly in the sink. Wrapping them up in a ball, he dropped them into a plastic grocery bag, tied it off, and dropped it into the gym bag full of clean clothes he'd made his secretary drop off. Sitting down on the lid of the toilet, he pulled a fresh, dry pair of clean white socks out of the bag. He pulled them on and slipped his feet into his tasseled loafers.

Slinging the bag over his shoulder, Paul walked out of the room to go get breakfast and a cup of coffee. And to throw out his trash. He made sure to cleanse his hands at the sanitizer station right outside the room before he went. MRSA. It's all over places like nursing homes and hospitals. Staph infections are usually nothing to worry about. Unless they invade deeper into your body, getting into your lungs or bloodstream or bones. He chose not to think about it, instead reflecting on the good times as he stepped out into the sun.

Those thoughts lasted until he found Carol's boyfriend in the parking lot leaning against his car.

Paul's step stuttered and he hesitated a second before resuming his stride. Wildman appearance or not, Paul had taken Krav Maga classes. He wasn't going to let this hipster shithead intimidate him.

Glenn took a deep drag, the red ember of the cigarette burning hot in the shade of the covered lot before fading again. His face darkened as the ember cooled and he blew the smoke out, waiting a moment, steadying himself. The man looked like his muscles were made of inch-thick coiled spring. He took a breath before speaking. "I brought you something. A little piece of art I thought you might like to see before it goes on public display."

"I don't want any more of your paintings in my house."

Glenn reached into his messenger bag. Paul's stomach tensed as he waited for the artist to pull a gun. He tensed up, ready to dive at the man's midsection. He wasn't going to just stand there and let the asshole shoot him. When the wildman pulled a silver disk in a white paper sleeve out of the bag, he half-relaxed.

"What's that?"

"It's for you, Goddard. A video installation piece."

"I don't get it."

Glenn's mouth turned up on one side in a kind of

humorless smile. "You ever go to a museum and walk into a room where they're playing a looped video of a rotting peach or a man in drag changing a truck tire? That's a video installation. I have a friend who does them."

Paul stepped up to Glenn, held up his key and said, "Not interested. Now get off my car so I can go change my clothes before Carol wakes up." His head was beginning to ache and he wanted nothing more than to be back in his apartment taking a hot shower while his socks turned to ash in the building incinerator.

The wildman persisted. "You're going to be interested in *this*. Believe me. My friend, the video artist, he has this thing about 'outsider perspective'."

Paul wanted to throw a punch through the air quotes Glenn fingered on either side of his face. He stood still and waited the man out. No sense getting arrested for fighting with the contents of the bag on him.

"He likes to film intimate situations at a distance. You know, dinners, quiet nights cuddling on the couch . . . parties. He climbs up telephone poles and ties these little tiny cameras to them so he can film through windows from across the street. If he didn't show the videos in museums, he'd just be a peeping Tom. But it's art when he does it. Oh, and he gets permission. If you'd shown up to the party with everyone else, you'd have gotten a copy of the likeness rights waiver. Still, we didn't want you to be unaware what you'd gotten into. I thought you should have a look-see before the big premiere."

"I told you, I'm not interested."

"On the news."

Paul's stomach tightened again and he found himself taking a step back from the man and his unmarked DVD.

"Finally piqued your curiosity, huh?" He dropped the disk on the ground and lit a fresh cigarette. "Watch it or don't. It'll be on at six and probably again at eleven. I'd try to catch it on your player though. You might not get another opportunity."

"Fuck you."

Glenn the wildman laughed a single explosive syllable before pushing off the side of Paul's BMW. "Our girl told me about your dark side, but I didn't let it sink in all the way. You know how people talk about their exes. That's on me. This," he said, spitting on the paper envelope. "This is all on you." He walked into the shadows of the parking garage, smoke drifting lazily in his wake. Paul thought about leaving the disc on the ground, but at the last minute snatched it and jumped into his car. He drove through the city in a daze, glancing from time to time at the DVD glinting on the passenger seat.

In his condo, he stood with the Blu-ray remote in hand, afraid to press PLAY. His phone started ringing not long after he arrived home. He didn't answer. Instead, he stared at the blank screen as if it was a black hole that might suck him in if he woke it.

Eventually, he started the disc and watched the image of the deck outside Glenn's studio appear crisp and clear and large as life on his plasma television. People filed in to the apartment appearing and disappearing into the space beyond the glass doors separating them from the outdoor landing. They laughed and poured drinks and talked. The only sound on the video was that of an occasional car passing by out of frame or an airplane overhead.

Paul fast-forwarded through the next hour of video. Eventually, he saw himself appear at the door and he let the film resume normal speed. He watched himself make a drink, talk to Carol and Glenn . . . and then the deck.

All those things he remembered about that night appeared differently on camera than in his recollection. His hand slipping off the handle of the door looked like what it was: a rear elbow strike. His lunge to catch her, a braced forearm shove. And the deliberate shift of hands, from a firm life-saving grip to a tenuous grasp on soft fabric. Most damning, however, was his face as she fell.

All those memories from a different perspective took on new life and his stomach tumbled at the thought of a single moment gone too far. An impulse that he didn't fight and a choice, once made, irrevocable. Made doubly so by his "tending" to Carol in the hospital.

The video ran on. The sounds of screaming and shouting and a siren growing louder until it filled his apartment, filled his head.

The phone rang again. And then the knock at the door.

He thought of the gym bag with his socks tied up in a shopping bag sitting in the foyer. In his haste to see the video he hadn't rushed first to the garbage chute at the end of the hall. Instead it sat by the door, harboring whatever he'd put into his wife's body to keep her from ever telling anyone what was so clear on the video. What anyone with eyes could see. What everyone would see when the evening news ran it alongside video of him being led into a courtroom in handcuffs. When they recounted the details of his trial and sentencing. When some expanded cable crime channel recounted his story as murder porn for shiftless people watching television in the middle of the day.

He walked to the glass door in his condo and slid it silently, easily open. Walking to the low wall at the end of his balcony, he peered at the street twelve floors below and imagined the last moment of quiet, pure panic right before hard ruin. Before he broke his bones on the concrete and city landfill beneath.

Instead, he chose to focus on the good times. At least for eleven floors until there was nothing left of him to remember.

BLOOD OF THE VINE

Becca slumped down in the seat with her feet on the dash, trying not to feel concerned that Ione was dancing and singing along to a song blaring through the stereo while driving her car at breakneck speeds along the winding, rural Pennsylvania highway. She tried to distract herself by checking her e-mail. Although the smart phone screen was hard to see in the daylight, the message from the detective assigned to her case was clear enough: there was insufficient evidence to make an arrest. Chris was free. She recalled what the cop said when Ione had first dragged her into the police station: *If you'd come to us that night it'd be different, but without any physical evidence, it's just your word against his.* The detective had looked a little sad and her tears convinced him to "conduct some interviews." It was the least he could do, he'd said. Apparently, the least also included sending her an e-mail instead of calling when he decided to shit-can her case. She closed her eyes and tried to remember what it had been like to live in the time before her life hit the brakes.

Her shoulder banged painfully against the inside of the passenger door as the car jerked harshly into the left lane. "Sorry!" Ione shouted over the music. She quickly regained control, changed lanes again, and resumed banging the steering wheel to the beat instead of gripping it. *You need to get away, darlin',* she'd counseled. *Get away from school, stress, and Chris. Get some real food in you—not this processed cafeteria shit, y'know? You need to have, like, a healing experience.* Ione had been hounding her to come visit the collective farm or whatever it was that she grew up on. It hadn't really interested Becca until Professor Hess posted her grade for Information Architecture. Then, running away seemed like a great idea. *Just a few days without anyone giving me sad looks or acting like I'm some kind of evil whore. Who knows? It might actually be fun to go make bricks out of cow poop or whatever it is they do on a hippie farm.*

"You're going to love Corinth. Everyone's so cool and it'll totally get your mind off of everything. Just remember, people are a little serious about religion where I come from, so don't be freaked out, okay? They can get intense, but nobody's going to judge you. It's just a bunch of stuff about eternal life and the blood of this and that."

"I'll try not to flip out," Becca said. "If we make it."

Ione stared at her for an uncomfortably long moment, somehow able to keep the car on the road navigating by peripheral vision. "Didn't you get anything out of Professor Tate's class? We need to embrace the Dionysian aspect of our consciousness, or some shit, you know?"

"I don't think 'or some shit' was part of that."

Ione held up a hand signaling that conversational subject had played out. She'd made her declaration and now it was time to sing louder and dance harder. "53rd & 3rd! I love this one!" Becca hunkered down a little lower in the seat. The pressure on the back of her neck felt good. She imagined herself submerged in a hot bath and wondered what the Jesus hippies in Corinth, Pennsylvania thought of girls who passed out drunk and lost their virginity to frat boys.

"Nonie!" The shriek awoke Becca and she kicked against the dash for a moment like she was caught in a live trap.

Ione hugged the woman leaning into the open driver's side window. They seemed to melt together, their matching black hair forming one long mane that absorbed the bright light of the day. The odor of patchouli invaded the car. The women parted and Becca noticed how alike they looked. She could be an older sister—or maybe even a twin. *Ione never mentioned a sister.*

"Mom, this is Becca. The one I told you about."

Mom!

"I am so pleased to meet you. I'm Chari." Becca held out her left hand to shake. The woman's hands were rough and strong but with slender bones and a cool dryness that seemed impossible in the unseasonable heat. "Why don't you guys park this thing behind the house and come inside for some lunch."

"Jesus! Your mom looks young," Becca whispered as they pulled away.

"It's not Jesus that keeps her looking that way."

Becca wasn't sure what to make of Ione's response. She didn't want to start the week off by insulting her best friend's mother. She changed the subject. "I thought you said this was coal country. This place looks like it could be Martha's Vineyard."

"Yeah, we've done a lot to keep it the way it was before they started tearing everything up for industry and commerce and shit. No McDonald's or anything. A couple of mining companies have come sniffing around, but we won't sell. After a while, they stop coming back. We like our village the way it is." Becca tried to imagine how a town of peace and love fundies could have run off big coal businesses. *That's the power of prayer, I guess.*

"It's beautiful." Becca tried not to act too smitten but found it hard. Corinth was everything that her own home town wasn't—green, bucolic, quiet. Even though she wasn't even out of the car, she felt a sense of belonging creeping its way under her skin.

Ione pulled the ancient Volvo around behind the house and killed the engine. It pinged and popped and knocked as it came to rest. Becca slipped on her shoes and let herself out.

Ione started pointing out nearby buildings. "Over there is the general store, across the street from that is the Beddows' restaurant—it's real casual-like—and around the corner we even have a little art gallery that Anna Freeman keeps expanding every year. She's the only one with paintings in it, but people really like her stuff."

"What about that place?" Becca jabbed her thumb over her shoulder at the building looming in the distance behind them.

"Oh, the Barn? That's kind of like the heart of the whole town. It's our meeting house and church and town hall all rolled into one." Although Becca had expected there to be a barn, she wasn't prepared for its actual appearance or the view surrounding it. "You'll get to see inside tonight. We're having a big festival to mark the equinox. It's one of only two nights a year that day and night are equal. That's what 'equinox' means. It's Latin for 'equal night'." Ione grabbed Becca by the hands and dragged her into the house.

Inside, Chari was setting a table for lunch. "I'll bet you two are hungry," she said. "It's a long drive from Boston; you must have been up before the sun." She put her hands gently on Becca's shoulders and guided her into a chair facing a window looking out on the Barn. Becca stared at a mural decorating the side of the building depicting grapes and a spilled wine glass surrounded by a wreath of leafy vine.

"Do you guys grow grapes out here or something?" she asked, greedily shoveling a forkful of seasoned eggs and cheese into her mouth. Chari lightly stroked Becca's cheek with the back of her cool hand. Becca flinched a little at the oddly familiar caress before relaxing. Although she'd just met Chari, her touch was so affectionate, so tender, that Becca almost closed her eyes and leaned into the woman's embrace.

"We make wine here, dear. Now eat your lunch. Tonight's a big night and you'll need your energy." As soon as she said it, Becca realized that she would love a nap after her meal. She hadn't done much but ride in a car down from Boston, yet she felt exhausted. Fatigue had been gnawing at her for weeks, but this felt different—like the pleasant half-drowsiness just before falling into restful sleep at night. She blinked away her drowsiness and tore into the food in front of her. Ione had said that getting away would be good. She felt like a new woman already.

After lunch, Becca felt a surge of energy and suggested a walk through the village instead of a nap. Ione gladly led her around, continuing to point out landmarks as they passed. "There's Rob Hardy's shop. He fixes shoes and does leather stuff. And that's Denny Wheatley's house. And that's April Morrison's place. She's like our doctor, I guess. Keeps everybody going during cold and flu season." The whole town seemed to be outside and most people that Ione pointed out paused from hanging grapevine garlands over their doors to wave and smile. The village's warmth was a welcome departure from the deep black water she felt like she'd barely been treading. Becca wanted to run from door to door, introducing herself. She stuck by her friend instead, managing her excitement. *Life hasn't changed. You haven't changed.*

"Why is everybody decorating? I thought you said the party was in the Barn tonight. "

"It is. But sometimes things overflow. It can turn into, like . . . a street festival. We have two really big celebrations a year; there's this one in the spring and then the other one in the fall. Everybody dresses up, comes out, and we tie one on. It's a way to 'foster unity' as my mom likes to say."

"She's intense. Is she the mayor or something?"

Ione laughed. "Or something. She leads the town council and keeps everything going when they aren't meeting. She's more like a town mom."

"This place is great."

"We're pretty proud of it." She said. They walked a few feet and Ione continued the tour. "We have a one-room school over on the other side of town. Mrs. Blackmun teaches all the grades except for high school. For that we have to take a bus over to Monroeville. It's a long ride, but it actually works out okay. The village is so small that practically everyone is related to everyone else in some way. There's got to be some way to meet new people—bring in new blood, you know."

As if on cue, Becca's phone buzzed in her pocket with a text from Chris. Meeting new people wasn't always as awesome as she expected it to be. Sometimes, it involved going to the pharmacy for an emergency pill—going to the police to file a report. She deleted the message without reading it. However the detective's interview had gone, she couldn't imagine that Chris had come out of it feeling good about her. She imagined she'd be receiving lots of messages from him in the future. If she was lucky, he'd be satisfied with gloating and not move on to threatening.

"That's not why you're at B.U., is it? For an M.R.S.?" Becca laughed, trying not to let recent history sour the pleasant vibe of her getaway. Ione's mouth curled up in a sneer.

"No. I'm actually studying for my degree. Mrs. Morrison needs help and a day or two off a week. I'm going to be her apprentice as soon as I finish my studies. Not everybody from the country comes to the big city just to land a man, Bec. It's the Twenty-First Century. I'm a modern woman."

"I'm sorry. I didn't mean . . ." Becca grabbed her friend's

hand and held it clutched against her chest. "I'm just jealous of what you have here, I guess. I don't see why anyone would ever leave this place. I wouldn't for anything."

Ione smiled broadly, displaying her large, slightly yellow teeth. The skin around her eyes wrinkled, and for a second she looked much older than twenty-two. She looked a hundred and twenty-two. And then, in a blink, she was young again. "I was hoping you were going to say that. My mom and I both think this place would suit you. And, you know, we need a librarian."

"Do you even have a library?"

"We do. Mrs. Beckham who ran it died last year after an accident. We need someone to take over for her."

"Wow. How do I apply for that job? I mean, I'm sorry to hear about Mrs. Beckham."

Ione laughed. "You can apply tonight. But if you're going to do that, we need to get you something suitable to wear for an interview." She pulled Becca forward along the lane and around a corner. "Up here," she crowed. "Mrs. Davies will have what we need." They ran up to the front steps of an unassuming little house. Before Ione could knock, the door swung wide revealing a woman who appeared much too young to go by "Mrs." anything.

"Hello, girls." She gasped and held out her hands, palms up. Ione took them in hers and kissed the woman on both cheeks. "Ione, is this the one you've been telling us all about? Is this Becca?"

"It is. Bec, this is Mrs. Davies."

"Pleased to meet you." Becca stuck out her hand to shake and was pulled in for a light kiss and tight hug. She felt her breath slip away. Mrs. Davies relaxed her hold and Becca resurfaced, taking a deep breath. The aromas of clean laundry and fresh bread drifted out from inside the house.

"Come in. Let's get you outfitted."

"How did you know I needed something to wear?" Mrs.

Davies took a step back, looking the girl up and down. She grinned and shook her head slightly. It didn't feel like judgment or criticism. If anyone else had done it—if one of those bitches from the sorority had done it—she'd have felt embarrassed and defensive.

"It's your first time; you'll need a fresh peplos."

"A pep-what?"

Ione nodded into the house. "You'll see." Mrs. Davies ushered the young women in and closed the door behind them. The smell of bread closed in around Becca like a warm blanket. *I think I could just lie down right here on the carpet like a cat and fall asleep.*

"Would you like a glass of wine while I fetch your dress?" Mrs. Davies grabbed a decanter off a table beside the door and began pouring the deep purple liquid into bright clear glasses that looked as fragile as eggshell.

Ione jumped at the offer. "Please!"

"Thank you, but I don't really—"

"It's okay, Bec. It's just a glass of wine." Ione laughed. "And another. And another!"

Mrs. Davies said, "If you take wine away, love will die, and every other source of human joy will follow."

Becca laughed at the somehow familiar line—*was it Shakespeare?*—and nodded her head. "Okay. I'll have some, please." Mrs. Davies served the girls their drinks and retrieved her own glass from the mantle.

"Stin ygeia mas," she said.

"What does that mean?"

"To our good health," Ione answered.

"Oh. Definitely. To our good health!" Becca sipped at her glass. The wine was rich and velvety on her tongue. It tasted like sour cherries, sweet vanilla, and earth. "It's delicious," she said. She smiled and took a healthy gulp. Ione laughed again and clapped her on the shoulder. "That's the way. Opa!"

Mrs. Davies slipped away without Becca seeing where she

went. She took another swallow and wondered if she drank too fast whether she'd be allowed to have another glass. She didn't want to be rude by appearing greedy. As if reading her mind, Ione emptied her own glass and fetched the carafe from the table. "More?" Before Becca could politely pretend to refuse, her glass was full again. She drank without complaint.

Mrs. Davies reappeared with a wooden cutting block covered in cheeses, a full olive dish, and small slices of toasted bread in one hand and a long white drape of cloth with purple edging hanging over her other arm. She set the block on the table next to the decanter and touched Becca's shoulders, lightly moving her away from the door and fully into the house.

"Well, I just can't get over what a picture of loveliness you are," she said.

It sounded so strange to Becca to hear someone not much older than she was talk like a friendly old grandmother. But the wine was normalizing the oddness of the encounter somewhat. She took another drink and a feeling of warmth spread from her belly up into her chest like a familiar seducing caress. She felt herself blush as she attempted a modest—if slightly ironic—curtsy. "Thank you."

"Now, let's get you out of those clothes and see how this looks." Mrs. Davies held up the "dress." It was a rectangular bolt of cloth with knotted buttons at each end of the top seam. The muscles in Becca's shoulders tightened up and she clenched her empty fist. She forced herself to relax. Ione was there guiding more wine to her lips as Mrs. Davies began working the buttons on Becca's blouse.

"It's okay," she whispered. "We all wear them. It's tradition. It's part of the festival." Mrs. Davies smiled broadly and, for a moment, that grandmotherly essence seemed to emanate from her whole body.

Becca took another sip, relaxed, and allowed herself to

be undressed. "Okay." At some point, Ione refilled her glass a third time. Her cell phone buzzed in her pocket on the floor—a million miles away.

Becca wanted to hike up, shift under, and pull closed the "dress" that Mrs. Davies had given her, but there seemed to be no good way to do it. The rectangle of fabric was fastened at her shoulders by knotted buttons—that Becca feared would simply pop undone—leaving a plunging scoop in front, and was tied around her waist with a narrow woven belt. Except where the belt held it together, the dress was open on the entire right side. Ione and Mrs. Davies had both convinced her (with a little reason and a lot of wine) that keeping her underwear on would look silly. Ione walked beside her in a similarly cut purple dress. Carrying their regular clothes in paper-wrapped bundles carefully tied closed with twine, they bounced up the street not caring who stared when the breeze whipped the loose, lower end of the dresses open. Naked underneath, Becca felt a little sexy, a lot exposed, and oddly empowered.

They bounded up the steps to Ione's house and burst inside, giggling drunkenly. Chari greeted them in the kitchen with more hors d'oeuvres and wine. "If you two don't look like you're ready to tear the night apart!" Becca blushed again. Ione handed her mother a paper bundle.

"Mrs. Davies asked me to bring you this."

"Isn't she sweet?" Chari stripped off her clothes before opening the package. Standing naked in the bright late afternoon sun, she leisurely untied the string, unwrapping her dress. Becca tried not to stare, but the woman's olive-toned body was hypnotic. *Ione is a senior, like me, which makes her twenty-two or twenty-three. That's got to make her mom at least thirty-nine if she had her when she was a teenager or something. Jesus! I hope I look that good at thirty-nine.* "I didn't know we had to wear togas," she said, trying to break the spell cast by Chari's skin.

"It's a *peplos*, dear. A toga doesn't fasten like this. And we do like to stand on ceremony. We've worn these for . . . well, I don't like to admit how long." She whipped the garment over her shoulders and wrapped it around herself. She buttoned it with practiced efficiency without looking while Ione helped fasten her belt up underneath her bosom, creating an empire waist that left the dress slit from Chari's ankle all the way up to her bust. Becca felt the urge to reach out and caress her naked hip. She controlled the urge by gripping the stem of her glass with both hands and taking another drink. Chari looked at her, tilting her head as if she'd felt the girl stroking her with her mind.

"That's the spirit, Becca." She pulled her thick black hair up into a loose bun on top of her head and tied it off.

"Shall we get started?"

"I feel like I'm almost finished," Becca replied, staring into an empty glass and wondering whether she'd drunk an entire bottle by herself yet. The memory of a stranger at a frat party handing her a red Solo cup flashed in her mind. The recollection only punctuated the blackout that followed upon that event. She smoothed her peplos down, self-consciously trying to close the side slit a little. She'd sworn only two weeks ago that she'd never touch another drop of alcohol. But that was the nature of promises; whether others made them to her or she made them to herself, they were always broken.

Chari took her glass and Ione slipped her hand into Becca's. They walked through the house, out the front door, and down the street away from the barn. As they made their way up the avenue, women and men from the village started filing out of their houses to follow. Eventually, they rounded a corner and started toward the barn. Becca looked over her shoulder and saw all the people she'd waved hello to on her first walking tour assembled in a crowd behind them. An excited hum of conversation bounced off buildings and floated up into the flowering white and yellow and green trees.

"Why am I the only one wearing a white whatever this is?" she asked. The warmth in her belly was slowly being replaced by a nervous tightness. She was finding it hard to swallow.

"What?" Ione asked, leaning in.

"White. I'm the only one in white. Everyone else is wearing red or purple."

"You're our *virgin*, honey," Chari said. She pulled the girl closer and they walked in a clumsy embrace.

"But I'm not a—" Ione held a finger to Becca's lips and shook her head slightly.

Becca thought of asking what to call the knee-length garments the men wore and whether they were naked underneath as well, but forgot when the transformed Barn loomed up in front of them. In the dying evening sun, the building flickered and danced in the light of burning torches surrounding the perimeter. The spilled wine mural seemed to extrude from the side and hover, shimmering in the air. They circled around to the front of the meeting hall. A pair of men rushed ahead to pull open the massive doors draped in the same grapevine hung all over town. They passed through the portal, the odor of fresh flowers from the trees outside drifting in after them.

Inside, the place was like no barn Becca had ever seen or heard of. It looked like the Museum of Fine Arts or an ancient church. Long tables along the far walls bowed under the weight of the feast set out. Fresh fruit and vegetables piled in colorful pyramids next to shiny meats almost glowing with dripping juices—beef and lamb and pork and everything Becca could imagine filling her suddenly achingly empty stomach with. *How can I be hungry? I've been drinking and snacking all day.*

The crowd surged past the trio of women and formed a circle around a dais in the center of the great hall. They all locked arms and the din of conversation died to a low silence that seemed to throb and hum as though all the beating hearts of the town had settled into a single rhythm. The massed citizens parted for Chari and the girls to step through. Although Becca shyly tried to take a position far from the center of attention on the outside of the circle, Ione pulled her through the opening and onto the low steps, whispering, "It's all for you."

Chari stood at the top of the dais, raising her hands over her head. She spoke with booming authority and her voice echoed through the great hall. "The god has blessed us again with good fortune and plenty."

"All hail the slain and the risen god," murmured the chorus en masse.

"The god has blessed us with a community of love and happiness."

"All hail the slain and the risen god."

"The god has blessed us with everlasting life."

"All hail the slain and the risen god." The steps of the dais seemed to pitch and roll as the voices of the town washed over Becca. Ione's grip on her hand tightened. She hadn't expected a spiritual revival meeting. She leaned into her best friend as drunkenness and religious fervor threatened to overwhelm her.

"And now we bring new life into our community. My new daughter, Becca, now stands as an offering to you. Will you accept her sacrifice?"

"Wait. What?"

"All hail the slain and the risen god," the chorus crowed.

"And for this gift of life, I present these gifts of plenty." Several men broke away from the circle, gathered up instruments haphazardly piled in a far corner of the hall, and started playing. The beating drums drew the breath from Becca's lungs and her heartbeat kept pace, hammering in her ears. The crowd swayed back and forth and began to circle the dais, rushing faster 'round as the beat became more frenetic. Becca's head swam and the room spun. The singing grew louder and the dancing wilder until the revels seemed ready to tear the hall to the ground. Their furious motion threatened to sweep Becca down the steps and away like a leaf fallen in the ocean. Ione grabbed her around the waist, hugging her tight. "Stay with me. Dance with me," she breathed into Becca's neck. Before she could say anything, Becca realized that she had no choice. Ione dragged her into the swirling village and they ran and danced and if they passed close to a table of plenty, they lashed out with shiny hands, tearing at meat and fruit and mashing it into their mouths.

Chari stood atop the dais and whispered, "The goat," her voice somehow carrying above it all.

The doors to the great hall creaked open to reveal a confused-looking man in jeans and an athletic jacket peering through. From the portal he watched as the crowd slowed and stopped, panting and pulsing in time to the music. He saw Becca and a look of relief washed over his face. "There you are. Jesus! This is wild. Ione didn't say it was going to be an orgy."

Rage flowed through Becca's body. "What are you doing here, Chris?" she growled. She wanted to scream. She wanted to accuse him of being the beast he was. She wanted to tear him apart. Ione held her back.

He pointed to Becca's side. "Ione said you were sorry for that shit with the cops. She said that you wanted to make it up to me."

"Make it up to you? To *you*?"

The crowd took a step forward—a single collective

footstep that echoed through the hall like a thunderclap. Chris took an involuntary step away.

Chari upended her glass and announced, "Though himself a god, it is his blood we pour out to offer thanks to the gods. And through him we are blessed."

"ALL HAIL THE SLAIN AND THE RISEN GOD!" the crowd cried, saturating the floor of the Barn with bloody red wine.

"What is going on?" Chris said. "What is this? Ione?"

"Prepare for the roaring voice of the God of Joy," Chari shouted, pointing to the woods beyond the clearing behind the boy.

The chorus took another thunderous step forward, "All hail, Dionysus!" they cried.

Chris turned and bolted for his car as the men and women of the town surged after him. Becca stood quivering with fury as they flowed around and away from her. Chris fumbled his keys. He glanced down quickly as the assembled madness closed in upon him, then abandoned the keys to the growing darkness of twilight. He ran.

Howling, Ione dragged Becca after the congregation.

Becca felt the pull of the woods ahead of her in her guts and in her loins. She ran. Her heart pounding with adrenaline and anger and life. She felt exhilarated as she caught up to the townspeople at the tree line. Branches caught at their clothes, tearing them. Her own peplos ripped away in the dark. She advanced, pushing past people and trees and brush, not caring about the welts and scratches the branches left on her pale skin.

She ran Chris down.

He stumbled and she fell on top of him, naked and screaming. She ripped at his clothes, rending them like tissue. She tore at his flesh, ripping him open.

The crowd descended upon them. Chris screamed as they grabbed and pulled his limbs in compass directions. His joints popped and tendons and ligaments snapped.

Ione and Chari finally arrived in the grove where the bacchants had felled their prey. They stood and watched as Becca rode his lurching body like Artemis in a stag-drawn chariot. She whipped her arms and hair and grabbed Chris's exposed ribs and tore, bellowing and tossing chunks of him high above her. Pieces of the boy dangled from the trees—dripping garlands raining wet red life down upon her. He wailed and fell silent. A great cheer went up from the crowd as they feasted and danced and ruined a man, pulling him apart.

From where she knelt in the young grass, Becca looked over at Ione and Chari. Her gore-streaked face beamed like a little child's on her birthday. She had never felt so filled with life. There wasn't a single part of her that was numb anymore; she felt every inch of her body.

Ione beamed at her best friend. It hadn't been hard to convince her of Chris' fictitious treachery. Becca needed to fill the blackout with any detail, no matter how wretched, and Ione kicked the naïve boy into the abyss. A goat, bleating in the darkness, to bear the sins of the modern world and birth a new innocence.

Swelling with pride, Chari hugged her daughter tightly.

Behind them loomed a man draped in plum robes tied with vine. He smiled through a wild beard wet with dripping wine, his eyes almost glowing in the moonlight. "Welcome home, my daughter," he said. "Welcome home, Bacchae."

LOOKING FOR THE DEATH TRICK

The cutoff denim skirt rode up over Honey's hips, exposing her ass as she bent over to get the attention of a driver slowly passing by. Although the men she signaled couldn't see from where they sat, Comfort and his top-earning girl—his bottom bitch—Chai, insisted she show ass *every* time she leaned into a car window. "For the customers still rollin' up," Comfort said. She did what she was told and didn't try to pull the fabric down, flashing her ass and pussy at the girls waiting behind her. It didn't bother Honey too much to show pink, but the other girls were always looking for a way to get ahead, get closer to top of the food chain. It wasn't like the movies; they weren't a sisterhood or a tribe. If she unconsciously displayed some modesty, word would move up the food chain and she'd pay for not marching in perfect step.

She didn't have much of a figure, but a lot of guys liked the girl-next-door look. That skinny, hasn't-quite-grown-out-of-being-a-tomboy-but-is-trying look worked for her surprisingly well. She had long, dishwater-blonde hair and wore "natural" make-up. Her tight camisole tops left her shoulders bare so the johns could see her freckles—if they could tear their eyes away from her nipples. Many of the men who trawled the block were looking for something familiar they couldn't have at home. The neighbor's daughter. The babysitter. The day care teacher. All forbidden fruit, juicy and ripe and hanging low on the tree waiting to be plucked and fucked—if only it wouldn't wreck their lives. She looked the part. All except for her hands. They were bony with big blue veins and she chewed her cuticles, leaving most of her fingernails with blood crusted around them. She kept her hands out of sight as much as possible.

She filled a niche in her pimp's business model. The suburban tourist. Comfort tried to convince her she was doing a public service. Saving other girls from what had driven her out of the 'burbs into his embrace. She was a protector, Comfort said. "Keepin' those innocent at-home bitches from gettin' preyed upon. You a one-girl rape pre-vention program, Honey."

He called her Honey because she was his "golden girl." "My ray of sunshine at night," he'd say, his words fat with hollow praise that filled the empty spaces in her heart.

Other girls on the stroll didn't have the luxury of looking like a type. Or rather, they looked like the type they were: drive-through convenience. A quick suck or fuck in the alley for someone with a hard-on in a hurry. Those girls wore tight lace outfits not much more concealing than lingerie. A few kept it even simpler, opting for a bra and thong under a big coat. Drive by and they opened their petals like moon flowers, blooming in the light of the streetlamps.

The car slowed and Honey got a glimpse of a face in shadow. White. Middle-aged. Athletic, going to seed. What she looked for was whether a john made eye contact. And how. If he looked her in the eyes, she could get him to stop. If he looked too hard, she might not be able to get him to stop when it mattered. It was the john angry with his wife or girlfriend who wanted to pin a working girl to prove something to "those bitches" who was trouble. The men needing to express power and virility were the ones who liked to hear Honey gag, hear her gasp when they shoved it in dry. Those were the ones who all wanted to ride bareback.

They paid extra for that privilege.

So did she. Usually with abrasions and tears.

The man beckoned her with a thick finger. She stood up, not pulling the skirt down, making sure he got a good look at her bald pussy as she walked toward his car. Honey leaned over again, resting her forearms on his windowsill. "Wanna date, Daddy?" she asked.

His face contorted briefly before his neutral expression returned. The change had been so subtle, so brief, that Honey couldn't tell whether she'd imagined it or not. Either way, it made her regret approaching the vehicle. She was preparing to shove off the car and let him roll on down the road when he said, "How much?"

"It depends, lover. What do you want?" she asked, delivering her line, locked into the role that the Director expected her to perform. He had to tell her he wanted to fuck for money if they were going to continue the play.

"I want the blue discount," he said pulling back his sport coat to reveal the gold badge clipped to his belt.

"I seen fake badges before."

"This one's the real deal." When she didn't respond, he added, "I can take you off the stroll for the night, book you and let you go in the morning, or you can come with me for a few minutes and get paid the rest of the night. Either way you're getting in the car." His expression didn't change again—he kept his mask in place—but the last sentence held all the threat the fleeting shadow that had passed over his face promised a second earlier. Another man saying one thing and meaning something else. *Get in the car or I'll give your pimp a reason to tune you up for lightening his roll.* It was like they had their own silent language always running under what you could hear them saying.

She opened the door and slipped in.

"Good girl."

"Whatever," she said. "Pull around to that alley so Chai

don't think I'm a rat."

"Chai?"

"You know Comfort, but not his bottom bitch? You ain't vice."

"Nope. Homicide." He put the car in gear and asked where she wanted him to park. She silently pointed toward the alley a half block away. He pulled into the gap between buildings and drove until she told him it was good enough. He backed the car into a berth next to a dumpster and killed the lights, but left the engine running. The smell of trash fermenting in the humid heat of the night floated into the car through the vent. She thought about pushing the recirculation button on the air conditioning, but had learned long ago about messing with a john's controls. Instead, she hoped his cock smelled clean. Sometimes the odor of the garbage dumpster was preferable to that of the man in the driver's seat.

Honey knelt on the seat, leaned over, and ran a hand over his crotch, squeezing gently, trying to work him up so she could get back on the track under the relative safety of the streetlight. He grabbed her wrist and set her hand back in her own lap. "I said I want to talk."

"About what? You too cheap for therapy?"

"About this guy." He pulled a photograph from the inside pocket of his jacket and handed it to her. She reached for the overhead light switch. He deflected her hand, pulling a small penlight from his pocket and shining it on the picture. "You seen him?" he asked.

"No. I don't know. All y'all look alike to me."

"Where are you from that 'all y'all' is something people say?"

"I'm from up that block," she said, pointing out the window.

The man sighed heavily and said, "Fair enough. Take another look at the guy. Study his face real hard. You recognize him or not?" He shone the light on the glossy paper, trying to get an angle that didn't obscure the image with glare. It was a grainy black and white, but taken from a close angle. The man in the picture had a goatee, oddly shaped sport sunglasses, and wore a baseball cap. His mouth was open, but it wasn't to say anything. It just looked like he breathed with his lips parted.

The creep in the photo was as familiar as anyone else she'd ever seen—white guy with a chin beard and a Red Sox cap. Almost every single john who rolled down her block looked like him. She said so.

"This one is special," the cop said.

"Nobody's special."

"He is. Believe me. You see this guy, you call me." He handed her a business card. A gold shield like the one he'd flashed at her was embossed on the card next to the logo for the Boston Police Department. Beside the shield it read,

LIEUTENANT DETECTIVE
WILLIAM P. DIXON
HOMICIDE UNIT

The precinct address was listed on the bottom left opposite his office number, fax, and direct dial. "What's the P stand for?" she asked.

"Pepper."

She laughed. He didn't even grin.

"What's *your* name?"

"Honey."

"What's the name your parents gave you?"

She blinked a few times. He hadn't asked for her "real" name—"the name your parents gave you." Honey was as real as a name got for her any more. "I was . . . my name is Mindy."

"Well, Mindy, you keep that picture. You see this prick, call the number on the back of my card." She turned the small white square over. He'd written a cell phone number on the reverse side in blue ink. "Give me a description of his car and the plate, but *do not get in*. You listening?"

"I hear you," she said, playing with a strand of her hair.

"Help yourself, Honey. I've got only so many eyes I can put on the stroll."

"You mean you don't want to spare none for the track."

"I'm out here, aren't I?"

She chewed on the end of her hair for a moment before asking, "Where am I supposed to keep all of this shit?" She indicated her outfit. No pockets; barely any fabric. She spread her legs slightly, giving him another look, wanting to see his expression change again. It didn't. He shook his head.

"Keep it out. Show the picture around. Let everyone know, any working girl who gets in this freak's car is turning a death trick. You hear me?"

Her breath caught. He'd said he was homicide, but all she'd cared about when she got in was that he wasn't vice. He asked again if she was listening. She nodded and stared a little harder at the image. "He's killing working girls?" she said when she was able to find her breath.

"Sometimes."

"Sometimes he lets them go?"

"Sometimes he murders citizens too. But he mostly sticks to 'low-profile targets.' Do you know what I mean when I say that?"

"No one cares if he does one of us."

The cop didn't say anything.

"Why me?"

"What do you mean?" he asked.

"Why did you pick me? You should be talking to Comfort's bottom girl. She's the one who runs the track. She can get the word out." Honey waited for him to tell her that he endangered her by jumping the chain of command because she looked smarter than the other girls. Friendlier and more likely to understand. She listened for the lines Comfort used when he explained why she was destined to out-earn all his other bitches except Chai.

He let out a long breath and said, "Because you look like the girls we find behind the dumpsters."

She sat staring at him for a long minute. He cracked his window and lit a cigarette, letting her have all the time she needed to picture herself lying lifeless behind a stinking trash bin, bled out and stiff. Dixon offered her a smoke. She shook her head, refusing.

"You're organic Honey, huh?" he said replacing the pack on his dash. "You keep that self-preservation instinct. Use it out there." He took one more deep drag. "You need me to drop you?"

"You don't know nothin' about The Game, do you? You gonna get me hurt worse than a bad date." His forehead wrinkled as if he didn't understand. "A bad date," she repeated, as if it was self-evident she meant a violent john. When he didn't seem to be getting it, she said, "Nobody ever drives me home. Especially not no cops. I ain't s'posed to talk to you."

"Then you better get going." He pushed the button on the door handle unlocking the car, but not moving to open her door. Electric chivalry.

She held out a hand. "Forty."

"A blow job on this block is twenty," he said.

"*Now* you think you know something, huh? You kept me longer than it'd take to blow."

"I have stamina."

"Not with me. No one has that much stamina."

He handed her sixty dollars and said, "Buy something to eat."

Honey snatched the money and let herself out of the car, trotted for the end of the alley. She hesitated at the sidewalk, glancing over her shoulder. The detective's car remained where he'd parked. She turned the corner and listened for a moment, waiting for the sound of him driving away. If he left, she didn't hear.

She stared at the man in the picture, memorizing what she could see of his face. Dixon didn't know anything about how she worked and survived. Taking the picture around the block was more likely to get her marked as a snitch than it was to be taken seriously. Still, she figured he might know a thing or two about the kind of people who got off on killing girls like her. She decided to take his word for it that he was looking out for her. Comfort would understand that she was looking out for him by warning them.

She was his golden girl.

Comfort's fists left Honey with an ache in her guts that reached up her spine and down into her bowels. She lay on the sidewalk, crumpled up like the detective's photograph. Chai spit on the picture before kicking her in the crotch with the wedge toe of her platform shoe. Honey's back arched and her cry echoed against the monolithic brick factory wall opposite the park. Comfort gave her another punt in the guts with his Timberland, silencing her. "You a snitch? You a snitch?" his bottom bitch yelled as she tore up the detective's business card. She threw the pieces in Honey's face.

She wanted to tell them she wasn't. She wanted to say that she was looking out for Comfort's girls by showing them the picture, but she couldn't get enough air in her lungs to give volume to her words. She whispered "I'm sorry," in between shallow breaths.

"Goddamn right you sorry. Gonna be more sorry if you don't get correct. You don't talk to five-oh. You don't open that mouth except to suck a dick. You feel me?"

"Ye—" Chai kicked her in the stomach as she tried to agree. She nodded.

Comfort said, "You learnin'. You got an hour to get back on the block, or else I'm callin' up a party. Get some motherfuckers to jump on the train." He stomped off, leaving Chai to finish explaining what was expected of her.

She squatted in front of Honey and flicked the crumpled picture at Honey's face with a dragonlady fingernail. "If you see this iceman, you come to me. I'll get Comfort and *he'll* take care of it. You don't go to the police for shit, you hear?"

Honey nodded. Chai stood up and brushed the hair out of her face, preening for her return to her man's side. He wouldn't tolerate her looking disheveled. She was not his most expensive piece of jewelry, but she was the prettiest. "You got forty-five minutes to get up and earn." She sashayed away, making sure that the other girls on the block saw she was queen.

Rolling over, Honey sobbed and held her stomach. It hurt so bad she worried she might be bleeding internally—that the two of them might have ruptured something. But she couldn't go to the hospital. She couldn't go anywhere except maybe around the corner to the "pharmacy." L'il Bentley would have something to get her through the night. She'd give him the twenty she'd stuffed in her shoe for an Oxy. It might not get her through the night, but it'd get her back on the track and in the game. She pushed up onto her hands and knees, waited until the cramping and nausea subsided enough to stand on her feet, and staggered off to find the dealer, leaving the picture where it lay. If Comfort or Chai found it on her, there would be no amount of Oxy that could dull what they'd do to her.

It was days before she could stand fully upright without

cramping. Days during which it was a welcome moment to lean over and rest her elbows on the doorframe of a john's car and ask, "Wanna date?" Still, she did it. Pushed through the pain until she'd skimmed enough to afford a pill or two.

She wasn't earning as well as she had been before the beating. But Comfort didn't say anything to her about the money or how she looked. While he was always reciting mystical-sounding shit to the people hanging around him, he didn't say anything to her at all anymore. One of his street soldiers asked why she was looking so used up and he thumped the book he always carried around, *The Art of War*, like some street corner preacher about to drop the word of Almighty God on an acolyte hungry to be fed the gospel of original pimping. "Once upon a time in China, the Emperor asked General Tso to make all his hos into an army," he said, holding court. "So the general, he lined all those bitches up and put the Emperor's favorite in charge. He tell them, 'turn left,' and when they didn't do shit like he said, he beheaded the bitch in charge. What do you think those hos did when he promoted the next one to bottom bitch and said 'turn left'? I tell you, they turned the fuck left." He laughed and nodded his head toward Honey. "She was an up-make-you-comer. Look at her now. That's what happens to snitches and bitches who don't do what they told." His golden girl was now his object lesson on how to keep the troops in line. And when she looked at him hungrily, she was left to starve.

Chai, in turn, was leaving Honey with less of her own money at the end of the night, claiming that it wasn't Comfort who was going to suffer if she wasn't working hard enough. Honey was doing the best she could, but as much as it hurt to stand up and even breathe, it hurt worse to fuck. And her increasingly despairing look was driving away the johns. If it wasn't the sleeplessness caused by the pain, it was surely the physical effects of the painkillers. The Oxy had left her looking pallid, with dark gray bags under her eyes. She tried to compensate with make-up, but she ended up looking . . . "trashy," her mother would have said. She was beginning to look like a junkie. Like a whore.

The man behind the wheel of the car looked her over as she asked him for a date, his face turning down with disappointment and contempt. Without a word he goosed the gas and the Mustang lurched off. The edge of the window frame banged Honey in the temple and she went sprawling to the ground, long skinny legs kicking out instinctively, shoving herself out of the way of the car's rear wheels before they crushed her legs. Before another man left her alone to suffer.

She picked herself up and staggered to the street. She didn't bother to pull down the tight jersey skirt bunched up over her hips. Another girl on the block laughed as Honey held her stinging face and sobbed. A long purple bruise was going to make her even less attractive. She could already feel the side of her face growing hot, swelling. Although, she didn't see how that could make business worse.

Another car slid up the block and stopped a few yards away. The girl who'd laughed wiggled her ample hips as she tottered on too-high heels toward the open window. Honey watched as she curved her spine to the side so the john could see both her cleavage and the curve of her bare hip while she set up the deal. She stared, watching the woman twitch her hips, listening to the crack of her cackle as she amused herself with her wit. But she wasn't opening the door. In a moment, if the john didn't agree to the terms she offered, she'd shift from flirty to furious. Screaming "faggot" while kicking backward at his car with her heels like a donkey, trying to dent the door or at least scratch the paint so he'd have something to explain when he got home to the missus. Punish him for not helping her make her ends.

Honey glanced at the john. Her heart beat hard in her chest and she lost her breath. He looked like all the others.

Goatee, Oakley Half Jackets, and baseball cap with a big white B shading his face. His mouth hung open, but not in a way that suggested idiocy. He looked hungry, like someone had just set out supper. He wanted to taste. He was a wolf who wanted to gobble the girl up and take her inside himself where she would be his forever, like in a fairy tale.

Honey thought about her huntsman, Detective Dixon. He told her to call him and he'd come running. He'd barge into the cottage and slay the wolf and rescue the girl.

She thought about Comfort and Chai. The bottom bitch had said to call her and Comfort would descend on the wolf like angry villagers protecting their lambs.

The man nodded and moved his head, indicating the girl should get in. What was her name? Something like Crystal or Quartz . . . or Ruby! That was it. Ruby—pulled open the door to climb inside.

Honey shouted, "Wait!" Tottering toward the car in the heels that she used to be good at walking in, but had become uncertain in as her back had been made weak and crooked, she called out for the man to stop. "How about a double date?" she shouted.

Ruby stuck her hand out the open window and stuck up her middle finger as they drove away. The car slipped off into the darkness, pulling around into the alley. She ran after it. Huffing and out of breath, she rounded the corner in time to see the silhouette of the man pull his hands away from Ruby's face and lay her limp form gently against the seatback. The red taillights of the car flashed as he stepped on the brake before putting it in gear and then they dimmed and he drove away.

"Wait!" she screamed, knowing he couldn't hear over the sound of the engine, Honey calling out after, "Not *her*! Me! Take ME! I'm the one you want!"

She memorized the license plate and make and model of the car. She tried to file everything away in her mind, making sure every detail was there to be recalled, despite the fog of her dulled Oxy brain.

The next time he rolled up the stroll, she would know it was him before she even saw his face. She'd see the car and she would be at his window, smiling and showing him that she was everything he'd ever wanted: the girl next door, the babysitter, his daughter, anyone as long as he let her in the car and took her away. He could do anything he wanted to her, as long as he took her away for good.

Except, of course, she knew he wouldn't come again. He'd move on to another track in another part of the city. He'd hunted this ground. He'd go looking for a new girl who was fresh and everything he desired. Not her. Not anymore.

She fell to her knees. The concrete dug into her shins and scuffed her skin and added another set of blemishes that tarnished her looks so no one would ever want her again.

Not even a killer.

THIS LAST LITTLE PIECE OF DARKNESS

Ms. Cassandra Blaine
1982 Grantham St.
Stamford, CT 06513

3 April 2017

Dear Ms. Blaine,

I write to express my sympathies for you on your father's sudden passing. I saw news of the accident on television and read in the paper of his upcoming memorial service. You don't know me, but I know too well what it's like to lose a parent, and I hope what I have to share below might help put the pain of your loss in a context. I am not sure exactly how to begin, but I do know when: 1979. That was the year that broke my mother. And I suppose that's as good a place to start as any.

My mother was twenty-nine that year, and worked during the day as a receptionist in the front office of an auto repair garage. She was a single mother and I was a considerably self-sufficient eight-year-old "latchkey kid." From reading your father's obituary, I understand you're only slightly younger than me, so I'm sure you remember that phrase, even if you were lucky enough not to have to be as independent as I was at that age.

We usually only saw each other in the early morning, and at dinner before she would head out to the bar. I would jump out of bed as soon as I heard water in the bathtub start to flow. She took long showers, and I took that time to have breakfast ready for her when she emerged from the bathroom in her terrycloth robe, a towel wrapped around her head in a damp turban. I'd pour a bowl of dry cereal for myself and set it on the table next to a sweating carton of milk, then stage a slice of bread in the toaster before carefully cutting a grapefruit and separating the slices from the rind and each other, the way she liked. If it doesn't sound like much of a breakfast, it was the seventies, mind you, and there was "no such thing as too thin." In any event, when the creak of the pipes in the bathroom signaled she was done, I'd push down the lever on the toaster. Mom liked her toast golden—not too done, but crunchy. I buttered her toast to my own taste, which meant too much margarine. She didn't complain, but she didn't always finish if it was too sodden by the time she sat down. For the same reasons, I never poured my milk until she came in to eat. I could have finished it while she was showering, but that would mean less of a reason for her to sit with me while I ate and she had the first cigarette of the day. I could barely taste my Cheerios through the smell of her Virginia Slims, but it didn't matter. Breakfast was a ritual, and while it wasn't much, I felt a sense of pride at having made it for the two of us. I'd make small talk, telling her how Scotty Goudsward up the block had gotten in trouble for using his lunch money to buy comic books, and now we couldn't play, or how Jamie Levine had tickets to the circus because she loved horses, but the elephants scared her. She'd rest her head in a hand and reluctantly eat slices of grapefruit in between drags and listen.

She was often tired and nauseous in the mornings. I knew what a hangover was, though I didn't exactly know what it was called back then. I'd had a doozy of one the year before at Thanksgiving when, after the rest of the family left the dinner table to go watch football, I finished off the wine left behind in everyone's abandoned glasses. It wasn't much, but at seven I was a lightweight, and it got me drunk enough to pass out in my grandparents' guest bed. Everyone thought it was hilarious, except my grandpa. He was the sort of guy who never laughed *at* another person. Later, my head pounded and I felt sick as we walked in silence out of Grandma and Grampa's house to the car. It never occurred to me that the reason my mother seemed so ill in the mornings was from a similar cause. All I knew was that making breakfast served two purposes: it relieved her of the burden of doing it— which she remembered only *some* mornings anyway—and it ensured time at the table with her. I made a meal, and she made time—a bargain in my mind, with me coming out ahead on the trade. A lot of kids took that time with their parents for granted, but not me. I was often reminded that I was a burden, though I tried to be less of one.

After breakfast, she'd finish her cigarette, unravel the towel from her head, and go back into the bathroom to get ready for work. I'd linger near her as long as I could, smelling the heat coils in her blow-dryer, the chemical perfume of her hair spray and the sweet scent of an eyeliner pencil as she softened the tip with a lighter. I loved those smells. I used to hold my breath to see if I could make them last. When she went into her room to get dressed, I'd rush back into the kitchen to make myself a bologna sandwich. I didn't have money to buy lunch at school; the cafeteria didn't accept our food stamps, and Mom didn't fill out the paperwork for "free lunch," so I ate a lot of bologna. She had to leave for work before it was time for me to catch the bus, so I usually got a hug and a kiss on her way out the door and a reminder not to miss the bus again. I made sure the house was locked up tight when I finally left for school. Once, I'd forgotten, and one of her ex-boyfriends had let himself in. He'd waited until I went to school and came in and trashed the place. He tipped over the shelves and smashed her records. He slashed open her pillows and then stopped in the middle of everything—or maybe he did this first—to make a pot of coffee which he poured on all of her clothes and her bed. He left my room alone. It was already a mess and it looked kind of like the rest of the house, so the police thought he'd vandalized that too. But he hadn't touched a thing of mine. I knew he hadn't wanted to hurt me. Still, he did, and I never forgot to lock the front door again.

I locked up every night too, not just out of fear, but also because the sound of her two a.m. fumbling at the lock usually woke me up and I could squeeze in an extra minute's attention in between shuffling out into the hallway and her ushering me back to bed. If I was lucky, she was alone, and she'd come in to tuck me under the covers and give me a whiskey and cigarette-scented kiss on the forehead. Nights she returned by herself were better than ones in which she brought someone home. If she had company, I would get a quick hug, and she'd say, "Go back to bed." I'd ask who she was with, and she'd tell me it was a "friend," while he looked away at the records on the shelves or down the hall into her bedroom. She'd turn me by my shoulders and nudge me away. I'd walk back slowly while they went in her room, and I'd listen for the click of the doorknob push lock echoing in the hallway that let me know she was home, but I was still alone. Still, those nights a man followed her into her room were better than the ones where she slept somewhere else. Mornings I woke up to find her bedroom door open and bed still made were a taste of the kind of total loneliness I feared so badly, it just being the two of us. I'd run to the front window and look for her car in the driveway and when it wasn't there, I imagined the worst—a robbery gone wrong, a car accident . . . the end of that movie she'd told me I was too young to watch.

Being slightly younger, you may not remember *Looking for Mr. Goodbar*. I shouldn't remember it either, but you can imagine that was an inescapably appealing title for a naïve boy who loved reading Roald Dahl and wanted to see a spiritual sibling to the tale of a boy who wins everything he ever dreamed of. I dreamed of candy that never lost its flavor and winning a life where Mom never had to work again. One night, the movie title appeared on our stolen cable channel along with the words COMING UP NEXT, so I stayed up to watch while I waited for her to come home. *Goodbar* wasn't what I'd expected and, while boring and mostly beyond my comprehension, I watched the whole thing. It seemed like a peek behind the curtain of my mother's secret night life. The one where she met her girlfriends for drinks and sometimes brought other friends home to spend some of the night... but not *all* of it. And though I only half-understood the ending, it terrified me in a way watching the violence in midnight showings of *Alien* on HBO didn't. Drooling silver-toothed monsters weren't real, but the singles bar "friends" were. And now there was the possibility in my mind one might stab her to death. Nights she didn't come home, that final scene strobe-flashed behind my eyes, the clicking and Diane Keaton's screaming echoing in my ears and I imagined my mother lying still, red and ripped apart in some stranger's bed, and cried myself to sleep.

You'll be relieved to know, that never happened. I'm sorry if this letter upsets you. I'll understand if you feel the need to skip to the end. Although, I hope you'll bear with me. It's taken me a long time to work up the nerve to write this letter, and all I ask is your indulgence a little while longer.

The night I want to tell you about, I remember waking to the insistent sounds of my mother's long-suffering bedsprings. They pierced through the hollow wall separating my room from hers. Like I mentioned above, most nights I awoke to the sounds of car doors slamming and my mother fumbling to get the door unlocked while her beau pulled and pawed at her. But not that night. That night, they were extra quiet and I'd missed her passage through the apartment entirely. I missed the headlights in the windows, the sounds of the car doors slamming, the scrape of her key, and the hiss of the draft guard dragging across the tile. I missed the hushed urgency of her telling the man who'd brought her home to be quiet and not wake her son, and his inevitably slurred, "You have a kid?" while she encouraged him not to worry about it. But I didn't miss the bedsprings. *That* was impossible. They were like far away shrieks, though they were just on the other side of the wall, and I hated them so much—even though they meant, at the very least, that she had come home, and we'd have the morning together. I hated what I knew they meant.

I remember stepping out of bed, my foot slipping on the litter of dirty clothes on the floor. I got my balance and tiptoed across the mess toward the door. Stopping to listen at the wall for a moment, the shrieking springs were familiar, but underneath was something new. Something more insistent. My bladder ached with fullness. I crept to the bathroom and lifted the toilet lid with too much urgency, banging it against the tank. I heard a man say, "What's that?" She replied that it was nothing, just her son. Me. He asked how old, and she said I wasn't a problem. Just a baby. That upset me. I was eight years old, not a baby. I would have protested, but I heard more whispering, and I forgot the slight. My mother's voice raised slightly, and I heard her say, "No," followed by the crack of a palm on skin, and a yelp.

I let go of the elastic on my underwear and ran to the bedroom door pulling up my pajamas. "Mom?" I said. I knocked softly. "Mom?" There was a pause while everything went silent and she asked me through the door what I wanted. She was out of breath, and I felt terror cramping in my belly. I asked if she was okay. I said, "I thought I heard something."

"I'm fine, Jude," she said. "Go back to bed." I heard the man whisper something, but I couldn't understand him. His tone was forceful. She was silent. Normally, she and her friends laughed. They giggled quietly and they whispered to each other things that sounded like encouragement. "Like that," they'd say. "Right there." Not that night. That night they were quiet, and then the springs started and I heard her breathing. Hard and fast like she was afraid.

"Mom?"

The sounds stopped again, and she shouted, "Get to bed, Bradley Julian!" She had used my full name. Scared, I ran into my bedroom. I slipped on a shirt and fell, bouncing my head off the floor. I lay still and listened to the silence. My head ached and I wept. And then the sounds. Harder, more insistent, her sobbing, "No. Stop." And then another hit—this time, the meatier thud of bone on bone. And sobbing.

I pissed in my pajamas.

I'm sorry if this is a lot to take in. I'm almost done. It'll all make sense in a minute.

Cold and wet, I rolled over and started searching the floor for a dry pair of underwear. The creaking rhythm of the bedsprings increased and I heard my mother start to vocalize louder. I abandoned my search and crept back to the door, wet pants clinging to my legs. I needed to hear what she was saying. "No . . . no . . . no . . . no" punctuated by his grunting.

"Mom," I whispered from my bedroom doorway.

"No."

"Mom?"

"No!"

His voice. "Shut up!" He was commanding her, not me. They couldn't hear me and my little boy's voice, high pitched and timid. She did as she was told and shut up and I began to cry. I crawled to her door and knocked lightly. The creaking and breathing continued. I squeaked out another "Mom?" Everything stopped.

"What, baby?" she asked, out of breath.

"Are you okay? I . . . I heard . . . something." Silence. I repeated my question. "Are you okay? Why are you saying 'no'?"

I heard urgent whispering from the man in my mother's bed, and she added, "Go back to bed, Jude."

"What's happening?" I asked. She told me that she had gotten a call from her friend, Ross, but she dropped the phone and the cord got tangled up and she was telling him "no" so he wouldn't hang up. "Now go in your room and shut the door!" The man whispered something and she added, "Don't come out again, okay? Promise?"

I didn't know what to say. "I can't sleep with all the noise," I explained truthfully, hoping that the man might listen to me, if he wouldn't to her. Another beat. A sob.

"That's all over, baby. We'll be quiet." I did as I was told and crawled back to my room. She lied. The noise resumed, louder and more insistent than before. I sat with my back to our shared wall. I sobbed and wished that it was a dream. I didn't know what was happening, but I knew this was unlike any other night that had come before. And I knew there wasn't a damn thing in the world I could do to stop it. I had no idea then what *it* was—not until a few years later—but I knew it was wrong and that I was perfectly hopeless in the face of it. Afraid and weak, wet with pissed-in pants like a baby, I was the opposite of every boy in every book I'd ever read. I couldn't save myself or my family. No one was coming to whisk me away to adventure and freedom. There was no such thing as candy that never lost its sweetness. And there never would be.

Eventually, the sounds slowly wound down to silence. Nothing dramatic, no crescendo, just a growing, sad quiet that felt like all the gravity in the universe. A terrible few minutes passed before I heard the lock on her door pop open. I scurried on my hands and knees to my own door to peek out and watch my mother head into the bathroom with her robe pulled around her like always. Except she didn't emerge. *He* did. I watched him walk away from me down the hallway into the living room, stopping in the moonlight shining through the front windows to dig in his pockets. He was backlit and I remember thinking of him as a big piece of darkness that had come apart from the night. He couldn't be real. And then he found his keys and let himself out our front door, looking at me over his shoulder as he pulled it closed behind him. Not a phantom; just a man with a long mustache and cruel eyes.

I sprinted to the door and threw the chain and the deadbolt. I twisted the knob lock and pressed my back up against it, holding it closed. With my back to the door I saw my mother standing in the doorway to her room, also watching him go—head down, eyes up, hugging herself. His car engine sounded like a monster. The headlamps blasted into the apartment, lighting up my mother in the hallway. Illuminating her split lip. I put my hand up to shield my eyes from the light filling the room, but she didn't. She watched him drive away. When the lights faded and the rumble of his engine grew softer as he peeled out around the corner, she stumbled into the bathroom and shut the door, locking it. I walked up to the door and knocked lightly. "Mom?" I whispered. "Mom?" She didn't reply. I could hear her crying behind the door.

I gave up, and started back to bed. Just inside her room I noticed a small, dense spot, darker than the rest of the floor. I picked up that little piece of darkness the man had left in our house and took it.

If that was difficult to read, I suppose it's no consolation to know how difficult it was to write. Please be patient just a little while longer. I'm almost done, and then I have a single favor to ask of you.

As you can imagine, things changed. She cried a lot at first. We stopped having breakfast together; she had trouble sleeping and got out of bed late, rushing out of the apartment without eating to get to work on time. I thought she'd stop going out to the bars, and she did at first, but that only lasted a couple of weeks. Her friends came over and insisted she "get back on the horse" and not "let one bad apple spoil the bunch," as if the man had merely stood her up on a date. I suspect she wasn't open with her friends about what happened. I don't know what she had told them, only that one of them offered to get her own boyfriend to cut off his balls if she ever saw him come around the club again. Afterward, she started going out again. She *did* stop bringing home boyfriends. Instead, she brought *all* her friends home. They'd stay up late listening to records and smoking out of tin foil—smoke that didn't smell like Virginia Slims—and they sniffled a lot, like they all had colds. They were loud and laughed the way my uncle laughed the time I got drunk on Thanksgiving wine and passed out. *At* me. I stayed in my room. I stole a slide lock from a hardware store to install on my door.

In the mornings, I stepped around their bodies, made myself a quick breakfast and sneaked out early to go wait for the school bus. I was never late for school again.

A few months later, I came home to find my mother slumped over on the sofa, a needle dangling out of her arm and her skin pale as moonlight. I called 9-1-1 and they whisked her away as quickly as I was taken into "protective custody." My grandparents couldn't take me and my uncle wouldn't, so for a few years, I bounced through a series of foster homes with varying ability to deal with a child possessed with as deeply entrenched "anger issues" as I had. I'll spare you the details, other than to say that when they allowed me into the apartment to collect my clothes and a few things—"not too much; we can't take it all"—I took that little piece of darkness and kept it with me always.

His wallet.

I took it hoping that someday, someone would ask me for it. Ask for the story and what happened. They'd come and take it, relieving me of the burden of holding on to what was inside. No one ever did, though, and I've been carrying it my whole life. Discarding a little bit at a time, here and there as I grew older and realized that I didn't need the actual wallet or the canceled CITGO card or a picture of an unsmiling girl posing in a halter top and short shorts against a red '68 Mustang—although that last, I carried for a very long time, only throwing it away after I was married. Once I got divorced, I missed it a little, but it was gone, and you can't get back what you throw away.

Which brings me to the favor I want to ask of you.

Along with this letter, I have enclosed your father's driver's license. I've held on to it for the better part of forty years and when I saw his obituary, I realized it was time to let go of this last little piece of darkness. My hope is that you will bury it with him, but the choice to keep it is yours.

Always,

Brad

Bradley "Jude" MacLean

REMINISCE

Marc's corner wasn't the best, but it was his and he didn't have to defend it. All the major intersections in town were taken by groups of panhandlers who banded together to secure their spots and look out for one another. They covered all four directions of traffic—one at each crosswalk—hitting the WALK button every time a light turned green and two of them had to retreat back to the safety of the median or the sidewalk. Marc didn't have a team of friends to rely upon. Not since Kandahar. No one to look out for meant no grieving families to explain your failures to.

Instead, he found the stop light near the underpass. There was no crosswalk button and traffic wasn't heavy, but it was steady in the morning and evening and it provided cover from both the sunlight and rain when he needed it. Press Street above was much busier, but his road wound around to the same place—the mall—so it was a popular cut-through for shoppers when travel on Press got too hairy. Stand-still traffic was a nightmare for a guy asking for change. No one wanted to get stuck for minutes staring awkwardly at the same sad sack with a cardboard sign. Similarly, once he either got a buck or a snub from a motorist, that relationship was over. He relied on a steady stream of people who hadn't already read his sign and made the choice whether or not to "donate."

He wore his desert camouflage BDU trousers and boots

with a clean, plain t-shirt. You didn't want to look too combative. Something about a blue t-shirt said "at-ease" to people with a little change rattling around in their cup holders. His sign told a simple story too: WOUNDED VETERAN. HONORABLY DC'D. SOBER & DRUG FREE. ANYTHING WILL HELP. GOD BLESS! Although he didn't have a faith to speak of, he knew that he had to offer something in exchange for people's money. A smile, gratitude, and an assurance that people were getting a reward for their change. They were being good Americans giving thanks for service rendered to the nation. They were doing good for someone who'd fallen on hard times. They were earning favor with The Big Guy. Marc made no pleas for mercy or offers to Work For Food—no one believed that line anyway. Only one man had ever stopped to offer Marc work and was such an asshole about it, it was clear he was just trying to prove a point to his passenger. Marc wasn't looking to barter, or for confrontation. Jobbing as a day laborer might not net him enough to eat well through the day if the boss was a cheapskate and it would burn up all his available time to make ends meet before he had to head "home." It was in by eight p.m., out by seven a.m. at the Night Mission. There he was guaranteed a shower twice a week and, if he was sober, they would rent him a locker in which to keep a few possessions. He used the shower as often as he could, but didn't take them up on the locker. Too many got broken into by other guys. Instead, he kept everything he needed—two changes of clothes, a travel mug, a can opener, his favorite book, and his DD 214 discharge certificate in a protective plastic sleeve—in his tan, pixilated camo rucksack.

At the far end of the underpass stood a lonely roadside memorial. It was a chintzy Styrofoam cross with a bunch of plastic flowers stuck on with wire. On the ground around the cross lay a few weather-beaten toys. Stuffed bears and dogs with floppety ears. The laminated card pinned to the memorial read: Andrew Ballard. 11/25/1990 – 01/01/2012. Marc guessed he died in a car crash. Like Marc's friend, Nat Coleman. And Norman Steahm. And Dimi Walter. He stayed as far as he could from the memorial. Not only did it distract people from his sign, it also just didn't feel right to him to beg for money on the same ground where someone died. It felt exploitative. Other people might not care, but he did. He gave the kid respect and distance.

The light turned red and Marc stepped out into the street, walking down the meager row of waiting cars, holding up his sign. Most people just stared straight ahead, watching the light, keeping an eye on him with their peripheral vision, wondering if he was going to knock on their window. He tried to make eye contact with everyone but didn't force it. Ahead, he saw a car window slide down and a hand with a dollar bill reach out. Marc jogged up and said "thank you" before reaching for the cash. The man behind the wheel smiled and told him to stay strong. Marc said, "I'm trying." The window slid back up with a low hum and he cut across back to the sidewalk, heading for the other angle of the intersection that would soon be stopping. Turning around, he saw someone had parked a minivan up on the sidewalk while he was grabbing his dollar. That sort of thing could put a real hurt on his earnings. If it looked like he could afford a car, he didn't need to ask for pocket change. Beyond the minivan he saw a man walking under the bridge toward his rucksack. Marc got that feeling like he did back *in country* right before climbing into a helo to fly out over the darkened mountains where the hajjis waited with their surface-to-air rockets. If he lost that bag, he lost everything.

He didn't want to fight this man, but he would to protect his last remaining things. He'd fight for that bag and the DD 214 and the well-worn copy of Eddie Bunker's *Dog Eat Dog*. Everything else he could replace. But the bag and the paper were his lifeline—they got him in places and occasional discounts on food and clothes. And the book. Well the book was the last thing he owned that he didn't *need* to survive. Stay sane, yes, but not to survive.

"Hey!" The man from the minivan stopped and turned. Marc slipped his hand into the back of his belt, trying to look like he had the tools to protect his things. It was a bluff. He'd long ago sold his .45 so he could afford to get that bad tooth pulled. Someone else had stolen his C.K.R.T. knife while he slept at the Mission. *They should have done me a favor and slit my wrists when they took it.* He squinted to see what he was up against. The man was armed with a . . . stuffed bear.

The man held up his hands. "Sorry. Is this your stuff?" Marc closed the distance, letting his empty hand fall back to his side. "I didn't mean to worry you or anything, I'm just here to . . ." The man trailed off.

"No. I'm sorry. I didn't realize . . ." The man stared at Marc for an uncomfortably long time with glistening, wet eyes. It had been almost eighteen months since Andrew Ballard had died, but Marc knew better than most how the ghosts of the dead stuck with you. They rode along just out of sight only speaking up when the comfortable silence let you think you could let your guard down and forget how much you missed them. Right when you thought you'd left them behind, they pulled up to the corner in the passenger seat of some stranger's car. Their laughter carrying over the sound of idling engines as you walked back to beg some more.

"You . . ."

Marc held up his hands. "Look, I'm just trying to get by. I never touch . . . those things."

"You look just like him. A little more tan, but you look . . . just like my son."

Marc stared down at his boots. He supposed as often as he heard how he resembled this person or that one, that he had "a familiar face." But he didn't want to look like this man's son. He just wanted to collect enough quarters to go get something for lunch.

"It's like you're—"

"I'm sorry," he said as he folded his sign and stuffed it into the rucksack. "I've got to go." He hadn't let anyone run him off his corner before, but he couldn't face this man and his grief. He zipped up the bag and shouldered it, turning to leave. The man caught him by the elbow. Marc pushed down his first inclination to yank his arm free and shove—the conditioned response once you've spent a night or two on the streets—and paused instead. "I'm really sorry for your loss," he said.

"My name's Ron. Could I buy you lunch?" Marc felt like his boots had sprouted roots. His stomach growled audibly. "Come on. Let's go get something to eat," Ron said, guiding him back toward the minivan.

"Don't you want to leave that over there?" he said, pointing behind them at the memorial.

Ron looked at the stuffed bear still in his hands. He shrugged and said, "I can drop it off when I bring you back."

Marc's stomach felt so empty, so hollow. He stopped walking. "I . . . No offense, sir, but I don't usually go places . . . with people. I'm . . ."

Ron laughed quietly and held up the toy. "It's weird, right? It feels kind of strange for me too. I really just want to buy you lunch. Honest." He turned the bear over in his hands, absently waving a stuffed arm up and down. "I'll bring you right back here when we're done. I promise." Marc hated to watch the man beg. He'd made peace with his own pride, or had at least sublimated it so he didn't feel its sting every single time he asked if someone could spare some change.

When Marc didn't reply, Ron offered more. "I'll give you a hundred dollars if you'll just spend an hour with me in a public place. Get a hot meal in your stomach and some money to spend however you like. Up front." Shifting the bear under his arm, he pulled out his wallet and counted out five twenties. Holding them out, he said, "It feels better than leaving another stupid bear on the corner." Ron looked at the toy in his other hand. "He was a grownup. I don't know why I keep bringing him this shit."

Despite his reticence and the feeling that this wasn't going to go as easy as a simple lunch, the sight of a hundred dollars got Marc's feet moving again. He took the cash and walked around to the passenger side of the van. He looked in the windows before opening the door. Guys had tried to pick him up before. He never went. *But this one—Ron— doesn't want a blowjob; he just wants to spend a little time with the ghost of his kid. It's not going to go the way he wants, but I could use that hundred bucks. I could use it to get a haircut and a shave, maybe buy a nice button-up shirt and a tie and try to fill out a couple of job applications. A hundred dollars could be just what I need to get a fresh start.* Marc decided that he could be a ghost for an hour and climbed into the van.

Ron stared at Marc across the table while he ate. Marc wanted to ask if he could have the untouched food on Ron's plate, but he reckoned it wouldn't be polite. Not with one burger already in his belly and a bunch of twenties in his pocket. He polished off the last of his fries and wiped his mouth with the cloth napkin. It had been a long time since he'd eaten anywhere with a *cloth* napkin. Ron had offered to buy him a beer but Marc declined. Ron took a drink of the one he'd ordered for himself as he slid his full plate across the table. "Here," he said. I'm betting you wouldn't mind helping me finish this. I'm not all that hungry." Marc thanked him and dug in, trying to ignore the man's stare. The more he focused on the food, the more he could pretend that he wasn't on display.

"I'm real sorry about your boy," Marc said, setting down the burger. "I'd like to see a picture if you've got one. You know, since we look so much alike." Ron had balled up his fists and it looked like it took some concentration to open them up and lay them flat on the table. "Look, I'm really sorry," Marc said. "I didn't mean to upset you." He hadn't asked to do a side-by-side comparison to remind Ron that he wasn't actually the dead boy. But then, the guy looked like he might need reminding.

"No. It's all right. It's just . . . hard, you know?"

"Yes, sir, I do. I lost some of my brothers when an I.E.D. took out our transport." He left out the part where he drove right past the suspicious wreck on the side of the road because they were all anxious to get back to their racks after a long night.

"Andrew turned twenty-one the month before and he wanted to go out with some friends on New Year's Eve and celebrate. They say they didn't see him leave the party."

Marc reached across the table and touched Ron's hand. The man didn't look like the sort who worked with his hands. His clothes and haircut and car all said accountant or insurance adjuster. The scrapes and yellowing bruises on his knuckles said something else. Marc couldn't think what'd make those marks other than combat, but Ron seemed too nice to be a brawler. *Don't pry. Who knows how he deals with grief. Who'd have thought what it did to you?* "I'm really sorry. You don't have to—"

"Impact threw him out through the front window. We had to have a closed-casket funeral." Ron gave Marc's hand a squeeze and then dried his eyes with his unblemished napkin. "What I was saying before about saying goodbye— you know they talk about 'closure' and how it'll help you heal? We couldn't even see our son in the morgue. There wasn't enough left of his . . . he was unrecognizable. We described a tattoo he had on his shoulder to the police and they confirmed it was him. We took him to one of those um, reconstruction guys. You know what I'm talking about. But they said it'd be better to just leave the coffin closed before we buried him. They said he'd never look the way we remembered." Ron shut his eyes. For the first time that afternoon Marc felt like he wasn't on display. Instead, it was like he was seeing a show. He wanted to get up and walk out while the man couldn't see him go. Just slip away and skip the end. But he'd made a promise.

An hour in a public place.

Ron opened his eyes and folded his hands like he was about to say a prayer. "My wife and I . . . we, uh . . . Marc? I really appreciate you coming out to lunch with me. It's been . . . nice." Ron cleared his throat and looked Marc right in the eye before he said, "Could I convince you to come home and have dinner with us?"

Marc sat up straight in his chair. "Oh, I don't think so."

Ron reached out quickly and caught both of Marc's hands in his. "Maribel. My wife, Mari. She cooks like a whiz and I know that this has helped me a lot. I'd just like her to get the chance to see you and fix you a meal and say goodbye at the end of the night. Tell you what, I'll double your money and get you a nice hotel room wherever you want. I'll even call you a cab to take you there. Come for dinner and you'll never see us again. I promise. It would mean so much to her, I know." Ron sat up and smiled weakly. He pulled his hands back and rested them in his lap. "I must seem so desperate. I'm sorry. I know you're not Andrew and it's not fair of me to ask you to do these things. You just finish up your burger there and I'll take you back to the underpass."

Marc thought about all his dead friends. None of their families had the chance to say goodbye either. One day they were video-chatting with their boys half a world away and the next they were getting a knock on the door from a chaplain. *Gold Star Families. Like it's some award that's given out for giving up your kid. You get a gold star!* He faked a grin and said, "It's been a long time since I had a home-cooked meal."

"You can't even imagine how happy she's going to be to see you."

"I hope so." Nerves got the better of Marc and he lost what was left of his appetite. "I guess I'll take that beer now."

The Ballard house sat at the end of a long, secluded lane lined with old growth trees. It was completely unlike the places Marc had always lived growing up in the city. They pulled into a long driveway and Ron shut off the ignition. "We're home!" Marc thought it was a weird thing to say since he'd never been there before, but let it go. He was just glad to get out of the van. The air fresheners hanging from the rear view stunk the thing up. Something else lingered underneath the fake pine perfume. At the same time, Marc was sure that he didn't smell all that great after three days of whore's baths in the 7-Eleven bathroom sink.

"This place is really out here." He felt like saying something when Ron took the on-ramp for the highway, but didn't. It didn't seem polite.

Ron jingled his keys with excitement and said, "I suppose I should have mentioned that."

Marc was already thinking of making his escape. He was pretty certain that an invitation to stay the night was coming next. He resolved to hold firm to the offer of the cab and hotel. *Don't get taken advantage of. You got two hundred dollars, a hot shower, and a private bed coming. Dinner is all you owe.* Still, he figured there would be other offers. Hey! I'll triple your money if you come out in the back and play a little touch football after dinner. Stay for breakfast? Another hundred if you come visit grandma in the home. *Nope. This is it!*

Ron hopped out of the car and practically floated up the front walk. He opened the door and shouted inside, "Mari!

We're here. Did you get my text?" Despite losing his son in an accident, he seemed to have no qualms about using his phone behind the wheel. He stepped through the threshold and moved aside, swinging his arm to say come-on-in. Marc followed him into the house. The pleasant aroma of roasted meat floated down the hallway, eddying in the foyer around them. Ron shut the door and flipped on a light. A woman's voice carried through the house.

"I got it. I made a pork roast. I hope your friend isn't a vegetarian."

Ron winked at Marc and shouted back, "I'm pretty sure he isn't." He hung up his windbreaker next to a navy blue jacket with a crimson letter B embroidered on the back. Ron took that one down and held it. "Heh! Andrew loved baseball. He played in high school." He got a mischievous look in his eye and offered it to Marc. "You want it?" he asked. Marc held up his hands to ward off the jacket. Ron stepped forward with it. "It's not quite summer yet, and it's better than just a t-shirt." Ron raised his eyebrows as if to say, *It's harmless. Putting on a dead man's jacket won't kill you.* Marc took the coat. He thought about stuffing it in his bag, but decided to play along instead and slipped it on. Although it was a little snug in the shoulders, it fit well. Ron practically beamed at him for a moment, then took Marc's elbow and led him down the hall.

The kitchen was immense. Mari stood at the sink at the far end with her back to them. She turned her head slightly and said, "There's beer in the fridge. Or, if you prefer, I'll open a bottle of wine."

"Beer's fine, ma'am."

"Ma'am? Just who in Creation did you bring home, honey?" She turned with a knife in hand, wiping the other on the front of her apron. Mari's mouth dropped open and the knife slipped from her fingers, spearing the floor in front of her feet. Marc felt blood rush to his face.

I never should have put on the fucking coat.

"Right? Can you believe it?" Ron asked.

Mari stood staring at him. "It's you," she whispered.

Ron walked over and took her hand. "Mari, this is Marc . . . uh. Jesus! Look at me. I don't even know your last name."

Marc held out his hand. "Marcus Welsh, ma'am. Pleased to meet you." Ron gave Mari a gentle shove forward. She took Marc's hand in both of hers, giving it a gentle squeeze. "I'm sorry," she said. "It's very nice to meet you." Marc tried to pull his hand away, but Mari wouldn't let go. She turned to her husband and said, "Dear, would you grab the skillet and sauté up those mushrooms? I'm going to take Marcus to open a bottle of something special." Ron nodded and grabbed down a pan hanging from a hook over the sink.

"It's Marc, please. And a beer is just fine."

She smiled. "Let's go in the other room so you can make yourself at home."

Marc intended to ask to get cleaned up before dinner as Mari pulled at him. He was interrupted by the ringing of the pan that made the floor pitch and rise up.

Marc wanted to rub at his eyes to try to push back the ache hanging just behind them but couldn't move his arms. *Did he really hit me with a fucking frying pan?* He leaned his head back and felt a tight constriction at his throat. He forced himself to calm down and breathe. A sharp jolt of pain shot through his skull as a flash of light erupted in his eyes.

"It's perfect," he heard Mari say, clapping excitedly. "Just perfect!"

Marc heard a muffled groan to his left. Through bleary eyes he looked over at the young woman tied to the chair next to his. She wore a pearl-beaded, white silk gown and a veil over her face. He looked down and saw that he was dressed up in a black tuxedo with a gray vest. He guessed that the tightness around his throat was a bow tie. "Wha's goin' on?" he asked. His bleary voice barely carried and he tried to repeat himself a little louder as the blinding flash went off again.

"Just in case," Ron said. In the background, Nat King Cole sang about L.O.V.E. and what it stood for. Mark repeated his question a little louder to be heard over the music. Ron answered. "We just wanted to get a picture of the bride and groom before the night wears on and you two don't look as perfect as you do right now." The girl beside Marc groaned again and her head lolled to her other shoulder. Marc looked at his surroundings. He sat next to the girl under a wicker archway draped with white and silver garlands, plenty of glitter, and white balloons. He was tied down with zip ties and a bungee cord around his chest. The cord had a little stretch in it, but the zips held him fast. He tried moving his feet and felt plastic straps holding his ankles as well.

"I think it's about time to be getting ready to throw the garter, Andrew. Michelle looks very tired." Mari stepped in front of the spotlights blinding Marc. She walked up to the girl, roughly yanked the veil out of the way and shoved a rag in her tear-streaked face. The girl struggled weakly in her chair and whined a little before slumping over.

"Stop it! Stop! What are you doing?" He bucked against his restraints, but struggling didn't do anything more than send pin-pricks of pain radiating into the backs of his hands and fingers as the ties dug into his tendons.

"Sh sh shh," Mari said. "I think she's had a little too much excitement. Did you guys overdo it with the champagne?" She smiled and winked and let go of the girl. "Naughty, naughty. You're not going to have anything left for your wedding night if you don't pace yourselves." She winked conspiratorially and licked her lips.

"You're out of your fuckin' mind. Let us go!"

"Don't you talk to your mother like that!" Ron yelled from behind the camera. He doused the spotlights and turned the overheads back on. Marc looked around in a panic trying to get a sense of where he was. Gray windowless walls surrounded him. In the far corner, a wooden workbench stood underneath a pegboard covered in tools. Opposite that, a stairway led up into the darkness. *The cellar. We're in the cellar.*

"Do you want to get the induction picture now?" Ron asked. Mari stood up and walked back to her husband.

"I'm not sure his clothes are going to work. They're too worn and ratty." Marc looked behind them at another staged scene. This one resembled the set for the photo he'd had taken after completing Basic: a blue backdrop with an American flag and the Marine Corps standard hanging from poles on either side. Beside that scene stood a coffin on a bier draped with another flag.

"Wh-what is all that?" Ron held up a finger to shush him. Marc shouted as loudly as he could, his head pounding. "What the fuck is all that?"

"Shh, dear," Mari said. "We only have two more memories to go. We wish we could do more, but sadly you gave all for your country. We're so proud of you, Andrew. You meant everything to us."

"Andrew Ballard died in a car crash, you fucking freaks! He got wasted and pulped his head against an overpass! My name is Marcus Welsh!"

She ran over and beat at his chest with her fists. "My son died a hero in Iraq! He saved his whole platoon!" Ron walked over and pulled the hysterical woman off of Marc. He shushed and hummed at her, trying to get her to calm down. Marc realized that wherever he was, he wasn't going to get out by shouting for help.

"See what you've done to your mother? I haven't seen her

this upset since we first heard." Ron pulled a pistol out of his pocket and aimed it at Marc. "I'm sorry, son, but it's better than you coming home like some broken shell of a man. War is hard on us all."

"You don't know a fucking thing about war! I'll show you war! When I get out of this, I am going to—" The sound of the shot stifled the rest of his threat. Marc had been shot once already in Afghanistan. It felt like being punched hard in the chest. He remembered how he'd struggled to catch his breath as his lung filled with blood and they dragged him to the medivac. He felt none of that now. Just the same pain in his head. He opened his eyes and saw Ron standing closer, pointing the gun at his heart.

"*That* was a warning. I don't want to skip right to your funeral, but we will if you make me." Marc felt the rag pressed against his nose before he noticed that Mari had slipped out of sight. *Hold your breath. Hold it. Play possum.* He did his best not to inhale the fumes of whatever it was—ether or chloroform. Despite his best effort, it still got through and his vision blurred. He slumped down, hoping that she'd take the rag away from his mouth soon.

As soon as he blacked out, she did.

The voices were distant and faint and faded in and out with his pained consciousness; still, he managed to catch a few words. *Everything is going to be all right. I heard what he said. Just take a deep breath and relax.* Then it faded back away into the fog. For a fleeting moment Marc thought that he was back at Walter Reed. Then he remembered the camera flashes. And he felt it then. The anger. The fury of having survived war—having survived homelessness and despair—only to die in a suburban basement, anonymous and alone. Except he was neither. He was worse than anonymous.

He was being made into someone else.

Marc peeked out through slitted eyes. He couldn't see his captors. Their voices were distant. *They're in another room.* He opened his eyes fully and looked around to make sure he was truly alone. They'd dressed him in his freshly washed and ironed BDU's. *They keep switching me up like a fucking Ken doll.* At least, he figured, it'd be easier to get away in these clothes than in a tuxedo.

Plastic zip ties still held his arms firm to the chair. He pulled up hard against them. The wood creaked but didn't give. The plastic straps cut into the backs of his wrists making his hands tingle painfully, but he kept at it. The elegantly arcing Swedish chair didn't offer any joints near his wrists or ankles that he could loosen and the bungee at his chest prevented him from leaning forward to chew at them. Ron and his bitch had thought these things through. His only hope was brute force. Break the ties.

He shoved his arm forward, trying to create a better fulcrum, and levered up with his forearm. He was fairly certain that the strap would give before his ulna and radius. His head ached as he exerted himself, trying to stay quiet, trying to keep an ear out for the couple's return. They kept bickering off in the distance.

"I don't see the point."

"Fine! Just get on with it then."

He pulled and pried, pushing through the pain. Keeping on, knowing that if he stopped—if he took a minute to relax and let his consciousness wander—it would be all over.

And then, one snapped.

His arm swung up wildly, hitting the flag behind him. Marc didn't wait to process what had happened. He'd have the rest of his life to be thankful that a quality assurance worker in some zip tie factory missed one. If he didn't focus and get back to it, the rest of his life wouldn't last as long as Mari's bottle of ether with the cap off.

Pulling at the other wrist tie, he realized that his luck was only in once. This one held. He scanned the room for something within arm's reach he could use as a tool or a weapon. There was nothing. The only things near him were the twin flagpoles standing behind him. He reached back over his shoulder and tilted the American flag forward, looking to see what topped the pole. An eagle. He carefully brought the pole around in front of him so he could inspect the ornament closer. *Please, not plastic. Please, not plastic.* The eagle was cool and heavy in his hand. *Metal!* Although it was gold-colored, he was certain the bird was made of aluminum. It didn't matter. If it broke, that was just a more ragged edge to saw through his bindings.

Holding the flagpole between his knees so it wouldn't clatter away and draw attention, he quickly unscrewed the ornament and went to work on the other tie, prying and poking with the wings of the bird—the eagle perched upon a globe, making its talons useless. It was slow work that had him wishing they'd chosen a spear tip or a Fleur de Lis as a topper instead. Eventually, however, the zip snapped apart with a satisfying pop and both his hands were free. He undid the cord tied around his chest and bent down to break his leg ties.

The noises drifting in from the other room dulled and Marc tried to work faster. Whatever they were doing sounded like it was wrapping up and he didn't want to be around when they got back on task. He broke the last tie and stood up. The room swam. He willed himself not to pass out. He couldn't tell whether the pain in his skull was the result of the frying pan or the shit in the rag they kept stuffing in his face. Neither did his brains any favors. He reckoned an E.R. visit was in his future, if he had one.

His rucksack was stuffed under a work bench at the far end of the room. He crept over to it and slid it out carefully. Resisting the urge to open it and take an inventory of his things, he slung the bag over his shoulders and fastened the clip in front before searching the surface of the workbench for a weapon.

Ron's tool collection wasn't expansive, but it was sufficient. Marc grabbed a long Phillips head screwdriver and a mid-sized claw hammer. Neither were what he'd prefer in a gunfight, but both were better than nothing.

Creeping toward the stairway leading up to freedom, he spied the room where his captors were getting ready for their next tableau. It was positioned directly opposite his goal, hidden by a peg-board partition on which a few odds and ends hung—small extension cords and cables. He'd almost walked out in front of it, exposing himself. He crouched and peeked around as discreetly as he dared. Both Ron and Mari were in plain sight. Ron looked like he was doing up his pants. In front of him on a table lay the girl they'd used as a prop in the wedding photo. Mari groused at her husband.

"It's enough to understand the context in the photo," she said.

"No. We have to *know*. It has to be real."

"But it's not his. And it's too early to even tell if she's pregnant. You just wanted to—"

Ron slapped Mari across the mouth before giving her a look that was an equal measure of frustration and pity. "I want everything to be perfect. I want to be a grandparent. Don't you?"

"Yes," she said, holding her stinging cheek.

"Well, this is how it's done." Mari opened her mouth to reply, but Ron interrupted by showing her his hand, ready to respond to her protests with his reddening palm again.

Marc took cover behind the pegboard wall. Although he couldn't see the pistol that Ron had brandished before, he couldn't assume that it wasn't within easy reach. What had seemed a difficult proposition before—escape up the stairs—had become more complicated. Although he still felt weakened and fuzzy from the dope in the rag, he couldn't just slip away; he couldn't leave the girl behind. He formed a quick plan and steeled himself. *Blitz Ron and take the gun. Eliminate the primary threat before taking out secondary targets.*

He thought about what it meant to kill them. What it meant was a fresh start. He'd save the girl. Call the cops and explain that it was self-defense. She'd back his play. He'd be a hero. Go on TV and tell his story. Maybe someone would see him and listen to his story and offer him a job. He could get his life back. Get back on track. Get better.

He peeked around a second time to take a better appraisal of the room and try to locate Ron's weapon. His breath caught in his lungs.

Behind the couple on the wall were a dozen framed photographs. A young boy in a soccer uniform, kneeling in front of a ball . . . crying. A different boy, similar-looking but not the same, stared fearfully out of another picture wearing a black gown and mortarboard cap. A scroll of paper was stuck in his fist tied closed with the now-familiar zip ties. In another shot, a child, maybe five or six, sat holding a brightly colored present and shrieking in front of a Christmas tree. Still more pictures showed random scenes from the life of a boy depicted by a cast of similar-looking people. *People who all look like me*, Marc realized. A couple of terrified kids at prom. A screaming child with an Easter basket. In the center of it all, a pair of beaming parents holding a silent infant. Andrew Ballard's whole life immortalized in pictures. The boy seemed not to exist at all except by proxy—except by pain and fear. Each milestone in his ersatz life was the capstone in someone else's.

Underneath it all on a shelf stood a gray box with a brass plaque on the front—a crematory box. *That's him. That's the fucking kid!*

He leaned back behind cover, steadied himself, and took a deep breath before bursting into the room.

Immediately his plan went to hell.

Still woozy from the blow to the head and the chloroform, he stumbled over a step and fumbled his weapons. The hammer and screwdriver clattered uselessly away. Ron and Mari spun around, twin looks of stunned surprise on their faces. Marc clumsily regained his footing, but his angle of attack was way off. Instead of hitting Ron, he took out Mari first, driving his shoulder into her ribs and slamming her back against the table. Mari screamed. Ron raised the pistol and fired. The sound was like a bomb going off in the small room. Marc pushed himself off the woman and pressed forward, swinging his forearm out to hit Ron's gun hand and drive the weapon's aim away long enough to get in close. Ron got off another shot. Another miss. *You're not going to get lucky three times!* Marc pushed in close, controlling the handgun and hit hard. Ron's eyes bulged in shock and panic as his windpipe collapsed under Marc's driving forearm. Marc swung up and brought his fist down hard on Ron's weapon arm. The gun clattered away as he pulled the bigger man's legs out from under him and took him to the ground. Together, they fell in a heap on the floor. Marc scrambled up onto Ron's chest and began to pound at his face.

Mari lurched toward the men. She grabbed Marc by the hair and pulled his head back with a hard jerk, screaming incoherently. Despite seeing her weather the crack she took from her husband before Marc plunged into the room, he hadn't accounted for her being able to take a hard hit and recover fast. Complicating matters, his initial burst of adrenaline-fueled energy was waning fast. The pain and dizziness and nausea were all coming back stronger than before as he struggled with the couple. He felt Ron slip out from under him as she dragged him off her husband.

He twisted under her arm, pinning her hand to his head with his own. He was readying to drive a hard kick into her stomach when he felt her other hand plunge the knife into his guts.

She has a knife. I didn't see a knife.

Fire burned through his midsection as she shoved the blade deeper in. The feeling made him want to vomit. It made him want to let go of his bladder. He wanted to sit down and give up. An image of his parents in black funeral clothes flashed in front of him and he wanted to say that he was sorry. Say he missed them. Say that he didn't blame them for anything. It wasn't their fault.

It was too late to wish for third and fourth chances. He'd blown his second. And that was all he got.

The claw end of the hammer stuck in Mari's skull. Her eyes dilated and rolled before she dropped, pulling the knife out of Marc's stomach as she went. The girl in the black dress fell to her knees behind her, tugging weakly at the handle of the embedded tool. Ron stepped up to her, bloody drooling mouth hanging open as if to ask what she'd done. He placed the barrel of his recovered gun to her head. Marc fell back and fumbled and grasped at the crematory urn on the shelf beside him. Prying at the lid off the metal box, he shouted as loudly as he could through the pain and the shallowness of his remaining breath.

"Don't you pull that fucking trigger!"

Ron looked at him with an idiotic blankness. If he had an expression, Marc couldn't read it through the swelling rising up from the beating he'd given him. Ron pulled back fat, split lips in a dripping red grimace and hissed, "Let him go."

Marc threw the ashes in the man's face.

The girl swung a fist into Ron's balls and he doubled over, firing the gun into his wife's limp thigh. Marc grabbed the knife out of the dead woman's hand. Pulling Ron by the hair, he jammed the blade into the man's neck, and again, and a third time, before twisting and grinding like he was trying to saw through the neck of a Christmas goose. Ron's gun fell to the ground and his body followed.

Marc looked at the knife and threw it into the corner before wiping his wet hands on his pants. The square urn lay beside him, the glinting plaque on the front facing up. Through bleary eyes, he read the engraved inscription: *Andrew Raymond Ballard. Our son. 11/25/1990.* He glanced back up at the picture wall. A collage of anguished semi-familiar faces stared back at him in a bleak farce of his life passing before his eyes.

1990? All these kids. None of them are him.

He looked up at the picture of a younger Ron and Mari holding a pale, silent infant. Seated together, they stared into the camera wearing smiles that looked pained. *Maybe one was him. Maybe he was stillborn.*

Marc looked down. Blood stained his pants and was beginning to pool on the ground, muddying the spilled ashes in front of him. The girl crawled over Ron and Mari's bodies and through the ashes to wrap her arms around Marc and lean against him, crying into his chest. He held her and brushed her hair back to kiss her forehead to reassure her that everything was going to be all right. But he didn't believe it. He wanted to ask her to go upstairs to find a telephone, to call for help. He needed an ambulance. They both did. He couldn't find the breath to give voice to his fear that he was bleeding to death.

At that moment, it felt better to just sit right there and hold each other. For a little while anyway, it seemed right to be still and alive in the present.

KHATAM

Even though the chair in the delivery room was unforgiving, Amahl welcomed the chance to sit. Although it had been Mira who labored and bled, after twenty sleepless hours he needed rest. He would have easily fallen asleep on the bare floor, but then he couldn't hold his son.

The light of the buzzing fluorescent bulb above them blanched the baby's dusky skin with brightness. The boy's inky hair absorbed the light like the characters in Mira's charcoal drawings. Beneath the antiseptic scents of polymeric disinfectant, bleach, and isopropyl alcohol, the scent of his baby was there. Deep underneath the iron smell of blood and spilled amniotic fluid and a hint of something else. Something that reminded him of the autumn evening in which they'd conceived the boy.

An uncharacteristic quiet had settled in the neighborhood. Traffic stopped. The men downstairs circling small tables on the tea house sidewalk fell silent, foregoing their gossip as they sat huddled around hookahs, sipping hot drinks and smoking. Mira's curried breath was quickened by the same anxious desire he felt. His beloved. His Mira. Since she had begun tracking ovulation cycles and periods of fertility, sex had almost become a chore. That night, in the sticky heat of a quiet humid evening, it had been like it was when they were first married: oceanic. They made love as exhaled smoke from the café diners below drifted in through their windows, flavoring the night.

A few weeks later, the good news: "I'm pregnant." She announced it quietly, as though the fact was too fragile to be spoken. She placed his hands on her still-flat belly and said it again, a little louder, before kissing him. "*We're* having a baby." Pregnant with the knowledge, Amahl moved through their apartment with more deliberation; a greater purpose filling him as he nested, preparing the room in the center of their home for the arrival of the baby. Preparing for a new life. The child's. His own. His family's.

The smell called to mind the image of Mira standing in the spring market, full and flushed, smiling at him over a fiercely craved date plucked from the bag before she paid—too eager to wait until they got home. She smiled as she bit her prize in half, one hand resting on the belly containing their son—due to join then in only three more weeks. "Happy now?" he asked. She laughed, tearing through the body of the dried fruit with her teeth. Behind her, at the opposite end of the alley, the bomb exploded, blowing a wave of fire and blood and hot metal through the long corridor, thrusting her into his arms. Together they crashed through the fruit cart from which she had picked her dates, landing in the dirt and the syrupy remains of ruined pomegranates and figs crushed beneath their entwined bodies. Mira's breath on his face— the herald of the creation of their son—was wet and stank of copper. Groaning, she rolled off of Amahl and onto her back. He glanced up at the shrapnel that had streaked through the spice-tinged air to nest in the wall just above their heads, thankful that it had missed them both. To his right lay the man who had sold them the fruit; the blast had not spared him.

Mira gasped, clutching her belly. Amahl felt a wet warmth plastering his pants to his legs. He sat up to see the stains soaking the front of Mira's dress. "My water," she said. "My water broke. Oh god, Amahl. The baby!"

That was twenty-four hours ago. *Gone in an instant*, he

thought, cradling the infant his wife had borne. The nurses had given him a set of scrubs to replace his burned, bloody clothes, but the stench of smoke was in his hair, his pores—a smell that, until twenty-four hours ago, had reminded him of the night of creation.

"Mr. al Adin." The nurse stood in the doorway, wringing cigarette-stained fingers. "Your wife is out of surgery and is in recovery. I imagine you'll want to be there when she wakes up." He walked over to the new father and held out his hands to take the child. Amahl shrank back from the man's reach. He did not want to give his son up to the nurse *or* to the ground. *I'd give anything for him to grow old, and for me to be buried instead.* But of course there was no one to accept his offer. The life he was given couldn't be bought or traded, although it could be stolen in a burst of fire and a cloud of smoke.

Amahl gazed down at the baby cradled in his arms. He wiped at his tears, feeling a slow realization swell up and envelop him like a cooling tide. *Once I was an infant, helpless in my father's hands.* Closing his eyes as he held the boy against his chest, he imagined what his father had felt twenty-seven years earlier. *This is how much he loved me.*

He kissed the baby softly on the forehead. "Thank you," he said, and stood up to take him to meet his mother.

ABOUT THE AUTHOR

BRACKEN MACLEOD is the author of *Mountain Home*, *White Knight*, and most recently, *Stranded*, which has been optioned by Warner Horizon Television. His short fiction has appeared in several anthologies and magazines including *Shock Totem*, *LampLight*, *ThugLit*, and *Splatterpunk*. He has worked as a trial attorney, philosophy instructor, and as a martial arts teacher. He lives in New England with his wife and son, where he is at work on his next novel.

ACKNOWLEDGMENTS

First of all, I owe a huge debt of gratitude to Brett Savory, Sandra Kasturi, Michael Rowe, Adrian Van Young, and my entire ChiZine family. Without your constant support and confidence in my work, I would not be where I am today.

To all the people who've read these stories in one form or another before publication, KL Pereira, Errick Nunnally, Christopher Irvin, Jan Kozlowski, John Mantooth, Adam Cesare, Thomas Pluck, Todd Robinson, Scott Goudsward, Tony Tremblay, Anthony Rivera, Sharon Lawson, Ken Wood, John Boden, Ron Earl Philips, jOhnny Morse, Jack Bantry, and Jacob Haddon, thank you for making them better.

To my influences, colleagues and friends, Christopher Golden, Chet Williamson, John Dixon, Paul Tremblay, Jonathan Maberry, Brian Keene, Nicholas Kaufmann, James A. Moore, John Skipp, John McIlveen, Charles Rutledge, Tony Tremblay, Kealan Patrick Burke, Dana Cameron, Kasey Lansdale, Joe Lansdale, Elizabeth Bear, Amanda Downum, John Goodrich, Ed Kurtz, Andrew Vachss, and Dallas Mayr, you all inspire me to work harder and be better at what I do. Thank you.

Finally, and forever, my abiding love goes to my wife, Heather, and son, Lucien. Life with them is the dream from which I never wish to wake.

PUBLICATION HISTORY

"Still Day: An Ending" is original to this collection.

"Something I Said?" was first published in 2015 in *Protectors 2: Heroes*.

"Pure Blood and Evergreen" was first published in 2013 in *Ominous Realities*.

"Ciudad de los Niños" was first published in 2013 in *Reloaded: Both Barrels*.

"The Blood and the Body" was first published in 2015 in *Wicked Tales*.

"The Boy Who Dreamt He Was a Bat" is original to this collection.

"Blood Makes the Grass Grow" was first published in 2015 in *Thuglit*, Issue 16.

"Some Other Time" was first published in 2012 in *Femme Fatale: Erotic Tales of Dangerous Women*.

"Morgenstern's Last Act" was first published in 2015 in *Eulogies III*.

"All Dreams Die in the Morning" is original to this collection.

"Mine, Not Yours" was first published in 2013 in *Anthology: Year Two*.

"Thirteen Views of the Suicide Woods" was first published in 2014 in *Shock Totem*.

"The Texas Chainsaw Breakfast Club *or* I Don't Like Mondays" was first published in 2014 in *Splatterpunk*.

"In the Bones" was first published in 2014 in *Widowmakers: A Benefit Anthology of Dark Fiction*.

"Blood of the Vine" was first published in 2014 in *Shroud*.

"Looking for the Death Trick" was first published in 2015 in *Locked and Loaded: Both Barrels Vol. 3*.

"This Last Little Piece of Darkness" is original to this collection.

"Reminisce" was first published in 2013 in *LampLight*.

"Khatam" was first published in 2011 by *Every Day Fiction*.